JUST DREAMS

L.J. TAYLOR

Waterview Publishing, LLC

Just Dreams
Waterview Publishing, LLC
ISBN 978-1-941778-00-5
©2014 by L.J. Taylor

This book is a work of fiction. The names, characters, dialogue, incidents, and places, except for incidental references to public figures, products or services, are the product of the author's imagination and are not to be construed as real. No character in this book is based on an actual person. Any resemblance to actual events, locales or persons living or dead is entirely coincidental and unintentional. The author and publisher have made every effort to ensure the accuracy and completeness of the information contained in this book and assume no responsibility for any errors, inaccuracies, omissions, or inconsistencies contained herein.

For information about special discounts for bulk purchases, please contact the author or Waterview Publishing, LLC.

Waterview Publishing, LLC
P.O. Box 398244
Miami Beach, FL 33139
www.ljtaylorbooks.com
Printed in the U.S.A

Dedication

This book is dedicated to my mother whom I lost last year and miss very much.

Acknowledgments

I'm going to keep this short and sweet and general for fear of leaving anyone out. First, I want to thank God for giving me the opportunity, the skills and the perseverance necessary to write this book. Next, I want to thank my friends and family for believing in and supporting me throughout this process.

I want to extend a special thanks to my beta readers – Courtney Green, Ericka Turk-Moore, and Anna Sarabia - for reading numerous drafts of this book and others and giving me honest (and sometimes hard to take) feedback.

I want to thank Valerie and Eric Valdes and all of the members of my writers group for encouraging me to keep my considerable behind in a chair and finish writing and editing this novel. I also want thank my outside editor for helping me to whip it into shape for publication.

Finally, I want to thank my significant other for his love and support, and his design of the cover.

CHAPTER I

"You can do this. It's just another client meeting." Kathy Brooks mumbled the words under her breath like a mantra.

Nerves had her loitering in the hallway instead of entering the conference room where her new client waited. She'd learned of the case only two hours before in a meeting with the managing partner of her law firm. He'd made her lead partner on the case saying it was time she came out from behind her senior partner's coattails and made a name for herself.

Lead partner. Kathy swallowed hard. She and her mentor, Steve Perdue, had tried cases together for the past five years. They had their respective roles down to a science. She dealt with the details. He dealt with the people. Together they made a highly effective team winning multimillion dollar jury verdicts and bringing in substantial fees. The very thought of having to deal with the people part of the practice made Kathy feel queasy. But she had no choice.

She glanced down at her navy blue pants suit and sensible pumps to make sure she looked the part. She transferred the legal pad, file folder and business card from her right hand to her left, took a deep breath, and opened the conference room door.

He was standing by the window, gazing out at the view of Biscayne Bay, his back to her. Tall and lean, he wore dress slacks and a shirt tucked into his belt. His long legs and taut rear-end filled out the slacks nicely. She caught herself staring and shook her head.

He turned to face her and, for a moment, time stopped. He had a caramel complexion, high cheekbones, and hazel eyes she could just drown in. She felt her smile slip for an instant before she recovered her composure.

"Mr. Morgan? My name is Kathy Brooks. I'll be the attorney helping you with your case."

She detected a glint of amusement in his eyes as he shook her hand. No doubt he was used to women falling at his feet with his looks.

"Please call me Charles," he said.

She gestured toward the conference room table. "Please have a seat, Charles. Can I get you something to drink?"

"No, I'm fine," he said.

He certainly was. She cleared her throat. What she needed to do was clear her head. She had a job to do and, as a client, he was off limits. To give herself a moment, she set her stuff down onto the table and headed over to the credenza to pour a glass of water. She carried the glass to the table and took a seat facing him. "So Charles, how did you hear about Gold, Rome and Harris?"

"My father's law partner is a friend of Bill Winters. His firm specializes in criminal defense. When he heard I needed an attorney for a wrongful death suit, he referred me to your firm.

I'm told you have an excellent reputation for aggressively pursuing these types of matters. That's exactly what I need."

Kathy nodded. "I see." She glanced down at her notepad then looked him in the eye. "There are a few things we need to talk about today. First, I'll walk you through what we can expect to happen in the case, then we'll talk about specific things like settlement --."

"Whoa -." He held up a hand, cutting her off. "Did you just say something about settlement?"

She stopped and stared at him. Clients didn't usually react so strangely to the mention of the word "settlement." Maybe he just wanted her to slow down and discuss the issue. She tended to speak quickly – especially when she was nervous. "Yes. We're bound to get settlement offers during the course of this case. A security firm like Peachtree, which has several government contracts, is going to want to get rid of this case quickly to avoid negative publicity. I need to know at what number you'd be willing to settle. You don't have to give it to me now. Just give it some thought."

Charles leaned forward in his chair, his hazel eyes shooting sparks in her direction. "I don't need to give it a moment's thought. That man's recklessness took away two of the most important people in my life - my wife and my unborn child. No amount of money can make that up to me. I want to inflict as much pain on that company as possible. I want my day in court. Do you hear me? There will be no settlement."

Even though he never raised his voice, the intensity with which he made the statement had Kathy leaning back in her chair - away from him.

She nodded. "Yes, I understand." She stifled a sigh. Any hope she had of settling the case short of trial just flew out the window. "Okay. Let's talk strategy. The first thing we're going to do is prepare a complaint – the document we use to file the lawsuit. Then we'll serve some document requests and written questions for Peachtree to answer under oath. After we serve the papers, we'll hold a press conference. They'll have twenty days to respond to the complaint and forty-five days to answer the discovery requests assuming they don't get any extensions of time. After that-."

Charles held up his hands forming the universal time-out signal. "Hold on. What do you mean extensions of time? Where would they get those from?"

Kathy felt a sinking feeling in the pit of her stomach. She prayed he wasn't one of those clients who didn't believe in granting reasonable extensions. "Well, it's not unusual for one or both parties in a civil lawsuit to ask for extensions of time on a court deadline. We routinely grant them so long as they don't harm the case in any way. If not, the court will usually grant them so long as they're reasonable and don't throw off the trial date."

He shook his head. "We're not giving any extensions. I want to get to trial as quickly as possible."

"Look," she said, "I understand your desire to resolve this matter quickly, but there are consequences to not extending basic professional courtesies in a case. They can range from making a case more expensive to pissing off the judge."

"Exactly. I want to make this case very expensive for Peachtree Consulting - in more ways than one. As far as we're concerned, money is no object. We'll stop short of pissing off the judge, but otherwise, I don't want to give these guys an inch. Look, if you can't handle this, I'll ask Bill to put someone else on the case."

What a jerk. She shot him a piercing look that tended to intimidate many of her opposing counsel and any witness who dared to lie to her on cross-examination. "Please don't mistake my looking out for your best interests for weakness. I assure you I can handle any type of case. Bill would never have assigned me to your case otherwise. It's my job, as your attorney, to let you know if the decisions you make could have unintended consequences."

He glowered at her. She met his stare and refused to back down. He sat back in his chair and crossed his arms. "Fine. We'll cross that bridge when we come to it." In the face of her silence, he gestured with his hand for her to continue. "So, go on. What else can I expect to happen?"

"You can expect them to be just as intrusive with their discovery as we're going to be," she said. "They'll serve you with document requests and ask you and anyone who ever knew your wife questions under oath. They're going to want to know everything about her to see if they can blame her for the accident. They'll try to claim that she was drunk or talking on her cell phone or texting while driving. Or they may claim she was sick and had a heart attack or a stroke or something and stopped short. They may even ask to exhume her body to test it --."

She stopped when she noticed the horrified look on his face. She remembered, too late, that Bill wasn't usually so blunt at the first client meeting. Something about the man had gotten under her skin causing her to dive into the sordid little world of "civil" litigation almost gleefully - as if she wanted to punish him for daring to believe she might not be cut out for it. She wondered if he knew what he was about to get into.

"Can they do that? Have my wife's body exhumed?"

She shrugged. "It's possible. It happened in another case we handled. We'd fight it, of course, but I can't guarantee we'd win on that issue."

He swore, got up and began to pace. She sat there and watched him. After a moment, he returned to his chair, and stabbed an index finger in her direction. "You do that. You fight those bastards tooth and nail every step of the way. But if we have to exhume my wife's body to prove she wasn't to blame in any way for the accident, then that's what we'll do."

"Okay," she said.

He picked up his water and took a sip.

She paused to give him a moment. She didn't know how this case would turn out but it promised to be an interesting ride.

***

Donald Peachtree, President and CEO of Peachtree Consulting, fumed in the reception area of his attorney's law firm. Weisman, Hoffman & Smith was a litigation boutique that made a lot of money handling sensitive matters for high profile clients. They were as well known for their prowess as defense attorneys as for their astronomically high hourly rates. They represented actors, senators, congressman, athletes, high-ranking corporate executives and corporations in civil and criminal cases all over the country. Their lawyers were tough and not above breaking the rules to achieve their clients' goals. Peachtree Consulting had hired the firm once before with good results.

Where the hell is Weisman? When he told his lawyer he wanted to see him, he expected the man to jump. As a retired colonel in the Marine Corps and CEO of one of the largest defense contractors in the country, Peachtree was used to men snapping to attention at his orders. And damn it, considering how much this law firm charged by the hour, he expected Weisman to jump the highest of them all. He slammed the delicate coffee cup into its saucer, stood up, and, with his back ramrod straight, marched up to the reception desk.

The receptionist stopped chattering into her headset and regarded him with wide eyes.

"Did you tell Mr. Weisman that I was here to see him, young lady?" he asked.

The receptionist nodded vigorously. "Yes sir," she said. Her voice was little more than a squeak. "I called him on his cell phone to tell him you had arrived. He said that he was on his way in and would be here shortly."

"That was fifteen minutes ago," he said. "Where exactly is he coming from – Outer Mongolia? Did he have a hearing this morning? Is he coming from the courthouse?"

She shook her head. "No, Sir. He . . . he's driving in from Coral Gables. You see, he didn't know you would arrive an hour early for your appointment, Sir. We weren't expecting you until ten thirty."

Weisman snarled. "Do you mean to tell me that he's in the habit of strolling in here at ten o'clock every morning? Is that what I'm paying you people for? This is unacceptable. I will not be kept waiting like this. Which of the other partners are available to meet with me now? Perhaps they will be more appreciative of my business."

"Oh no, Sir. It - It's not like that at all. I'm sure - - ." The receptionist stopped speaking abruptly when the elevator chime sounded. She looked past Peachtree and an expression of profound relief appeared on her face. Peachtree turned to see Stewart Weisman step off the elevator.

"Peachtree, are you terrorizing my receptionist again?" Weisman, a trim and impeccably dressed man in his late fifties, crossed the reception area. He stopped in front of Peachtree and extended his hand.

Peachtree ignored it. "I've been sitting here for more than thirty minutes. You know how much I hate to be kept waiting. Time is money, Weisman."

Weisman smiled and dropped the hand. "Ain't that the truth? And you're on the clock, buddy, so why don't we just go into my office and get down to business?"

Peachtree leveled a glare at Weisman that would have weakened the knees of several officers under his command. He barked out a short laugh when Weisman just stood there smiling back at him. He stepped up to the attorney and clapped him hard on the back.

"You've got balls, Weisman. I've got to give you that," he said.

"That's why you keep coming back," Weisman said. He gestured ahead of him. "Right this way."

They settled onto the whiskey colored leather couch in Weisman's office. Coffee, tea and pastries were set up on a tray on the coffee table. Weisman reached for the coffee pot and poured himself a cup. He turned to Peachtree. "You want some of this?"

"Yes, I'll take a cup," Peachtree said.

Weisman poured coffee into Peachtree's cup then set the pot down. "Cream? Sugar?"

"No just plain coffee. The way it should be," Peachtree said. He watched in disapproval as Weisman poured a liberal amount of cream and two sugars into his own cup.

"Okay," Weisman said. "Let's get down to business. I read the complaint and the discovery you sent me last night."

Peachtree took a sip of the coffee. It was damned good java. "The bastards served my agent at home in front of his wife in the middle of their dinner hour. They served me yesterday afternoon in the middle of a board meeting. Can they do that?"

"Unfortunately, yes. It's within their rights to have you served at work and your agent served at home. Next time, if you know someone is trying to serve you or your agents with process, just give me a call and we can arrange for me to accept service on your behalf. That should help to avoid any embarrassing scenes."

"What did you think about the complaint? Who is this Kathy Brooks woman?" Peachtree said.

"She's a partner at Gold, Rome and Harris – a law firm we've gone up against in the past. She's a good lawyer who normally works cases as second chair to her mentor, Steve Perdue. She doesn't usually take the lead like she's done here. Now, the complaint itself alleges a pretty straightforward wrongful death claim. They say that your man, Wilkes, was reckless when he crashed into the plaintiff's wife's car, killing her. They say that he was driving a company car and engaged in company business at the time he did it. Is any of that true?" Weisman took a sip of his coffee.

Peachtree picked up his cup and aimed a measuring look at Weisman over the rim. He took a sip while he decided how much to tell him.

As if reading his mind, Weisman sighed and set his cup down. "Look, I can be a much more effective advocate for you if I'm not blindsided with facts that come out later in the case or, worse yet, at trial."

Peachtree rested his cup on his knee. "You've worked on cases with my company in the past, so you know what we do, right?"

"Yes. You provide assistance and support to the federal government in operations all over the world."

"That's right - sometimes right here in the U.S. Wilkes was involved in an operation here in Miami that involved national security. You don't have the clearance for me to read you in. Let's just say that the operation involved stopping an act of domestic terrorism," Peachtree said.

Weisman nodded. He leaned back in his seat and crossed his arms. "I see."

"I don't think you do," Peachtree said. "The matter Wilkes was assigned to didn't come from the F.B.I., the N.S.A. or any other government agency authorized to operate domestically."

Weisman raised his eyebrows. "Oh. That could pose a slight problem. I don't know if you noticed, but the package you sent me didn't just contain a complaint. It also contained written discovery in which the plaintiff seeks documents and written answers under oath regarding what Wilkes was doing at the time of the accident."

"Of course I noticed the discovery. That's the main reason I needed to see you today. We can't possibly provide them with the information or the documents they're asking for. It's classified. That's not to mention the hell that would break loose if we have to publicly disclose that we and the client were engaged in unauthorized domestic operations. The F.B.I. and the N.S.A. have been gunning for the government to get rid of defense contractors like us for ages. They don't acknowledge that it's the all the inter-agency infighting and bullshit that creates the need for companies like mine to begin with. Can't we raise national security as grounds for objecting to the discovery or whatever it is you lawyers do?"

Weisman nodded. "We certainly will object to the discovery on several grounds, including national security, but that may not be enough to keep the plaintiff from getting it. We have to look at other methods for dealing with this issue, like getting the Court to enter a confidentiality order."

Peachtree stared at Weisman as if he had two heads. "A confidentiality order? You want me to risk losing my government contracts - my company's lifeblood - on a piece of paper? What happens if this Morgan fellow decides to ignore the confidentiality order?"

"He would be sanctioned by the Court for violating the order and receive anything from a fine to imprisonment to dismissal of his case," Weisman said.

Peachtree threw back his head and laughed. "You call that a sanction? In my world, if you get sanctioned, you don't come back. Now that's an incentive I'd trust a little more." He shook his head. "No, I'm not resting the fate of a billion dollar company I worked my ass off to build on a piece of paper or a possible fine. What are our other options?" he asked.

"Well, we can try to get the case dismissed, but the Court's not likely to grant such a motion. Another option would be to settle the case in the early stages to avoid discovery. If we can't get them to settle then we'll have to explore other options." Weisman looked at Peachtree over the rims of his eyeglasses. Since Peachtree had worked with him before, he didn't need to elaborate.

Peachtree nodded. "You just make this case disappear. I don't care how. Am I making myself clear?"

"Clear as crystal," Weisman said.

CHAPTER II

Kathy's heart pounded as she surveyed the mob scene in front of the Wilkie D. Ferguson, Jr. Federal Courthouse. It was a modern, artistic structure designed by one of the top architectural firms in the country comprised of two massive towers lifted three stories off the ground by large limestone columns and linked together by a blue-green glass curtain wall.

She stood in front of the door to the courthouse and played with the pearl necklace she wore on top of her grey pinstriped skirt suit and white silk blouse. Charles stood by her looking dapper in a brown suit, a gold-toned shirt and a tie that brought all the colors together. They made a nice looking couple. Reporters surrounded them, shouting questions and thrusting news cameras and microphones into their faces.

"Mr. Morgan, how does it feel to bring your wife's killers to justice?" one reporter asked.

Charles looked toward the reporter as if he were going to answer the question. Kathy put a hand on his arm and shook her head ever so slightly. "No," she said, her voice quiet. "Let me do the talking, remember?"

Charles nodded.

Kathy held up her hands in a gesture she had seen Bill use to get the reporters' attention. When they turned to her and stopped shouting questions, she began to speak.

"We have prepared a statement," she said. "My client, Charles Morgan, Jr., has filed a lawsuit against the defense contractor, Peachtree Consulting, and its employee, Thomas Wilkes, for negligence. Upon information and belief, Thomas Wilkes, an employee of Peachtree Consulting, was driving a company car at extremely high rates of speed on I-95, in reckless disregard of the safety of other vehicles, while engaged in company business. His gross negligence resulted in the death of my client's wife, Patricia Morgan, and their unborn child. We're seeking damages in excess of twenty million dollars. Thank you."

"Twenty million dollars? Mr. Morgan, are you, like so many other personal injury plaintiffs, in this for the money?" one reporter asked.

Charles' whipped his head toward the reporter, his eyes blazing with fury. Cameras flashed and made buzzing noises as their operators zoomed in for close-ups. "How can you put a value on a human life? Twenty million dollars is nothing. No amount of money could make up for what those bastards took from me," he said.

Kathy stared at him. What the hell was he doing? She had prepared him for this press conference and specifically instructed him not to answer any of the reporters' questions. And now, here he was, raving at them with the cameras rolling. Reporters started firing questions directly at him hoping to provoke a response and Charles looked as though he was about to give them more of a show. She needed to do some damage control and fast. She stepped in front of him, blocking him from the cameras. "This press conference is now over."

The reporters continued to shout questions as she turned to Charles, took him by the arm, and led him into the courthouse. They went through security, rode up to the 7th floor and headed into a small conference room just outside of the courtroom where the hearing would be held.

Kathy lit into Charles as soon as the door closed behind them. "What the hell was that?"

Charles turned to look at her. "What?"

"You know what," she said. "When we prepped for this press conference, I specifically instructed you not to make any statements to the reporters and to let me do the talking. And what do you do? You start ranting and raving in front of the news cameras."

"I'm sorry if I failed to follow your instructions or stole some of your limelight, Counselor, but that was something I needed to say."

"It's not about being in the limelight or being in control. It's about portraying you in the best possible light in the media. I don't give you instructions to be bossy. I'm doing my job which is to look out for your best interests. If you don't listen to my advice, then I can't be responsible for the results. It's easy to be sympathetic toward a grieving father and widower. It's just as easy to alienate people. When you see that footage later, with a cooler head, you'll see what I mean," she said.

Charles grinned. "Are you calling me a hothead?"

Kathy crossed her arms over her chest and glared up at him over the top of her glasses. They had slipped down her nose again as they were prone to do. "If the shoe fits."

Charles reached out and pushed her glasses back up the

bridge of her nose. She reared back and blinked at him.

"Hey!" she said.

He held up his hands. "Just fixing your glasses, Counselor."

"Don't do that," she said. "They're prescription glasses and very pricey. I'd hate to have to add a new pair to your bill."

He put his hands behind his back. "Ouch, your bills are high enough."

She chuckled. "And they're going to get even higher if you don't take my advice."

He grimaced. "Alright, point taken."

Kathy's paralegal, Jim, opened the door and poked his head into the room. "The bailiff says Judge McCarthy's about to take the bench," he said.

"Thanks Jim," Kathy said. She turned to Charles. "It's show time."

They left the conference room and entered the courtroom. The place was packed. Reporters, attorneys and bystanders filled the gallery and even the jury box. Kathy recognized several lawyers from her firm, including her mentor, Steve Perdue. He was seated in the front row of the gallery. She headed over to him.

"Hey Kiddo," he said.

"Hi there," she said. "Steve, this is Charles Morgan, Jr. Charles, this is my partner, Steve Perdue."

Steve held out his hand. "It's a pleasure to meet you. Sorry it had to be under these circumstances."

"Thank you. Nice to meet you too." Charles shook his

hand and then turned to Kathy. "Where do you want me to sit?"

"Why don't you sit right over there with Jim? When the judge comes in, I'll join you. Our hearing is right after the first one, so we should be called fairly soon," she said.

"Okay," he said. He left to take his seat.

Steve leaned over to talk to Kathy. "I saw the press conference. You need to put that guy on a leash before he says or does something to turn the public off. Did you prep him beforehand?"

Kathy felt her cheeks warm. "Of course I did. Do I look like a first year associate?"

Steve just waited.

Kathy took a deep breath and blew it out. "Sorry. I specifically told him to let me do the talking to the press and look what he did."

Steve chuckled. "We've all been there, Kiddo. Sometimes they just blow their tops no matter how much we prep them." He shrugged. "Hopefully, he'll see the error of his ways when he sees how they portray him in the news."

"I'll be sure to play the news clip over and over for him until he does," Kathy said.

"Now, now, don't go alienating the client so early in the representation. At least get to know him first," Steve said.

Kathy sighed. "I'm going to need pearls of wisdom like that throughout this case. Keep them coming."

"I've got a million of them," he said.

Kathy smiled. "I bet you do."

"Excuse me," a voice said from behind Kathy, "are you

here on the Morgan case?"

Kathy looked over her shoulder and recognized Stewart Weisman from the photo on his law firm's website.

"Yes," she said. "You must be Stewart Weisman."

"That's right," he said. He shook her hand and then looked over at Steve. "Hello Steve. Are you here to watch over your protégé?"

Steve smiled. "Hello Stewart. You'll learn soon enough that Kathy doesn't need my protection. It's usually her coming to my rescue."

Weisman chuckled. "Fair enough." He turned to Kathy. "We haven't had a chance to confer on the motions to be heard by the court today."

Kathy frowned. "Motions? The only motion noticed for hearing today is the motion to dismiss."

"Didn't you receive our re-notice? We added on a motion for protective order concerning the discovery," he said.

"Added on? When did you do that? My office never received any motion for protective order or a re-notice. Since you failed to provide my client with adequate notice on the motion for protective order, we do not agree to have that motion heard today. What did you have in mind with respect to the motion to dismiss?"

"We don't believe your client has stated a viable cause of action for gross negligence. Why don't we just submit an agreed order dismissing the complaint and giving you twenty days to amend it?" he asked.

Kathy smiled. Yeah right. He wished she was green enough to fall for that one. "Stewart, I'm afraid we'll have to reject that offer, such as it is. The complaint clearly states a claim and, if, for some reason, the judge believes otherwise, we won't need twenty days to amend it."

Stewart shrugged. "I guess we'll just have to take it up with the court."

"I guess so," she said. She turned to look at Steve. He winked at her.

"All rise!" The bailiff called the court to order. The noise level in the courtroom decreased from a low roar to near silence save for the sound of attorneys, reporters and bystanders snapping to their feet.

Judge Evelyn McCarthy, a statuesque redhead with her hair pulled back into a tight bun at the nape of her neck walked briskly into the courtroom and took her place on the bench. Cameras flashed and popped as she took a moment to survey the scene. She raised her eyebrows. "I see we have a full house this morning. We also have a full hearing schedule so there will be no time for theatrics or shenanigans in front of the cameras. If I detect even a hint of that, I will clear this courtroom of everyone except counsel and their clients." She rapped her gavel. "Call the first case."

While the first hearing took place, Kathy ran through her arguments in her mind. She felt a slight sense of panic as she replayed her conversation with Weisman in her head. She didn't doubt he'd try to get his client's motion for protective order heard this morning. She just hoped Judge McCarthy didn't let him.

"Charles Morgan, Jr. versus Peachtree Consulting and Thomas Wilkes," the bailiff called.

Kathy looked over at Charles and smiled reassuringly at him. He smiled back and nodded at her. She gathered her papers and her wits and left the gallery to stand behind one of the counsel tables.

"Please make your appearances," the judge said.

"Kathy Brooks from Gold, Rome & Harris for the plaintiff, Charles Morgan, Jr., your Honor."

"Good morning, your Honor. Stewart Weisman for the defendants."

"Thank you," Judge McCarthy said. "I see that we're here on a motion to dismiss. I don't usually hold oral argument on such motions, but I noticed there was no certification that counsel made a good faith effort to confer on the motion. I want to make it clear, to both parties, that this court expects counsel to confer on all motions prior to filing them with the court. Is that understood?"

"Yes, your Honor," Kathy said.

"Of course, your Honor. Let the record reflect that Ms. Brooks and I conferred this morning on both the motion to dismiss and Defendant's motion for protective order," Weisman said.

Kathy shot a brief look at him. He was a smooth bastard. She'd have to watch out for him. She turned back to the judge.

"Actually, your Honor, that's not entirely true. We did confer this morning, in this courtroom, over the motion to dismiss. At that time, Mr. Weisman informed me that he had filed a motion for protective order and noticed it for hearing as an add-on; however, my office never received the motion or any notice of hearing," Kathy said.

A frown appeared on Judge McCarthy's brow. She turned to her computer monitor and punched a few buttons. "According to the certificate of service on the motion, it was filed late last night." She gave Weisman a stern look. "This is clearly inadequate notice. There will be no hearing on the motion for protective order this morning. I am referring the motion to be heard by Magistrate Judge Jacobs at a later date. As for the motion to dismiss, it is denied. You need to know now that I will not tolerate sharp practices in my courtroom. I expect for attorneys practicing in this court to have conferred on motions prior to filing them or, at the very least, well in advance of any hearing. I also expect parties to provide each other with adequate notice. Otherwise there will be sanctions. Have I made myself clear?"

"Yes, your Honor," Kathy said.

"Completely, your Honor. My apologies to the Court and to counsel for any misunderstandings," Weisman said.

"This hearing is adjourned. Have a nice day, counsel." Judge McCarthy slammed down her gavel.

Kathy headed back to the gallery flushed with success. The feeling didn't last long. She could see, from the grim expression on Charles' face that she had a lot of explaining to do about the motion for protective order. She stopped walking when she felt a hand touch her elbow. It was Weisman.

"Counselor," he said. "May I have a word?"

"Yes." She turned back to Charles and held up a hand to tell him to wait for her. She then caught Steve's eye and inclined her head toward Charles. He nodded. She followed Weisman out of the courtroom and into one of the small conference rooms just outside.

"You did a nice job in there," he said.

Kathy smiled. Actually, he'd done a nice job on himself. They both knew the easiest way to piss off a judge was to be less than civil or to break protocol. He had done both. "Thank you. You too."

It was his turn to smile. "I wanted to take this opportunity to see if we can explore the possibility of settling this case. Peachtree Consulting is a large government defense contractor. They don't have time to deal with nuisances like this, so I've been asked to ascertain where your client's head is at in terms of resolving this matter."

"I'm not at liberty to discuss my client's thoughts on any subject matter due to that pesky little thing called the attorney-client privilege; however, I have been authorized to tell you that my client is not interested in engaging in settlement discussions at this time," she said.

"What do you mean he's not interested in settlement discussions? Everybody has a number. Look, you don't need to play games here to get a higher settlement offer. Just let me know the ballpark we're playing in and I'll see if we can make it happen," Stewart said.

Kathy felt her jaw drop. The nerve of this man to accuse her of playing games when he and his law firm were known to be the biggest game players around. "Contrary to popular belief, there are some people in this world who cannot be bought." She knew she had said too much when she saw the realization dawn on his face.

"Oh, so we've got ourselves a crusader here. Well, you be sure to advise your client that revenge can be costly – in more ways than one."

"What I advise my client of is none of your business. Look, if you've got a settlement offer to make, put it in writing and I'll pass it along. If there's nothing else, I have to go. I have a full plate today," Kathy said. She turned toward the door, then stopped and turned back when she felt a hand on her arm.

"There is one more thing," Weisman said. "Steve and I

have always had a cordial relationship even though we're usually on opposite sides. My clients have a vested interest in preserving their defense contracts. To do that, they've got to uphold national security interests. The discovery you served in this case is extremely broad and delves into areas best left alone. If this case doesn't settle, things are going to get ugly. Neither my client nor the government can afford to let certain top secret information, for which neither you nor your client have clearance, get out. I'm sure you have an idea how far the government will go to protect national security interests."

Kathy looked pointedly down at the hand that was still holding her arm. He released her. She looked up at him, her eyes narrowed into slits. "Are you threatening me, Weisman?"

Weisman crossed his arms and shrugged. A disingenuous smile spread across his face.

"Not at all, Counselor," he said. "I'm just discussing the potential ramifications of allowing this case to run its course. I'm sure you've watched enough television to know what happens when the government feels threatened. I just don't want to see you get caught in the cross-fire."

His words sent a pang of fear through her. Kathy, a lover of spy novels and action movies, could very well imagine what a government or rogue defense contractor might do to protect its interests. She couldn't let him see how his words had affected her, so she looked him dead in the eye. "Well, at least one of us has been watching way too much television. As I said, put any settlement offer your client wants to make in writing and I'll pass it along. Maybe we could reach an agreement."

On that note, she left the conference room and headed to the ladies' room down the hall. Once inside, she sank onto a couch in the small sitting area just inside the restroom door and replayed the conversation in her mind. There were no two ways about it. He had definitely made a veiled threat. She'd have to talk to Bill about this and figure out the best way to handle it. She took a deep, cleansing breath before standing up and heading back to the courtroom.

CHAPTER III

Donald Peachtree hung up the telephone, a scowl covering his face. So, Charles Morgan, Jr. was hell bent on revenge and had no interest in settling the lawsuit. Well, they'd just have to get that black bastard to change his mind.

He sat back in his chair. Normally, when he encountered an obstacle like this in the field, he just had it removed – swiftly and brutally. However, with all of the publicity this case had generated, he knew that wouldn't be the smartest choice to make at this time.

He had to be patient. He knew how to do that. He was a hunter. Sometimes he'd lie in wait for hours to get his prey. He knew the virtues of waiting for just the right moment and then pouncing.

He sighed. Sometimes he missed the old days when things were simpler. Back then, the public was only interested in containing threats to the country – not in the details of how such missions were accomplished. There weren't so many constraints, so much Congressional oversight, so many rules. It was almost impossible for the government to accomplish its mandate of protecting the people with all that tying it hands. That's where companies like his came in.

He sat there for a moment and came up with a plan. He didn't discount the settlement option. He firmly believed that every man had his price. Sometimes that price wasn't money. Sometimes a man needed to be persuaded to accept money in lieu of other perceived rewards or punishments. He would provide that persuasion.

A grin replaced the scowl on his face. He pushed the intercom button for his assistant.

"Yes?" The sound of Giada's low, sexy voice never failed to send a little rush of excitement through him. It reminded him of the things she could do to a man. He thought for a split second about calling her into his office then he shook it off. He had to take care of business first. There would be time for pleasure later.

"Giada find McAllister and send him in."

"Yes Sir."

A few moments later, there was a knock at the door.

"Come in."

McAllister strolled in. He was a tall, muscular, good-looking guy with blonde hair and green eyes women always went for. His laid back demeanor hid a man who was truly driven and exceptionally talented in both espionage and wet work. He was Peachtree's right hand man. He stopped to stand behind the chairs in front of Peachtree's desk.

"You wanted to see me, Sir?"

"Yes." Peachtree gestured to the chairs. McAllister took a seat.

"This is about the Morgan case. What intel have you gathered on him so far?"

McAllister shrugged. "Everything we have is in the file I left on your desk. He went into the Marines ROTC then he served for four years in the Corps. He worked as a corporate security specialist for a couple of years before becoming a novelist. He wrote some pretty good spy novels that became bestsellers. After his wife died, he began to write children's books. They made one of his books into a movie. He owns a condo in Key Biscayne and a boat that's docked at the Key Biscayne Marina."

Peachtree raised his eyebrows. "So, we've got a Marine on our hands. We'll just have to take that into consideration. In the meantime, I want you to arrange for twenty-four hour surveillance on this guy. I also want someone to check out his online activity. I want to know what he likes to do in his free time, what he eats for dinner, who he's seeing and what's important to him. Is that clear?"

"Yes Sir," McAllister said. He stood up. "Is that all?"

"Yes, for now."

McAllister nodded. "I'll get right on it."

"Good."

***

Charles sat at the conference room table reading an e-mail from his agent on his I-Phone when Kathy Brooks walked into the room. He looked up and was once again confronted by her beauty. She was a damned good-looking woman. At 5'8" (almost 5'11" in heels) she was on the tall side for a woman, with a curvy figure, a café-au-lait complexion, long legs, and full, sensuous lips that made a man's mind wander when she talked. She was dressed in a black pantsuit with a gold toned silk blouse and a necklace made of multiple strands of black beads at her neck. Her hair, as usual, was pulled up into a bun and her slightly flashy gold-rimmed Chanel glasses, were, for once, up on the bridge of her nose where they belonged. She looked like a cross between a sexy librarian and a businesswoman in a power suit. He wondered what she looked like with her hair down and those glasses off.

She smiled at him and extended her hand. "Hello Charles. How are you this morning?"

He stood up. "I'm fine, thank you. You?"

"Very well, thank you. Can I offer you some coffee or a bagel or something?" She gestured toward the coffee and breakfast set-up on the credenza on the side of the conference room.

He glanced over and contemplated the offerings. There were bagels, danishes, and sugar-laden little Cuban pastries called *pastelitos*. None of it appealed to him. "I'll take a cup of coffee."

Kathy walked over to the credenza, set up two cups and poured coffee into one and hot water into the other. She then reached into her pants pocket and extracted a teabag and a small green and white packet from inside. She dunked the teabag into the cup of hot water, then ripped open the packet and emptied its contents into the cup. She turned to him. "How do you take your coffee?"

"I take it black. What is that you just put into your cup?"

"I don't drink coffee. I drink green tea. That was a teabag and a packet of sweetener you saw me put in there," she said.

"So you don't use regular sugar or the pink or the yellow or the blue packet either?"

She laughed. "No, being the high maintenance gal that I am, I have to use something entirely different. It's called Truvia. It's made from the stevia plant."

"From the *what* plant?"

Kathy rolled her eyes and smiled at him. "Never mind. Here's your coffee." She put his coffee cup and saucer on the table in front of him before taking her seat. She stirred her tea. "I called you in to talk to you about the next steps in the case. But first, as your counsel, I'm duty bound to tell you that I received a written settlement offer yesterday from counsel for Peachtree," she said. She extracted a letter from a manila folder and slid it across the table toward him.

Charles skimmed it. They were offering him a million dollars to settle the lawsuit. He slid it back to her. "No deal."

Kathy nodded, approval in her eyes. "I thought you'd say that. Well, the next step is for the Court to rule on Peachtree's motion for protective order. In their motion, they claim that information pertaining to the work the driver was engaged in at the time of the accident is 'need to know' only. They say they're willing to stipulate that Wilkes was engaged in authorized company business at the time of the accident to avoid having to answer the discovery requests we served on them."

Charles took a sip of his coffee. He had reason to believe Peachtree was involved in illegal activities at the time of the accident. He needed to prove that to put Peachtree out of business. The best way to get that proof was through discovery in his civil case. Peachtree wouldn't be able to deny the authenticity of the documents it produced or the veracity of the interrogatory answers it provided under oath. He had to find a way to make that happen.

He looked at Kathy and debated whether or not to reveal

his ultimate goal. On one hand, if she knew the plan, she could devote her efforts to helping him implement it instead of being so focused on winning the lawsuit itself. On the other hand, she might react badly. As an attorney, he understood the possible conflicts she might face if she knew the lawsuit was only a means to an end for him.

He couldn't put his finger on it, but there was something about her that made him want to confide in her. He was probably just distracted by the attraction he felt for her. He hadn't felt this attracted to any woman since his wife's death. It felt strange to sit there working on his plan to avenge Patti's death while, at the same time, thinking about how attracted he was to the attorney helping him do it. He shifted in his seat.

No, he couldn't confide in her. He couldn't afford to let a pretty face, a sexy voice and an intriguing personality get in the way of his mission. He'd done that once before while serving on a mission in the Corps. It had nearly gotten him killed. He set his coffee cup back onto the saucer. "What are the chances the Court will grant Peachtree's motion?"

"I'd say about forty percent," she said. "The standard for civil discovery is very broad. We're entitled to discover things that might even arguably lead to the discovery of admissible evidence. The judge has to weigh our interest in receiving the discovery to prove our case against their supposed interest in protecting national security interests. I'm not buying the national security argument though."

"Why not? Peachtree is a well-known defense contractor."

"I know. But, so far, they haven't submitted any affidavits from government officials in support of the motion. They still have time to do that, but the fact they haven't yet looks a little suspicious to me. Even if the Court buys their national security defense, it will probably choose less drastic ways to protect the information than precluding us from receiving it at all."

"Less drastic measures? Like what?" he asked.

"Like entering a confidentiality order."

"What sort of restrictions would a confidentiality order have?"

"Well, the court could order that any documents produced by Peachtree that are designated as being highly confidential be provided on an 'attorney's eyes only' basis. In that case, I couldn't show you the documents. The court could also bar the press from the courtroom at trial and sequester the jury until they reach a verdict."

Charles leaned forward in his seat. "That's not what I want at all. We have to do everything possible to prevent that."

Kathy looked at him, a slight frown appearing between her brows. "Okay, but might I ask why? I mean, whether or not the public gets to sit in on the trial won't necessarily have an impact on the outcome of the case."

He shook his head. "Don't play dumb. I told you during our first meeting that I wanted to make this as public and painful for Peachtree as possible. I can't do that if the Court enters an order allowing them to keep all of their dirty laundry under wraps."

"Well, just so you know, it's very likely the court will enter a confidentiality order no matter how much we fight it," she said. "Confidentiality orders are pretty routine and you haven't given me a legitimate reason to not have one entered in this case. Your desire to embarrass Peachtree publicly is not a valid argument against having the order entered. You don't have the right to share information we obtain in discovery to third parties who are not involved in the lawsuit."

"What would happen if the information made it out into the public domain despite the entry of a confidentiality order?" he asked.

Kathy stared at him. "If you're planning to blatantly disobey a Court order, I must advise you against it. The consequences of such an action could be severe."

"What sort of consequences are we talking about?" he asked.

"The court could enter an order preventing us from being able to use any information leaked to the public to prove your case or it could dismiss your case altogether. The court could even fine or throw you jail for contempt. So please, please, don't even think about taking such an action," she said. "Nothing good would come of that."

"I never said I was planning to disobey an order of the Court. Anyone could be the source of a leak – someone at Peachtree trying to get the case thrown out, someone from your office, someone at the Court. Everyone wants their fifteen minutes of fame."

"Well, we'll just have to do everything we can to make sure that doesn't happen," she said.

They looked at each other – his gaze wide-eyed and innocent, hers narrow and suspicious. The tension in the room became so thick you could cut it with a knife.

There was a knock at the conference room door. Annette walked in carrying a document. Neither Kathy nor Charles broke eye contact. Annette looked curiously from one to the other before placing the document onto the conference room table in front of Kathy.

Kathy broke the stare first and looked up. "Thank you, Annette."

"No problem," Annette said. She glanced at Charles again and then left.

Kathy scanned the document. "This is a notice from the Court setting a hearing on Defendant's Motion for Protective Order on Friday morning at 10:00 a.m."

Charles pulled out his I-Phone and checked his calendar. "I'm available then."

"You don't have to be there," she said. "It's just motion practice. I can call you afterwards and tell you what happened."

So, she didn't want him there. Well, he had a right to be there and he would be. It was as simple as that. "I'll be there."

CHAPTER IV

At 9:30 a.m. on Friday morning, Charles and Kathy stood on the steps of the C. Clyde Atkins courthouse where the magistrate judges were housed. It was an older, more traditional courthouse building than the very modern Wilkie D. Ferguson, Jr. Courthouse.

Once again, news reporters surrounded them and shouted questions. This time though, Charles let Kathy do the talking.

"Do you think the Court is going to grant the defendants' motion for protective order?" one reporter asked.

"We certainly hope not. Liberal discovery is one of the bedrocks of our legal system. That's why the standard for seeking to prevent discovery is so high," Kathy said. "Now, if you'll excuse us, we have to go inside and prepare for the hearing. Thank you."

Charles and Kathy headed into the courthouse. They took a seat at the counsel's table on the right hand side of the courtroom. It was a smaller courtroom than Judge McCarthy's, decorated more traditionally in wood and polished brass.

Weisman, Donald Peachtree, Wilkes, and a man whom Kathy did not recognize, sat at the other counsel's table. Weisman rose from his seat and walked over to Kathy. "Good morning, Counselor. Mr. Morgan." He nodded at Charles.

Charles nodded back.

"Good morning, Stewart," Kathy said.

"Do you have a moment?" Weisman inclined his head toward the back of the courtroom.

"Yes." She got up and followed him into one of the small conference rooms just outside the courtroom.

"Has your client had a chance to consider our rather generous settlement offer?"

"Yes, he has. Your office should have received our letter by now rejecting it," she said.

He raised his eyebrows. "I see. Well, does your client intend to make a counteroffer?" He held up a hand to stave off any protest she might make.

"I know that you're not able to discuss your client's intentions with me. It's just that, my client has provided me with a certain amount of settlement authority. If we're able to resolve this matter now, we could announce a settlement to the Court and obviate the need for the hearing. So, is there an amount at which your client would be willing to settle this case?"

"I am not authorized to negotiate settlement with you at this time," she said.

He grimaced. "Okay. Well, moving on to the next order of business. Have you given any thought to withdrawing your discovery requests in light of our agreement to stipulate that Mr. Wilkes was engaged in authorized company business at the time of the accident?"

"Yes," she said. "We still need that discovery, so we reject the offer to enter into a stipulation. But thank you for the offer, though."

Weisman frowned. "I see. Well, I guess that's all for now." He walked over to the conference room door and held it open for her. He made a slight bow and swept his arm toward the opening. "After you, Counselor."

"Thank you," she said.

He followed her into the courtroom and they took their respective seats.

Charles leaned over toward her. "What did he want?"

"Later." She stood up as the door to the judge's chambers opened.

"All rise!" the bailiff called.

Everyone in the courtroom rose to their feet as Magistrate Judge Jacobs walked in and took his seat. He was a tall, burly, African-American man, with a full beard and a stern expression on his face. He cut an imposing figure in his judicial robes. "You may be seated." His deep booming voice resonated with authority. He looked down at the lawyers. "Counselors, please make your appearances for the record."

"Kathy Brooks from Gold, Rome & Harris on behalf of the plaintiff, Charles Morgan, Jr., your honor. Also with me is my paralegal, Jim Mann."

"Stewart Weisman here on behalf of Defendants, your Honor. With me is Mr. Donald Peachtree, the President of Peachtree Consulting, and the individual Defendant, Mr. Thomas Wilkes."

"We are here today on Defendants' motion for protective order," Judge Jacobs said. "I have read ----."

"Excuse me, your Honor," Kathy said, "but I don't believe the man sitting at the end of defense counsel's table has been introduced." It was normally a huge *faux pas* to interrupt a judge – especially a federal one - but she couldn't allow the opportunity to pass without forcing Weisman to introduce the mystery man sitting next to him. Weisman stared at Kathy blandly for a brief moment before addressing the judge.

"Oh that was an oversight, your Honor. This gentleman is David Bradford from the U.S. Attorney's office. He's here today in case your Honor requires testimony with respect to the confidential nature of the information at issue in the motion," he said.

"I object to the taking of any testimony from this witness your Honor. This hearing was not noticed as an evidentiary hearing and we had no notice whatsoever that it would be," she said.

Judge Jacobs looked sternly at Weisman. "She's correct, Counselor. This is not an evidentiary hearing and I will not entertain any testimony from any witnesses at this juncture. I have reviewed the motion papers and have a few questions. That's the only reason I set this oral argument. My first question is the basis for defendants' argument that information pertaining to the assignment Mr. Wilkes was working on at the time of the accident is confidential. My second question is whether the interests of national security can be served through less drastic means than precluding the discovery altogether. I'll start with counsel for the defendants first."

Stewart Weisman walked up to the podium located in between and a few feet in front of counsels' tables. "To address the first question, your Honor, we have submitted the affidavit of Mr. Donald Peachtree in which he testified that Peachtree Consulting is a government defense contractor that performs operations for the U.S. Government all over the world, many of which are highly classified. He and Mr. Wilkes have submitted affidavits stating that, at the time of the accident, Mr. Wilkes was engaged in duly authorized business of the company. In fact, he was engaged in a highly classified operation at the government's request. We brought Mr. Bradford here to testify that the U.S. government has an interest in protecting the information sought in some of the very broad ranging discovery served by the Plaintiff in the interests of national security. The dissemination of this highly classified information to the general public would be detrimental to national security interests. With respect to the second question - whether lesser relief would serve the same purpose – we submit it would not. A confidentiality order, no matter how restrictive, would still tend to place highly confidential information in the hands of persons without the necessary clearance to be read in."

Judge Jacobs' face was impassive when he turned to Kathy. She couldn't tell whether he had been swayed by Weisman's arguments or not. "Ms. Brooks, any response?"

"Yes, your Honor." She stood up and headed to the podium. Weisman stepped aside and took his seat.

"First," she said, ticking the arguments off on her fingers, "although counsel mentioned the words 'national security' several times during his argument, nowhere in the affidavits submitted by the defendants in support of their motion does it state that Mr. Wilkes was engaged in a mission vital to national security at the time of the accident. In fact, neither his nor Mr. Peachtree's affidavit states that he was working on a highly classified matter at the time of the accident. The only indication we have of that is argument of counsel, and, as we all know, argument of counsel is not evidence."

She turned to look at Weisman and watched as his lips

thinned. She then turned back to address the judge. "Second, as your Honor pointed out, any reference to the possible testimony of the assistant U.S. attorney today is improper and cannot be used as evidence."

Judge Jacobs turned to his computer and tapped a few keys. "The defendants' affidavits do state that Peachtree Consulting is a defense contractor for the U.S. government and that the information sought by Plaintiff in its discovery is classified. In light of that, and the fact that the defendants are willing to enter into a stipulation that Mr. Wilkes was engaged in authorized company business at the time of the accident, I'm inclined to grant the motion for protective order."

Damn. The judge was about to grant Peachtree's motion. She had no choice but to go to her fallback position and ask for less drastic measures even though she knew Charles would not be happy.

"Your honor, even if the Court believes that Peachtree has met its burden of proof, there are less drastic means of safeguarding the information than precluding its production altogether such as the entry of a confidentiality order." Kathy made the mistake of looking at Charles after she made that last argument. If looks could kill, she would certainly be dead. Didn't he understand she was fighting for their lives here? Oh well, she'd just have to deal with him later.

Judge Jacobs nodded. He picked up his gavel and rapped it. "Having reviewed the motion papers and heard the arguments of counsel, I have come to a decision. The Motion for Protective Order will be granted, in part, as follows. The discovery shall be produced subject to a confidentiality order. Those documents and information designated by the defendants as highly confidential shall be produced for 'attorney's eyes only.' If there is no other business, the Court is recessed." He rapped his gavel again, set it down and stood up.

"All rise," the bailiff called out.

Everyone in the courtroom rose to their feet. Voices erupted as soon as the door to the Judge's chambers had closed behind him. Reporters raced out of the courtroom - presumably to get to their cell phones and call their editors since only attorneys were allowed to bring such devices into the building.

Kathy returned to the table to face a furious looking Charles. When he opened his mouth, she held up a hand to cut him off. "Not here," she said, quietly. "And fix your face. There are a million cameras around here. Remember?"

He gave her a grim nod before standing up and heading out of the courtroom. Kathy turned to look at Weisman. She had expected for him to look smug with his little victory, but he was busy talking to his client who looked as furious as Charles did. She followed Charles out of the courtroom.

***

The next day, Charles met his father for lunch at the Grand Bay Hotel. They sat at a corner table where they could have a little bit of privacy. His father dove into his lobster with gusto. Charles narrowed his eyes. "Are you supposed to be eating that?"

His father looked as guilty as a schoolboy caught with his hand in the cookie jar. He held an index finger up to his mouth. "Sssh," he said. "Don't tell your mother." He looked around furtively, as if half expecting his wife to show up any moment and catch him eating the shellfish.

Charles laughed. "Dad, that's the stuff that gave you gout in the first place. Shouldn't you give it a rest?"

"Shouldn't a man be able to eat what he wants to? If I

let them keep me from eating my favorite foods, then what's next? Anyway, we're not here to talk about me. I invited you out to lunch to find out how you're doing. I've been following the press coverage on your case. You didn't look too happy on the cameras there, son. How's that law firm we recommended working out?"

"They're doing a very good job actually. The lawyer they've assigned to my case is pretty sharp and good on her feet."

"I saw her on the news. She's good with the press and she's not bad-looking either."

"Don't let Mom find out you're checking out my attorney."

His father laughed. "I won't tell if you don't, son. So, if the law firm is doing a good job, why are you so unhappy?"

"It's not the law firm I have a problem with or even how the case is going. It's working within the confines of civil litigation," Charles said.

His father looked at him curiously. "In what way?"

Charles swore under his breath. He could have kicked himself for that last statement. He hadn't told his father about his ultimate plan for Peachtree Consulting. As far as his father was concerned, this was just a wrongful death lawsuit and nothing more. He didn't want his father to worry about him like he used to do when Charles was in the Corps. But his father was a very astute man and, now that he'd mentioned the confines of civil litigation, he'd have to come clean.

"Well, Dad, my sources tell me that Peachtree's operative killed Patti and our baby while playing James Bond for the C.I.A. which had no authority to hire Peachtree to conduct operations on U.S. soil in the first place. I'm not in this for the money. I won't be satisfied with just winning the lawsuit either. I'm not going to be happy until Peachtree loses all of its government contracts and goes out of business," he said.

Charles Morgan, Sr. put down his fork and took a good look at his son. "I don't need to tell you that you've chosen a very dangerous path. Defense contractors like Peachtree are filled with ex-spooks and mercs. They won't hesitate to take you out if they perceive you to be a threat." Charles opened his mouth to speak, but closed it when his father held up a hand.

"I'm not finished. I know how much you want to get those bastards. I do too. Don't forget I lost my daughter-in-law and my future grandchild in that accident. That's why I was behind you a hundred percent when you said you wanted to sue them. But I don't want to lose you too. I couldn't bear that, son."

Guilt and love for his father warred with Charles' burning need for revenge. He didn't want his father to worry about him, but he had to do what he had to do. The big man would just have to understand that. "Look Dad, you know me. I can't just walk away from this and I don't appreciate you asking me to. Those bastards have to pay for what they took away from me. A verdict – even a large one – would be nothing more than a drop in the bucket for Peachtree. Their operative was engaged in illegal operations on behalf of the C.I.A. when he rammed his car into Patti's. I'm going to use the lawsuit to expose them for what they really are."

Charles Morgan, Sr. leaned forward in his seat, reached across the table, and gripped Charles' hand. "I know that when you set your mind to something, son, nothing can change it. But have you considered the consequences of putting this plan into action? If you expose an illegal government operation, you're not only exposing Peachtree but also the government agency that hired the company. That means you'll not only piss off

Peachtree but also the C.I.A. If they even get wind of your intent, they will not hesitate to put your sorry black ass out of commission," he said

Charles pulled his hand out from under his father's and sighed. His father had never understood him and never would. "I do understand. You're just going to have to accept the fact that I have to do this and trust that I have a plan to address that contingency."

"How exactly do you plan to address it?"

"Once the information is out in the public domain, the damage will have already been done. Taking me out then wouldn't be a smart move as Peachtree and the C.I.A. would be the most obvious suspects. Plus, they'll most likely be facing an investigation," Charles said.

His father sagged back into his chair and stared at him open-mouthed. "That's your plan? Are you crazy? What's to stop them from waiting a few months when the public forgets about the case and the investigation is over? Don't you think they'll want revenge? What's your plan for that?"

Charles shrugged. "I'll handle that like I would any threat if and when the time comes."

Charles Morgan Sr. shook his head. "No. I am not going to stand by while you go and get yourself killed thinking you can take on the world. Do you hear me? Now, if you'll excuse me, I have some plans of my own to make." He stood up, threw his napkin onto the table, and walked out of the restaurant.

Charles sighed. He'd just wanted to spend a little time with his father and maybe pick his brain a little about the case. He hadn't intended to scare the man half to death. Guilt rose within him as he replayed the conversation in his head. A small sliver of doubt about his plan began to rise as well. He hadn't told his father everything. He couldn't be sure who was listening.

He looked around the large dining room of the restaurant. It was mostly filled with business men and women wearing expensive suits while they wined and dined clients. The rest of the clientele was the leisurely set one tends to see in Miami during the day – retirees, tourists and young women who either didn't have to work or who worked at night. No-one seemed out of place. No-one appeared to be watching him either. But a good surveillance team wouldn't make its presence known unless it wanted to.

Feeling exposed, he got up, dropped some money onto the table and left the restaurant.

CHAPTER V

Kathy sat at the conference room table and looked over her outline one last time. She then picked up her Blackberry and tried to put a dent in the barrage of e-mail she'd received that morning. They were nowhere near trial yet, but, nonetheless, Charles' case was consuming the lion's share of her time. If she wasn't careful, she'd drop a ball or two. She couldn't allow that to happen.

In response to the court's ruling, Peachtree Consulting had decided to play hardball. They set Charles for deposition and tried to bury Kathy in paper. Fifty-five boxes of documents had come in. Jim and Kathy had worked for days reviewing them and they still hadn't made a dent. Kathy needed to assign an associate to the case. She hoped Charles would be okay with that.

There was a knock at the conference room door. Kathy looked up to see Annette leading Charles into the room. His eyes met hers. Her pulse jumped. What was this? Whatever it was, it needed to stop. The last thing she needed was to be this attracted to her client. It would only serve to distract her from the task at hand. She couldn't afford that.

Charles smiled at her. She smiled back, uncrossed her legs, stood up and held out her hand to shake his. He clasped it warmly. "Good morning, Counselor."

"Good morning Charles. Please have a seat." Kathy extracted her hand from his and turned to look at Annette, who stood there, smiling. "Thank you, Annette. Please hold all of my calls for the next few hours."

"Okay. Give me a call if you need anything. I've already arranged for lunch to be brought in." Annette continued to stand there.

"Okay. I will." Kathy caught Annette's eye and jerked her head a little toward the door. Annette cleared her throat and left.

Kathy turned to Charles who sat at the conference room table with an amused expression on his face. She raised her eyebrows. "You'd better watch out for my secretary. She's quite taken with you."

Charles grinned and shrugged. "I sometimes have that effect on women."

"I bet," she said. "Can I offer you some coffee before we get started?"

"I'll get it," he said. He got up and headed over to the credenza. "Do you want some tea while I'm up here?"

Kathy smiled. His question reminded her of something her father used to say about how it would be nice for her to find a "special friend" to make her a nice cup of tea from time to time. Well here was a man offering to do just that and he was off limits.

Why were all the good ones unattainable? They were either married, about to get married or, in this case, untouchable.

If only they could have met under different circumstances. It would have been interesting to see just how far it would go. Of course, he'd probably end up being a liar and a cheat like all the other men in her life.

"Yes, I'd like a cup. I just need some hot water. I have my teabag and my sweetener right here," she said.

She watched as he put two cups into saucers, poured out his coffee and her hot water and grabbed spoons and napkins. He placed her cup in front of her and took his seat. She made her tea. He took a sip of his coffee.

"So," she said, "I asked you to come in this morning for two reasons. One, defendants have set a date for your deposition and we have to get you ready for that. Two, defendants have produced documents and interrogatory answers in response to the discovery we served on them. Unfortunately, -."

He put down his coffee cup and sat upright in his chair. "They produced documents and answered the interrogatories? What did they say?"

She held up a hand to ward him off. "As I was saying, unfortunately, they've designated every single one of the interrogatory answers and the documents they produced as being highly confidential. That means they're 'attorney's eyes only' and I can't show them to you or tell you what they say."

Charles' hands balled into fists. "That's ridiculous! You mean to tell me that every single one of those interrogatory answers and every page of those documents contains highly classified information? Come on."

Kathy shrugged. "I agree. It's utterly ridiculous for them to have designated all of the discovery responses as being highly confidential. We intend to challenge that. I've read the interrogatory answers. They're so vague and evasive that nothing in them could possibly raise national security concerns. Jim and I have gone through ten of the fifty boxes of documents they produced and, so far, we've yet to see a single document raising national security implications."

"The old bury them in paper trick." Charles blew out a breath and slumped back into his chair. "This would go so much faster if I could help you look through those documents."

"I don't doubt it," Kathy said. "But look, they've played this trick on the wrong law firm. We're used to dealing with large volumes of discovery. We've already scanned and loaded the documents into a document database program and made them fully searchable. Jim and I can log onto the system, access the documents on our laptops and review them anytime from anywhere."

Charles perked up a little. "Well at least that's something. So, how long will it take for you and Jim to finish reviewing those documents and for us to make our next move?"

Kathy grimaced. "It's slow going with just the two of us. It's going to take us at least another week just to get our arms around what they've given us so that we can complain about what they haven't. Jim is preparing a chart of the types of documents we have and what we can tell is missing. But he needs more direction from an attorney and, at my hourly rate, it's just not feasible. With your permission, I'd like to bring on an associate to help out. She'd be able to focus on the project and do it at a lower hourly rate."

He waved a hand. "I told you money wasn't a problem. Do whatever you have to do."

She smiled. "Let's hope you remember this conversation when you get our bill."

He returned her smile. "I'm more likely to remember it

in the event we win."

She grimaced. "No pressure. Oh well, I guess I'd better start earning my fee." She picked up a manila folder and extracted an outline from it. She then folded her hands on the table and gave him a serious look.

Charles' smile slowly faded. A small frown creased his eyebrows. "What?"

"Have you ever been deposed before?"

"No."

"Your deposition will probably take place in a conference room in Weisman's office. I'll be there, Weisman will be there, a representative of Peachtree and Wilkes might attend, as well as a court reporter and a videographer. Weisman will ask you questions under oath and the court reporter will take everything down. When you answer his questions, there are some important things you need to remember. First, no matter how upsetting or insulting the questions, do not, under any circumstances, go on a rant. Only answer the question asked. Nothing more."

He raised his eyebrows. "So, based on the fact that I lost my cool during the first press conference, you think I'm likely to go spouting off at the mouth during my deposition." He shook his head. "That's not going to happen. I learned my lesson when I saw the replay of that news clip. I promise not to lose my cool anymore - on camera or off."

"Good," she said. "Let's hope you're a man of your word, because that promise is going to be harder to keep than you can possibly imagine. I learned that the hard way when I was deposed in my divorce case. I thought I had it all under control ---."

"Wait – you're divorced?" he asked.

"Yes. Why do you look so shocked by that? Does my being divorced offend your sensibilities?"

"No. It's just that I imagined you as the quintessential career woman – dedicated to the law and duty and all that. I didn't see you as the marrying type. So what happened? Did working all hours of the day and night put a damper on things?"

She stiffened. "My personal life has no relevance here. What is relevant is that Peachtree is going to dig into your personal life with a vengeance during this deposition. The point I was trying to make is that, no matter how personal or offensive their questions might seem, you're going to have to answer them - candidly and without losing your cool. That is, unless I instruct you not to. The deposition will be videotaped and they have the right to play the video at trial. The jury will have the opportunity to see every expression on your face and hear every inflection in your voice."

"I see." He tugged at the knot of his tie as if trying to keep it from choking him.

"Not really," she said, "but you will. I've prepared an outline of potential deposition questions. We're going to run through them so I can evaluate how you answer them."

They ran through the list of preliminary background questions about education and employment. Kathy learned a lot about him. She hadn't known that he was an ex-Marine, for example, or that he and his wife had met when they were both serving in the armed services. She was a Navy nurse assigned to a Navy hospital overseas. They met when he was wounded and she nursed him back to health. It was a story straight out of a romance novel. Kathy couldn't help but feel a little envious. She got over that feeling quickly when he got to the year of Patricia's death.

"I was on the road all the time doing book tours and, when I was home, I was locked away writing the next book," he said. "Patti was complaining about never getting to spend time with me anymore. One morning, we got into a heated argument."

He paused, getting up to pour himself a glass of water. He sat down, set his cup onto the table and closed his eyes. "That was the last time I ever spoke to her. I told her to stop whining and that I was too busy to deal with her bullshit. I didn't even tell her that I loved her. "

Kathy knew the story all too well. It was the tale of many lawyers and other busy professionals whose jobs demanded too much of their time. She imagined that his arguments with his wife were not so very different from the ones she used to have with her ex-husband when she had killed herself working seventy or more hours a week to make partner at her law firm. Eventually, he stopped arguing with her and used her work schedule as an excuse to have an affair with his secretary.

Charles was so obviously in pain that Kathy put her hand over his to comfort him. "Patti knew that you loved her. You were under a great deal of stress. I'm sure she understood that."

He opened his eyes, turned his hand around in hers and gave her hand a gentle squeeze. "Thank you. I never told anyone else that."

She wiggled her eyebrows at him to lighten the mood. "We have ways of making you talk," she said, using what she imagined to be a Transylvanian accent.

He chuckled. "Let's hope counsel for Peachtree isn't as good at making me talk as you are."

She smiled at him, squeezed his hand lightly and then released it. "Okay. Although it's hard to imagine a line of questioning more intimate than that, the next set of questions are designed to deal with your claim for loss of consortium. Here, they get to ask you questions about your sex life with Patti – whether either of you ever had an extra-marital affair, which one of you prepared the meals, did the housework, and so on and so forth. Would you like to take a short break before we begin?"

He stared at her open-mouthed for a second. "No." The word came out in a croak.

Kathy smothered a smile and raised an eyebrow.

Charles cleared his throat and gestured for her to proceed.

"So, how would you describe your sex life with your wife?" she asked.

When they were done with that line of questions, the room seemed a little warm to Kathy. She got up to adjust the temperature on the thermostat on the wall. She knew it was completely unprofessional for her to be intrigued by her client's answers, but she couldn't help but wonder what it would be like to be married to the man. According to Charles, despite their arguments, he and his wife made love three to four times a week. And they were in their fifth year of marriage. They must have been very much in love and the sex must have been incredible.

Charles watched her adjust the thermostat. "I have a request to make."

"Yes?"

"Well, it's just not fair that you get to learn the most intimate details of my life and I don't get to learn anything about you," he said. "So, in the interests of fairness, I propose that we go out for drinks later on and you allow me to get to know you a little better."

She frowned. "Charles, are you asking me out on a date?

If so, I need to tell you that GRH has a very strict anti-fraternization policy. We're not allowed to date our clients. There are also ethical rules that come into play."

He shook his head. "No, I just like to know who I'm dealing with. It's not unusual for attorneys and their clients to network and socialize outside of the office. You and I have never even had lunch together and here we are discussing the most intimate details of my relationship with my wife. I just thought having a drink together after work might be a more conducive setting in which to get to know you."

It made perfect sense. Here she was accusing the man of wanting to take her out on a date when all he wanted to do was to get to know the person with whom he'd just shared his life story. If she were a man, she wouldn't think twice about the invitation. In fact, she'd probably relish the opportunity to do a little male bonding with the client over a beer after work. The fact that she was a woman who was undeniably attracted to him tended to complicate things. But she'd have to get over that if she wanted to be successful in bringing in business. "In that case, I'd love to have a drink with you after work. Why don't we meet at O'Shaughnessy's Grill on the Beach, at say, eight o'clock?"

He smiled. "Sounds like a plan."

***

Later that afternoon, Charles Morgan, Sr. stood up to greet his son's best friend. Tyler Fox was shorter than Mr. Morgan, with a darker complexion and a stocky build. The two men engaged in an elaborate handshake and gave each other a man hug. Mr. Morgan gestured for Tyler to have a seat. He then eased a hip onto the side of his desk. "It's good to see you, son. How long has it been?"

"Last Thanksgiving when I had dinner here," Tyler said.

He pat his stomach. "There's nothing like Mama Morgan's cooking."

Mr. Morgan chuckled. "I've got to agree with you there, son. Listen, I asked you to come see me today because I need your help."

"Anything for you, Mr. Morgan," Tyler said. "What kind of help are we talking about?"

"Well, you know the lawsuit Charles filed against Peachtree Consulting?"

Tyler nodded. "Yeah, he told me he was going to file the suit and it's gotten a lot of news coverage."

"Well, Charles told me the other day that he doesn't just want to get money out of Peachtree Consulting. He wants to bring the firm down."

Tyler frowned. "Bring them down? What do you mean by that?"

"He has this crazy idea that Peachtree Consulting was working for a government agency not authorized to conduct domestic operations when the accident happened. He wants to find a way to prove it and then leak that information to the public."

Tyler leaned forward in his seat. "Mr. Morgan, this is very serious business. If what Charles is saying is true, we've got rogue operatives hiring Peachtree to conduct unauthorized operations on U.S. soil."

"I know. I'm afraid he's going to get his fool self killed." Mr. Morgan rubbed his hands over his face then he stood up, walked around the desk, and sat down behind it.

"I tried to talk him out of it, but you know how he is. Once he's set his mind to something, nothing can stop him. You two are like brothers. Hell, you spent so much time at my house growing up I thought about claiming you on my tax returns. Can you talk to him? If you can't talk him out of it, can you at least get the F.B.I. to protect him?"

Tyler grimaced. "I'll talk to him. But you know how the F.B.I. is - strictly by the book. They're going to want to open up an investigation and they're going to want him to testify. Does he have any proof?"

Mr. Morgan shrugged. "He didn't say. The Court did order Peachtree Consulting to produce documents. Maybe there's something in there." He shrugged again. "Thank you for helping me with this."

"No need to thank me, Mr. Morgan. With all those great meals I've eaten at your dinner table over the years, it's the least I can do. Don't worry. I'll look into this."

***

That evening, Kathy walked into O'Shaughnessy's - a dimly lit Irish pub popular with off-duty Miami Beach police officers. Kathy liked it because it was in her neighborhood, the drinks weren't watered down and she felt safe. It also served up some pretty good food.

Charles was already seated at the bar with some sort of amber colored liquor in a low-ball in front of him. Kathy nodded and waved at some of the patrons who greeted her. She walked up to him, looked at his glass and raised her eyebrows. "Hi there. I see you've started without me."

Charles smiled and shrugged. "Well, you are five minutes late."

Kathy grimaced. "Sorry about that. At least five people stopped me on the way out of the office and traffic was terrible tonight."

The bartender set a glass of pinot noir onto the bar in front of her. "The girl works too hard, I say." He had a thick Irish accent. "You need to distract her more often. It's rare to see her out and about before nine of an evening."

Kathy put an index finger to her lips. "Now, now, Roarke, don't go telling the man all of my secrets."

Charles put his elbows onto the bar and rested his chin in his hands. "Please, feel free to tell me everything about her. She knows all about me."

Roarke chuckled, winked at Kathy and walked away to tend to his other customers.

"Why don't we get that table in the back over there? We can order something to snack on. I'm starving. I haven't had anything since lunch," she said.

"Sounds good."

Kathy picked up her drink and led the way over to the table. They took their seats, perused the menu and ordered some food.

Kathy settled back into her chair and turned to Charles. "So, what do you want to know about me?"

"Well, I've already learned more about you than I knew before," he said.

"Really? What have you learned?"

"That you like to drink red wine. That you like to hang out in this bar and know half the patrons. That you work late most nights. That tells me you're a dedicated professional who works long hours and comes in here to decompress. It also tells me that you live nearby, you don't cook much, you feel safe here and you're friendly."

Kathy raised her eyebrows. "That's very observant of you. I guess I need to be careful who I bring in here lest they learn too much about me. Tell me – how do you know I live nearby?"

"That's easy," he said. "You work in downtown Miami, but this bar's in South Beach. No-one who lives on the mainland would cross the causeway several times a week just to have a drink and some dinner. Besides, the Beach is a logical place for you to live. It's only fifteen minutes away from your office."

Kathy nodded. "That makes sense. I can see that. What else have you guessed about me?"

"I'll never tell," he said.

Kathy laughed.

The food came. Over dinner, they discovered they had more in common than either of them would have guessed. She discovered that he'd grown up in New York – just like she had. Only he'd lived in Long Island and she'd lived in Brooklyn. She learned that they both liked action movies; however, he didn't share her enthusiasm for spy novels.

"How can you like action movies and not spy novels?" she asked.

"I can suspend my disbelief for an action movie. It's not supposed to be realistic. But spy novels? They're totally unrealistic," he said.

"How would you know?" she asked.

He shrugged. "My best friend's an F.B.I. agent."

Kathy found herself enjoying his company immensely. He was funny and charming and oh, so sexy. She covered her wineglass with her hand when Roarke tried to pour more wine into it.

"Oh no," she said. "I've reached my limit. It's a school night."

Charles looked at her quizzically. "You're taking some classes?"

"No silly. I just meant that it's a weeknight. I have a hearing in the morning."

"Oh. Is it a hearing in my case?"

"No. Another one. And I still have some case law to look over before I go to bed. I hate to be a party pooper, but I'm going to have to leave soon."

"No problem." He signaled for the check. "Can I give you a lift?"

"You don't have to. I usually just walk. I'm only a couple of blocks away."

"It would be my pleasure."

Charles insisted upon paying the bill. She reached for it when the waitress dropped it onto the table, but he snatched it up first.

"What are you doing?" she asked. "This is on the firm – client entertainment and all that."

"No, I've got it. I haven't enjoyed good drinks, good food and nice conversation with a pretty lady in a while," he said.

Kathy frowned. "I'm not a lady, I'm your attorney."

Charles cracked up. After a second, she joined in. "Wow. Did I just say that? It's a good thing I turned down that third glass of wine. Lord only knows what would have come out of my mouth then."

"I'm going to have to get you drunk one day to find out," he said.

She shook her head and wagged her index finger at him. "No. No. It's against firm policy to get drunk with clients – you might leave a bad impression."

"Or a really good one," he said.

Kathy chuckled.

He paid the bill and they left. He drove a black, late model BMW. He opened the door for Kathy, closed it behind her and then walked over to the driver side and slid in. His car was immaculate - unlike hers which invariably had a layer of sand on it. Living close to the beach caused her car to get sandblasted often. She made a mental note to get it washed.

"Nice car," she said.

"Thank you," he said. "Now which way do I go?"

"Keep straight on this street and then follow the bend around until you see the entrance to Poinciana Towers on the left about a block up."

He whistled. "Poinciana Towers? The law business must be treating you well."

She laughed. "Don't get too excited. I don't own the unit. I'm renting."

"Renting? Girl, don't you know you're just paying someone else's mortgage? Why are you renting instead of owning?"

She shrugged. "I used to own a big house in Miami Shores but, after my divorce, I guess I just wanted to be footloose and fancy free. The thought of being tied down to one place and having a mortgage just didn't appeal to me. And then the real estate market crashed."

"All the more reason for you to scoop up a place now. You can get a good price on it. Before, they were way overpriced," he said.

"I know. I know," she said. "Bill tells me the same thing all the time. I'll buy when I'm ready to. Here we are. Just drive up to the entrance over there."

They pulled up to the entrance of her building. Charles unlocked the doors. A valet attendant opened Kathy's door. "Hello, Mrs. Brooks," he said in a heavy Cuban accent.

"Hello Ruben. Thank you." She climbed out.

Charles got out of the car and walked over to her side. Ruben turned to him. "You want me to park the car for you Sir?"

Charles shook his head. "No, I'm just saying good night to the lady."

"Okay." Ruben headed into the valet shack.

Kathy turned to Charles. "Thanks for dinner. I had a good time."

"I did too." He paused and looked into her eyes. She lowered her gaze and found herself staring at his lips. He leaned forward. For a second, she thought he was going to kiss her on the lips. He kissed her cheek instead. She felt her pulse jump at the brief contact.

"Good night," he said.

"Good night." Her voice was a little breathless.

CHAPTER VI

On Saturday afternoon, Donald Peachtree waited for his contact at TY Park in Fort Lauderdale. He had left his wife and children at a birthday party at a nearby cabana and wandered off to a bench next to the lake. He sat there watching ducks frolic as he tried to figure out what to say to Manning. A military man who'd seen more than his share of combat, Peachtree wasn't afraid of anyone. But something about Manning gave him the creeps. Maybe it was his quiet way of talking or his Zen-like calm manner. He didn't know. He just knew that if he didn't want to lose his government contracts, he had to find a way to end this mess as soon as possible.

He felt the hairs prick up on the back of his neck. He turned his head. Manning was standing behind him. "I keep telling you not to sneak up on me like that, Manning. One day, you might get yourself killed."

Manning, an unremarkable, clean cut, dark-haired guy of average height and build wearing jeans and a polo shirt, smiled. He walked around the bench, sat down next to Peachtree and looked straight ahead. "You let me worry about that, old chap."

Peachtree wondered how a Brit came to be an American spook. He should have been in MI-5 or something – not some secret government agency in the U.S. They sat there in silence. As it drew on, Peachtree shifted on the bench. He looked over at Manning who sat there watching the ducks. He never liked spooks. They tended to be odd birds who couldn't be trusted or controlled. "Look, I've got to get back to my family or they're going to wonder where I've gone. You're the one who called this meeting. What do you want?"

Manning watched the ducks for a moment more then turned his gaze to Peachtree. "It should be fairly obvious what we want to talk to you about, old chap. We want to know what you're doing to make that lawsuit go away. We've been watching the news coverage and following the progress of the case and we don't like it. Pay the man whatever he wants. This is not the time to be penny wise and pound foolish."

Peachtree's face reddened. "What? Is this my first day on the job? We're doing everything possible to make this lawsuit go away. We've already told him to make us an offer. The guy just won't settle. He's one of those cowboys out for revenge or something. We've already moved on to plan B."

"And what, exactly, is plan B?" Manning asked.

Peachtree grinned. "Plan B is to encourage him to settle. We find his pressure points and squeeze until he'd be happy to accept cash in lieu of revenge. My man is already working on that angle and we've come up with a few ideas."

Manning frowned. "Don't underestimate him Peachtree. He worked with some of our people on a few missions while he served in the Marines. He's smart and as tough as they come. He can also be ruthless. He once broke out of an Indonesian prison camp taking out nine guards in the process. If you press the bloke too hard, you might bite off more than you can chew."

Peachtree waved a hand. "My man McAllister can handle him. We can be pretty ruthless too. That's why you people hired us in the first place. By the way, McAllister brought me some pictures recently suggesting that Mr. Morgan and that lady lawyer of his might be engaged in more than an attorney/client relationship. We might be able to use that to encourage him to settle."

Manning nodded. "If your plan B doesn't work, we're going to plan C. There's too much at stake here to let Morgan find out too much. And another thing - someone at the F.B.I. has pulled your file. While there is no mention of your work for us in the official file, the last thing we need is for sister agencies to start poking around and discovering things by accident. We'd have a bit of cleanup to do then."

Peachtree was silent. Manning didn't have to say any more to convey the message. He knew what cleanup meant. It meant erasing the entire problem. If it came to that, he'd have to be ready to leave the country in a hurry.

He straightened his shoulders and looked Manning in the eye. "The only cleanup taking place here will be of Charles Morgan, Jr. if he can't be persuaded to settle. But don't worry. He will. Every man has his price. Sometimes it's just not money."

Manning nodded. "Glad to hear it, old chap." He stood up and turned to face Peachtree. "Enjoy the rest of the day with Melissa and little Amy. You'll be hearing from me soon." He strolled off.

Peachtree balled his hands into fists. How dare that bastard even mention his family? He hadn't risen through the ranks of the military allowing runts like that to shake him. He'd just have to do a little clean-up of his own when all was said and done. He took a few deep breaths and let the rage pass out of him. It was a little trick he'd learned during his work in the Far East. An angry man made mistakes. In his line of business, you couldn't afford to be angry. That, as far as he was concerned, would be Morgan's downfall. After he regained his equilibrium, he got up to join his wife and daughter at the party.

***

Later that afternoon Charles walked into an Internet café on Washington Avenue. He stopped just inside the entrance and scanned the room. People of all ages and types were huddled at computers doing everything from checking their e-mail to fixing their resumes to surfing the web. Others milled about chatting while they sipped lattes, cappuccinos and iced coffee from Styrofoam cups. Some were dressed in business suits. Others wore t-shirts and shorts. Smooth jazz blared from the speakers. The place had an almost party-like atmosphere.

One young woman wearing a pair of headphones typed furiously into what appeared to be a Word document, her face scrunched in concentration. A steaming mug sat next to the keyboard. Charles smiled, remembering the early days when he worked in Internet cafes and wore a similar expression. She was probably writing a novel.

He spotted his contact, Darryl, sitting at a table in a corner at the back of the café. Good. They'd have a little privacy. Darryl's dreadlocks were tied back with a leather strap. His eyes were glued to the monitor of his laptop as his fingers worked their magic on the keyboard. Charles wondered what he was doing. The monitor went dark as he approached the table preventing him from getting a glimpse. Darryl looked up at him.

"Ras clot!" he said. The irritated expression on his face did not clear when he saw that it was Charles who had interrupted him. He snatched up his cell phone and glanced at the time. "Chuh. You come early mon and mess up me ting. I was only a minute away from success."

"Success, huh? Big word for you. What were you working on anyway?" Charles asked.

Darryl looked around to make sure no one was listening. "Let's just say that I was doing a little fundraising for the cause."

Charles raised his eyebrows. "I see. Well maybe I can help you with that." He looked around the café. "Is there somewhere more private where we can talk?"

Darryl nodded. He packed up his laptop, grabbed his cell phone and led Charles out of the back door of the café. They crossed a parking lot and then the street behind it and headed into a small West Indian bakery. The smell of curry and other exotic spices permeated the air. An older woman manned the counter. Darryl nodded at her. She nodded back and watched them stroll through a door at the back of the shop. They walked down a short hall and made a left into Darryl's lair.

Computers, printers, scanners, cameras and other high-tech equipment were strewn throughout the space which looked as if it belonged in a lab instead of the back of a Caribbean bakery. Darryl put an index finger to his lips, took a seat behind a huge u-shaped console, and flipped a switch underneath it. A red light appeared on the console that soon turned green. Darryl looked up at Charles and gestured toward a seat in front of the desk.

"We're clean now, mon," he said.

Charles sat down. "I need your help."

"It's been a long time since ya' come here seeking my assistance. I thought you were out of the game," Darryl said.

Charles nodded. "Yeah, you're right. Officially, I am out of the game. But I still require your assistance. Is that a problem?"

Darryl grinned. "Nah mon. In my book that makes you a better client. I don't have to give you the government discount anymore."

Charles grinned. "Still enterprising I see. No. I don't qualify anymore for the government discount, but maybe you could cut me a little break for old time's sake."

Darryl nodded. "What ya' need?"

"I need to break into a law firm computer system and download documents kept in a database there. You probably heard about the lawsuit I brought against Peachtree Consulting, right?"

"Yah mon. It's all over the news."

"Well, Peachtree got a confidentiality order entered and produced documents to my attorney on an 'attorneys eyes only' basis. That means she can't show them to me. I need to see those documents. Her law firm keeps them in a database using a program called Concordance." Charles reached into his back pocket and pulled out his wallet. He extracted a card and handed it to Darryl.

"Here's the name of her law firm and her e-mail address. She's able to access the database by signing onto her law firm's network via the Internet. I've written the web address she used to access the network on the back of the card."

Darryl glanced down at the card and then looked up at Charles, his mouth twisted in a sneer. "That's all you need? This will be a piece of cake."

"They can't even suspect you've taken this information,"

Charles said. "That would put my attorney in a tight spot with the Florida Bar ethics committee."

Darryl nodded. "In that case, I might have to plan a little diversion." He put the card down on the desk. "This will cost you ten."

"Agreed. Shall we do a dead drop like the good old days?"

Darryl grinned. "Yes, just like the old days."

"I'm going to need instructions on how to use the Concordance database and a copy of the program," Charles said.

Darryl waved a hand. "I'll throw that in at no extra charge."

Charles blew out a breath. "Thank you, man. I knew you'd be able to help with this."

Darryl stood up, came around his desk and shook Charles' hand. "It's good to see you, mon. Don't be a stranger."

"Okay," Charles said.

They walked out of the office and into the bakery. The smell of the food and spices made Charles' stomach rumble. He turned to Darryl. "Can you hook a brother up with a beef patty and some coco bread?"

***

Kathy sat at her desk reviewing the index her paralegal had prepared of the documents produced by Peachtree Consulting. She would still have to review the documents themselves, but, from what she could see, Peachtree had failed to provide a single document describing the work Wilkes was engaged in at the time of the accident. She'd have to file a motion to get the Court to order the company to provide better discovery responses. Sighing, she put down the index, turned to her computer, typed in her password and pulled up a similar motion she had recently drafted in another case. There was no need to reinvent the wheel.

She had just started writing the introduction section when her telephone rang. It was Bill. What did he want? Kathy frowned and hit the line button. "Hello?"

"Kathy, I'm glad I caught you. Do you have a moment to stop by?"

"Yes, of course. I'll be right over." She hung up, saved her document and headed over to Bill's office. When she got there, his door was open. She hesitated before entering since Royce Evans, one of the law firm's banking lawyers, was seated in one of the chairs in front of Bill's desk. The two men appeared to be having a heated discussion. Royce's face was flushed. Bill didn't look too pleased himself.

Kathy knocked on the door. Royce closed his mouth into a thin line and tried to glare a hole into her.

Bill looked up and waved her in. "Kathy, come on in here and have a seat." He turned to Royce. "You and I will talk about this later." When Royce opened his mouth to speak, Bill held up an index finger to stop him. "Later." He inclined his head toward the door. Royce closed his mouth, rose from his seat, aimed another malevolent glare in Kathy's direction and stalked out of the office.

Kathy looked at Bill with wide eyes. "What? Why does Royce, with whom I've exchanged no more than pleasantries, suddenly hate me?"

Bill's face was grim. "Because he just got a call from a receiver he's representing in the Banco Superior bankruptcy who told him that he'd find another law firm to represent him if we didn't find a way to settle that Peachtree Consulting case you're working on,. Apparently, the receiver's getting pressure from the federal government on this one."

"But that's outrageous! They can't do that. It's completely unethical, not to mention unconstitutional. A party has the right to the counsel of their choice," Kathy said.

Bill looked at her the way parents look at children when they first learn the world isn't fair. "They just did." His voice was matter-of-fact. "And that's not all. I've received similar calls from attorneys in our D.C. and Tallahassee offices.

"But –."

Bill shook his head. "Where are we on the Peachtree case? Have they made any settlement offers yet? Have we?"

Kathy swallowed her protests. "They offered us a million dollars to walk away. Charles rejected the offer outright and refused to make a counteroffer. He told me that he has no interest in settling the case. He wants his day in court and he wants to inflict as much pain as possible on Peachtree in the interim. He seems more interested in revenge than money. Even though the lawyer in me knows that's not rational, I can't say I blame him, Bill. I mean, they did kill his wife."

Bill stared at her for a moment before speaking. Kathy squirmed uncomfortably under his gaze. Now that this case was going to cost the firm some clients, he was probably regretting his decision not to assign someone with more experience to handle it.

"Kathy, we don't have time for you to be going soft on the man. We need to get that case resolved, quick, fast and in a hurry or we're going to start losing substantial business. That's not something we can afford. *Comprende*? I need for you to get the client to settle the case. Do whatever you have to do. In the meantime, I'll check with the general counsel's office and see what our options are. Any solution he comes up with though will not be optimal for you. Do I make myself clear?"

Kathy nodded and stood up. "Very clear." Her tone was curt. "I'll see what I can do." She headed out of his office.

"You do that."

Kathy entered her office, slammed the door shut, stalked over to her desk and kicked it. She cursed when the pain set in. She'd forgotten she was wearing peep toe pumps.

She limped over to her chair and sat down. It was easy to blame Bill and Royce for her current predicament; but they were just the messengers. It was Peachtree and the government turning up the heat. She just needed to find a way to cool things down. The most obvious route was to get Charles to settle the case. But it would be unethical for her to coerce a client into a settlement he didn't really want.

What were her other alternatives? Did she have any? She wondered if Steve had ever run into a similar situation. With all his years of practice and his penchant for representing the underdog, he probably had. She turned to the telephone and dialed his number. He picked up on the first ring.

"Hey, Kiddo, what's up?" he asked.

"I need your help," she said.

"I'll be right there."

Kathy hung up the telephone and sat there staring into space. Steve found her like that a few minutes later when he stepped into her office.

"Close the door behind you, take a seat and put on your mentor hat," she said.

Steve smiled, closed the door and eased into one of her visitor's chairs.

"That's my favorite one to wear. What's going on?"

Kathy told him about her conversation with Bill and brought him up to speed. When she finished, he let out a long, low whistle and shook his head. "You've got a hot one there, Kiddo."

Kathy grimaced. "I know. Any ideas?"

He thought for a moment, the fingers of his right hand tapping the arm of his chair. Then he sat up, pulled himself to the edge of the chair and leaned forward. "It seems to me you have two ways of dealing with this issue - really three if you think about it. One obvious choice is to find a way to get the client to settle the case. Another choice is for the law firm to withdraw from representing him."

Kathy's mouth dropped open. She couldn't believe her ears. Outrage had her clamping her mouth into a thin line and shaking her head at him. "Those aren't real choices. You and I both know it would be unethical for me to trick or coerce or even put pressure on the client to settle the case to solve the law firm's problems. And we can't just abandon him because the government decided to turn up the heat. I can't believe you even suggested that."

Steve smiled. "I've taught you well, grasshopper. The third choice is to find a way to make the government relieve the pressure on the firm."

"How?"

"Well, the firm could go public on the issue by talking to the press or bringing a lawsuit for violation of its constitutional rights. Of course, if we go that route, we can all look forward to getting audited by the I.R.S. and we'd probably never be appointed to serve as counsel for trustees or receivers in federal cases ever again," he said.

Kathy rolled her eyes. "Oh yeah. That's a great idea. Bill and Royce would really love me then."

"But you might not have to go that far. Maybe you could just hint to counsel for Peachtree that we intend to file a lawsuit in the event we lose a client over this. That might be enough to get the government to back off - at least for a little while," he said.

Kathy smiled. "Now that's not a bad idea at all. I could use that time to try to find additional leverage against Peachtree. I knew you'd have a trick or two up your sleeve, you brilliant man."

Steve smiled. "Don't get too happy yet. Let's see if it works first."

CHAPTER VII

That evening, Kathy walked into O'Shaughnessy's and headed straight for the bar. She needed a drink after the day she'd had. Roarke poured her a glass of pinot noir and set it down in front of her.

"Thanks," she said. She picked up the wineglass and took a large sip.

"Rough day?" Roarke asked.

Kathy grimaced and set the glass back onto the bar. "You don't know the half of it and I can't tell you about it." She smiled to take the sting out of the words.

Roarke shook his head. "If you ask me, that job is taking years off your life. Are you sure it's worth it, lassie?"

"That's a good question Roarke. Sometimes, I wonder about that myself," she said.

"Wonder about what, *chica*?" Kathy's partner and friend Marisela - a fiery Latina from Cuba - slid onto the barstool next to her. She looked as if she'd just stepped out of the pages of a fashion magazine. Even though it was 9:00p.m., her suit looked crisp, as if she'd just put it on. She set her large designer purse onto the seat next to her and hooked the heels of her Christian Louboutin shoes onto the lower rung of the barstool.

Kathy glanced down at her boring gray pinstriped Jones New York pants suit and thought about going shopping that weekend. Maybe she could ask Marisela to help her pick out some new duds. "Roarke was just asking me whether the job is worth all the long hours and the stress."

Marisela rolled her eyes and took a sip of the mojito Roarke set onto the bar in front of her. "Hell no it's not worth it. But since we haven't found rich husbands yet and like designer purses and shoes, we have to keep working. Besides, it's a lot better than working for the government."

Marisela was a prosecutor in a former life. She and Kathy liked each other immediately and became fast friends when she joined the law firm. They both had a mutual love of designer purses, living on South Beach, and African-American men.

Kathy's stomach rumbled, reminding her that she hadn't eaten anything since lunch. "Can we move to a table? I'm starving."

"Good idea," Marisela said.

They grabbed their drinks and headed over to their favorite table in the back.

"So, how are things going? I haven't seen you much lately," Kathy asked.

"I know. You haven't been available for lunch much since you caught that new case. I haven't even seen you in here since you brought that gorgeous man in last week," Marisela said. She put a hand over her heart and fluttered her eyelashes dramatically. "Forget about me, how are things going with him?"

Kathy laughed. "Don't you mean how are things going with the case? You know I can't mess with him. I'd be breaking all kinds of rules."

Marisela twisted her lips and waved a hand as if she were swatting away a fly. "Please. With a man that sexy, there are always exceptions. Besides, that pesky detail wouldn't stop the men from trying to get close to a pretty female client."

"Yeah right. Those 'exceptions' will get me disbarred. You know as well as I do that the rules are different for us than they are for them."

Marisela snarled and muttered an oath in Spanish. "That doesn't mean we have to accept it, *chica*. I do not. Besides, rules or not, I bet you find it pretty hard to concentrate on dry legal issues with that *delicioso* man around."

Kathy sat back in her seat and grinned. "Girl, you don't know the half of it. There are times when I stop thinking about him as a client. Like the day you saw us come in here. I was prepping him for deposition and I asked him about his marriage, his relationship with his wife, their sex life. You know, all those questions they like to ask in personal injury cases to figure out what the damages should be. When he told me that he and his wife used to have sex three or four times a week in their fifth year of marriage, I was done." She fanned herself.

Marisela raised her eyebrows and leaned forward. "Wow. What else did he tell you? Did you ask their favorite position? Whether or not she had multiple orgasms? The size of his package?"

Kathy cracked up. "You are so crazy."

Marisela looked innocent. "What? This is very important information. It could be relevant to the case." She rolled her eyes when Kathy just sent her a bland look. "Fine." She threw her hands up in defeat. "How's the case going?"

Kathy rewarded her with a wan smile. "Not so great. Peachtree played the national security card and tried to block our discovery. The Court ordered them to produce the documents we requested but it also entered a confidentiality order. Peachtree responded by trying to bury us in paper and designating each and every document 'attorneys eyes only.' The client is pissed because that means he can't see the documents. From what I've seen so far, he's not missing much. Peachtree redacted the documents so heavily, I can't make heads or tails of them."

"*Cabrones,*" Marisela said. "You should drag their sorry asses back into court and seek sanctions against them for discovery abuses."

Kathy nodded. "Yeah, that's the plan. But, believe it or not, the discovery abuses are the least of our problems. They're playing hardball now. They got the federal government to put pressure on our other clients to put pressure on us to settle the case." She told Marisela about her conversation with Bill. "Did you ever run into this when you were a federal prosecutor?

Marisela nodded. "I was afraid you'd run into something like this when I heard you were going up against Peachtree Consulting. They work for a lot of government agencies and have contacts and allies everywhere."

"So what do I do? The client has no interest in settling this case. These people killed his wife. He doesn't just want money. He wants his day in court. How do I get the federal government to back off? Any suggestions?"

Marisela picked up a French fry, dragged it through a mound of ketchup, shoved it into her mouth, tipped back in her chair and chewed it thoughtfully. The French fries looked good.

While Marisela ruminated, Kathy reached over and snagged one off her friend's plate. The fact that Marisela didn't protest or tease Kathy mercilessly for eating junk food – something she hardly ever did – was a testament to how deep in thought she was. After a moment, Kathy heard a thunk. Marisela's chair legs had reconnected with the floor.

"Okay," she said. "The way I see it, the only way you're going to get the government to stop helping Peachtree is if you make Peachtree look so bad the government will want to kick them to the curb."

"How do I do that? " Kathy asked.

Marisela reached across the table and slapped the back of Kathy's hand. "How do you think? You dig, girl! A fancy defense contractor like that has to have a few skeletons in its closet. Get some investigators on that. Look for lawsuits filed against them, subpoenas served by government agencies like the S.E.C. or the I.R.S. Talk to employees they fired, former spouses of senior executives, executives who left to join their competitors - people like that. They want to play hardball, you play too. If you find enough dirt, they'll become a liability and the government won't protect them. But be careful. Defense contractors don't always play by the rules. If they see you as a threat to their operation, they might take it personally. I don't want to hear you had a car accident or fell down a flight of stairs or worse." She said what sounded like a quick prayer in Spanish and made the sign of a cross over her ample bosom.

Kathy sucked her teeth. "Yeah right. Stop that. You can be so dramatic sometimes."

She relented when Marisela continued to study her, a worried frown creasing her brow.

"Fine, I'll be careful. I'll even hire security if I think it's necessary. Thanks for the advice though. It will come in handy." She raised her wineglass in a toast. "To kicking Peachtree's ass."

"I'll drink to that," Marisela said.

"You'll drink to anything," Kathy said.

Marisela laughed. "That's true." She raised her glass, tapped it against Kathy's and took a sip.

***

The next day, Kathy met with Charles to tell him about her conversation with Bill.

"Can the federal government do that? It's tantamount to blackmail. Can't you just sue them?" he asked.

Kathy shrugged. "Suing the federal government is a lot harder than you think and won't really fix the problem. Sure, we might eventually get a ruling in our favor, but the lawsuit could drag on for a long time. With appeals, it go on for years."

Charles leaned forward, rested his elbows onto the conference room table and rubbed his hands over his face. He sighed and sat back in his chair. "Maybe I should get another law firm to handle this. If I do that, then maybe Peachtree and the government will focus their efforts on me and my new counsel instead of Gold, Rome & Harris."

Kathy stared at him. She couldn't help but be impressed by his desire to protect her and GRH. Most clients didn't give a rat's ass about anything but themselves. She was momentarily tempted to take him up on his offer as that would allow both her and GRH an easy way out of this mess; however, the moment passed. She'd never been a quitter and she'd be damned if she'd become one now. She shook her head. "No. We are not quitting. If you really don't think settling the lawsuit is in your best interests then we'll just have to go to Plan B."

He looked up at her. "What's plan B?"

"We don't file a lawsuit against the federal government. We just make it think we will. It's an election year. The government's not going to want the negative publicity a lawsuit would bring. The threat should get it to back off for a bit, giving us time to find some sort of leverage against Peachtree in the hopes of driving a wedge between them. If we can make Peachtree look bad enough, maybe the government will cut ties with the company instead of protecting it."

Charles nodded, a slow smile spreading across his face. "That just might work. Of course, Plan B is entirely dependent upon us finding something to use as leverage against Peachtree. How do you plan to do that?"

She shook her head. "I haven't worked that part out yet. We haven't finished reviewing the documents they produced and what we've seen so far doesn't help us. But a company like Peachtree is bound to have a few skeletons in its closet. I plan to put my associate and the firm's investigator on finding them."

"Let's hope they have enough time," he said. "Look, if Plan B doesn't work, I'll find new counsel. I don't want to be the cause of harm to you or your law firm." He put his hand over hers.

The warmth of his words and his hand felt like a hug to Kathy who couldn't, for the life of her, figure out why the gesture touched her so deeply. She needed to stop this. She couldn't afford to develop feelings for a client – especially this one. She withdrew her hand from his. "Thank you, Charles. We'll cross that road when we come to it. In the meantime, we have some work to do."

***

Later that day, Kathy sat at her desk poring over

Peachtree's answers to interrogatories. They were filled with objections and evasive answers and didn't provide much information at all. She'd already filed a motion to compel better answers, but the motion wouldn't be decided for at least another two weeks.

Peachtree had gone overboard with the objections as far as she was concerned. It had even objected to standard questions concerning lawsuits filed against the company in the past five years. Magistrate Judge Jacobs would surely slam them for that.

She wondered why Peachtree had refused to answer the question since lawsuits were public record. She could easily search for lawsuits filed against Peachtree via the Web. In fact, she often did that as a matter of course at the start of a new case. She liked to see if similar cases had been filed against a defendant she was suing or against her client if she was defending. She hadn't done that in this case because she'd been too busy. Now that she was lead counsel, she needed to learn how to delegate some of the tasks she normally handled while she handled the tasks Steve normally did.

She knew she should delegate the task of researching prior lawsuits to an associate; however, being the control freak that she was, she couldn't resist doing a quick search to see what she could find. She turned to her computer, pulled up Google and typed "Peachtree Consulting wrongful death" into the search box. Her eyes widened when several articles came up. She trawled through the ones pertaining to Charles' case and stopped when she got to an article about a case filed against Peachtree in New York. According to the article, a woman filed a wrongful death suit in state court against Peachtree when her husband was killed by a stray bullet during a shootout involving a Peachtree employee. The article reported that the matter was 'amicably resolved' and the lawsuit was dismissed. She printed it out and made a call.

A few minutes later, Erin - an African-American associate who had joined the firm two years ago - stepped into Kathy's office. Law was her second career. She'd worked for several years as an engineer in a prior life. She and Kathy were close in age and had similar interests in novels, movies and music. With so much in common, it was almost inevitable that they'd become friends.

"Hey girl, what's up?" Erin plopped down in one of Kathy's visitor's chairs.

"How much do you know about the new case I'm working on?" Kathy asked.

Erin smiled. "Well Annette told me about the tall, dark, and handsome widow you're representing. Office gossip and news coverage told me the rest."

"I'm going to bring you in," Kathy said.

Erin's smile grew wider. She rubbed her hands together in anticipation. "Yes! Working with you on such an exciting case and for such a fine client – what else can a girl ask for?"

Kathy frowned. "I wouldn't be so excited if I were you. I'm bringing you in on a limited basis for discrete assignments only. This case might be a career ender, not to mention dangerous."

It was Erin's turn to frown. "What's going on?"

"Peachtree Consulting and the government are putting all kinds of pressure on GRH to get the client to settle the case. He has no interest in settling – not for any amount of money," Kathy said.

Erin let out a low whistle. "That's a bit of a problem."

"You bet. As your friend and mentor, I want to keep your name out of this mess as much as possible. You don't want to be associated with this case if we can't find anything to get the government to back off. It could become very unpopular – especially if it causes the firm to lose business. The backlash could affect you too."

Erin sat quietly for a moment. "Given everything you just said, why are you asking me to do any work on the case?"

"Because I need someone I can trust. Peachtree and the government have unlimited resources. If they can put pressure on the law firm like this, they could easily bribe an associate to leak information or worse yet, sabotage the case," Kathy said.

"What kind of friend would I be if I didn't step in to help you when you so obviously need it? I'm in. But I'm not coming into this case half-assed. If I'm in, then I'm in all the way or not at all. Damn the consequences," Erin said.

"Okay, but I don't want to hear about it if you and I are out on our behinds looking for jobs as a result of this damned case."

Erin just smiled. "What do you need?"

"I need for you to run down any information you can find on this wrongful death suit filed against Peachtree in New York," Kathy said. She picked up the printouts of the articles and handed them to Erin. "Work with the investigator to track down potential witnesses and see if Jim can get copies of pleadings, depositions, affidavits, etc. from the court file or the opposing counsel. Also, see if there were any other lawsuits filed against Peachtree anywhere in the country. You know the drill."

Erin nodded. She jotted a few notes onto the legal pad she had brought with her. "Yes indeed. When do you need this by?"

"I need it yesterday. I don't know how much time we have before the firm starts losing clients. In that event, Bill might shut us down and force me to file a motion to withdraw from the case," Kathy said. "Plus, the end of the discovery period is coming up soon and we have a lot to do. This case is going to be all consuming. You're going to have to clear the decks."

"I'll get on this right away. Luckily, my other cases aren't so busy right now."

"Thanks," Kathy said.

CHAPTER VIII

Charles parked his car and walked into Elaine Gordon Park on 135th street. The park was an oasis from its decidedly urban surroundings. Men, women and children rode bicycles on the bike paths, unmolested by the cars that usually threatened to run them over. A young couple enjoyed a picnic under the shade of an oak tree. They seemed more interested in sampling each other than any food contained in the picnic basket sitting next to them on the blanket.

Charles appeared to stroll aimlessly through the park. In reality, he was looking for any signs of surveillance. He spotted a young guy with dark hair, sunglasses and a mustache walking behind him. He looked familiar. Charles stopped abruptly at a water fountain and took a drink. The guy pretended to head in another direction. Charles sauntered off. When he had put enough distance between himself and the operative, he ducked into a maintenance shack. He saw the operative pass by through a small window in the rusty metal door. He waited a moment breathing in the fumes of the noxious cleaning liquids to see if any other members of a surveillance team appeared. Seeing none, he slipped out of the shack and headed in the opposite direction from the operative.

When he was sure that he was no longer being watched, he headed toward an empty bench, shrugged off the backpack and sat down. He extracted a newspaper and opened it up. After a moment, he lifted his gaze and checked to see if anyone was paying him any attention. Seeing nothing untoward, he reached down with his left hand and slid it along the underside of the bench until he encountered what felt like a thick padded envelope. He pulled the envelope free and tucked it into his backpack. He folded the newspaper, donned the backpack and headed toward the park entrance. He passed a garbage can next to the playground and dropped the newspaper inside. He then strode out of the park and headed toward his car. Out of the corner of his eye, he saw the operative heading toward him, faced flushed, breathing heavily. Charles caught the younger man's eye, nodded and sent him a cocky smile. The operative's flush deepened as he hurried past.

***

Back in his home office, Charles extracted the package from his backpack and slit it open with a letter opener. Inside were two CD's, a manual on how to use the Concordance program and a handwritten note giving him instructions. He brewed some coffee, installed the program and uploaded the documents.

He skimmed the manual and then, with it open in front of him, experimented with pulling up documents, searching for them and reviewing them. Two hours later, he sat back in his chair and closed his eyes. He must have reviewed at least five hundred pages without finding anything remotely useful. His eyes burned from staring into the computer screen for so long. He could see why Kathy and her people were taking so long to review the documents.

He took a sip of his coffee and grimaced. It was cold and

down to the dregs. He got up to brew a fresh pot. He wasn't concerned that it would keep him up all night. In the Corps you learned to sleep when you got the opportunity to. He'd drop off to sleep when he was ready no matter how many cups of java he consumed.

He seasoned a steak and put it under the broiler and threw a pack of frozen broccoli into the microwave. All the while his mind worked on the task at hand. There had to be a more efficient way of extracting the information he needed from Peachtree's documents without reviewing each and every page. He thought about the types of documents that might contain information about the government agencies that hired Peachtree or mission details. He searched for documents containing the word "mission" and came up empty. He searched for the word "agency" and came up empty.

He thought for a moment. Peachtree and his employees were former military. They probably used military jargon in their protocols. He typed in the word "report" and came up with a thousand documents. He smiled. He was getting a little closer. His smile faded as he began to review the documents pulled up by the search. They were heavily redacted. He pulled up a report dated the day of the accident. The only parts of the report that were not blacked out were Wilkes' name, the date, a report of the accident and the fact that the report had been sent to someone named "Manning." Who was Manning? The name was vaguely familiar. Charles searched his memory. His eyes widened when the answer came to him.

He'd once run an op with a man named David Manning during his stint in the Corps. Manning was with the C.I.A. back then - a maverick who'd nearly gotten Charles' whole team killed.

The name took him back. He remembered peering

through the scope of his rifle out of the twenty-fourth floor window of an office building in Geneva and cursing at the circus taking place below. Swiss police vehicles blocked the entrance of the hotel across the street. From what he could see, the place was completely surrounded.

What the hell had happened? They had a foolproof plan. His men and the C.I.A. operative, Manning, were just supposed to make sure the mark left the hotel through the front entrance. They were to get in and out, undetected, and let him take care of the rest. Now, the Swiss police were on high alert. With all the big shots attending the conference at the hotel, they'd most definitely lock the place down and check the identity of every man, woman and child in there.

He wasn't worried about his men maintaining their covers. But if they were arrested and photographed, their ability to perform future operations would be severely compromised. As team leader, he couldn't allow that. It would be the end of their careers and his.

He pulled up the schematics of the hotel in his head. He and his team had gone over them dozens of times. There was no easy exit strategy once the building was cordoned off. The only way out was by air. Since there would undoubtedly be security on the roof of the hotel, they'd have to fight their way out.

"Rocking Horse to Royal Blue. Do you read me?" Keeping his voice low, he glanced over his shoulder. The Swiss executive whose office he was using for the operation was still sprawled across the couch where he had fallen after Charles had tranquilized him.

"Loud and clear, Rocking Horse. Go." It was Tyler.

Charles breathed a sigh of relief. "Mission abort. Repeat, abort the mission. Swiss police have cordoned off the hotel and are blocking the entrance. Do you copy?"

"Roger that," Tyler said. "What's our exit strategy?"

"By air. Get the team up to the roof in fifteen minutes and clear the runway," he said.

"Roger that," Tyler said.

Charles radioed command to call in the chopper then he broke down the rifle and packed it away. He checked the area around him, pulled out a clean cloth and wiped down any surface he might have touched.

He looked at the Swiss executive sleeping peacefully on the couch across the room. The tranquilizer would keep him under for two more hours or so. He picked up his leather briefcase and left the office.

The Swiss executive's assistant looked up at him and smiled. He smiled back at her. "Goodbye, Emma. Your boss took a call on his cell phone. He asked me to tell you not to disturb him."

Emma grinned. "It's probably his wife. She's away in America on business. They must be having a romantic conversation. You know what I mean." She wiggled her eyebrows.

Charles' smile turned into a grin. "Yes I do. My wife and I have those romantic conversations sometimes when I'm away. Well, it was a pleasure to meet you Emma."

"The pleasure was all mine. Have a safe trip home, Mr. White. Do you need for me to call you a taxi?" she asked.

"No need thank you. I have a car waiting for me downstairs." He walked away and pressed the elevator call button.

The telephone rang on Emma's desk. His heartbeat sped up as he watched her turn away to pick it up. He relaxed a little when he heard her tell the caller in French that Mr. Johansson was unavailable. As she took the message, the elevator arrived. He took it up to the top floor, exited the car and walked swiftly down the hall to the stairwell. No-one paid him any attention.

He climbed the stairs until he reached the roof access door. It was already propped open. He peered through the doorway and saw a young man smoking a cigarette on the roof. Charles stepped out onto the roof and joined him on the ledge. Apparently, it was a popular smoking spot. Ashes and spent cigarette butts littered the area.

The kid looked at him curiously. Charles smiled at him and used two fingers to make the universal signal for smoking a cigarette.

"Do you speak English?" he asked.

The young man nodded. "Yes."

Charles feigned a sigh of relief. "Thank God. My German is dreadful, my French lousy and my Italian non-existent. I've been in meetings all day with Mr. Johansson. I'm dying for a smoke. Would you happen to have an extra cigarette? I'd be happy to buy it from you."

The young man pulled a pack of cigarettes from his pants pocket and offered them to Charles. "Here. You don't need to pay me."

"Thanks." Charles extracted a cigarette, lit it with the lighter he found inside the pack and took a puff. Willing himself not to cough, he aimed a smile at his new smoking buddy. "That hit the spot. Thanks again." He put the lighter back into the pack and handed it back to the kid.

"You are welcome."

Charles scanned the roof for security. There appeared to be none. He could hear the faint whoosh of the helicopter approaching from a distance. It would be there in seconds. He turned to watch the young man. As the helicopter drew closer, the kid turned to look at it. Charles moved fast. He tossed the cigarette down and grabbed the kid in a chokehold, cutting off his air supply. He then gently laid his unconscious body down onto the rooftop.

He picked up his briefcase and ran to the helipad in the center of the roof. When the chopper landed, he climbed in and strapped on his headset. He then picked up the tranq rifle lying on the seat next to him, flipped off the safety and told the pilot to head to the roof of the hotel.

As they approached the hotel rooftop, Charles could see that his team was in trouble. They were pinned down in the northwest corner of the roof by Swiss police. He counted seven hostiles. The helicopter distracted the hostiles for an instant. It was all Charles and his team needed. He put three of them to sleep with his rifle. His team made short work of the rest. They then climbed aboard the helicopter one by one.

The hotel roof access door opened and more Swiss officers began to pour out. Charles and those members of his team already aboard kept them at bay as best they could, but they were outnumbered and outgunned. The police offers shot live ammo instead of tranqs. Charles ducked as bullets bounced off the side of the helicopter. One of them caught Tyler as he boarded the chopper. He fell, his legs dangling outside. Charles pulled him the rest of the way inside.

"Get us out of here," he shouted into his headset.

The pilot didn't have to be told twice. The helicopter lurched violently as it took off and made its way into the air. The metallic ring of bullets ceased as they increased their altitude and put some distance between themselves and the hotel.

"Are you alright, soldier?" Charles asked. "Where are you hit?"

"My shoulder," Tyler said, hissing through his teeth.

Charles extracted a pair of scissors from the helicopter's emergency kit and cut away Tyler's bloody suit jacket and shirt. He took a look at the bullet wound and smiled.

"The bullet went right through," he said. "You'll be okay." He applied pressure to stop the bleeding, cleaned the wound as best he could and bandaged it tightly. He then grabbed a sweat suit from a small suitcase tucked behind the seats of the helicopter and helped Tyler get into it.

"What the hell happened in there?" he asked once Tyler was settled.

Tyler grimaced. "Manning decided to take the mark out himself. A hotel maid walked in on him and screamed bloody murder before he broke her neck. Someone called security. They discovered the bodies and locked the place down tighter than a drum. It's a miracle we got out of there alive."

Charles cursed. He looked at the men on the chopper. Manning was not among them. "And Manning? Where is he?"

Tyler shook his head. "I don't know. The man is a ghost. He just disappeared."

Charles returned to the present, his mouth tightened into a grim line. If the Manning referred to in Peachtree's documents was the same guy who'd screwed up that mission and exposed his team, he'd have a lot of explaining to do. Peachtree Consulting would also have a lot of explaining to do. That is, if Manning was still C.I.A. A lot could change in eleven years. He could have left the C.I.A. and joined the F.B.I., the N.S.A., the

D.E.A. or any number of government agencies authorized to operate domestically.

He picked up the telephone and made two calls – one to his best friend Tyler and the other to leave a coded message for Darryl to arrange another meeting.

***

The next day, Tyler sat at his desk reading a file on Peachtree Consulting. The Bureau was already investigating the company which was suspected of conducting rogue clandestine operations. However, every time the Bureau investigated a suspicious operation, some government agency would vouch for the company.

Peachtree had been sued three times in the past ten years. All three of the lawsuits were settled quickly and the plaintiffs refused to give and/or claimed not to know any helpful information. The Bureau had even sent an operative to infiltrate the company; however, he turned up dead, under suspicious circumstances, before he could make any headway.

This was not good. Reading between the lines, Peachtree Consulting was as tightly knit and as organized as the Mafia. It had powerful government contacts and it wasn't above killing to maintain the status quo. What had Charles gotten himself into?

He picked up the file to look up the name of the case agent and grimaced when he found it. It was Michaels - the most rigid, by the book fool he'd ever met. He wouldn't break protocol if it meant saving agents' lives. He certainly wouldn't stick his neck out for Charles.

Tyler sighed. He'd just have to get himself assigned to the case. He was sitting there wondering how to do that when he saw Michaels cross the hall and go into the break room. Speak of the devil. He got up, picked up his empty coffee mug and headed toward the break room. When he got there, Michaels was refilling his water bottle. Another agent kicked the candy machine in an effort to get a Snickers bar that had gotten stuck halfway down to drop.

"Hey!" Michaels said. "Tampering with that thing is illegal. I don't want to have to arrest you, Stiver."

"That stupid machine took my money," Stiver whined. "That's the third time this week."

"You shouldn't be eating that stuff anyway, it's bad for your health" Tyler said. He stepped up to the machine and took some coins out of his pants pocket. "Move."

Stiver stepped aside.

Tyler inserted the coins and selected a Snickers bar. The second candy bar pushed the first one down and both candy bars dropped to the shelf below. Tyler retrieved them and handed them both to Stiver. "Here. Now, you've got two of them."

"Thanks, man." Stiver put one candy bar in his pocket, tore the wrapper off the other and took a huge bite out of it. Then he left the break room.

"You know you're just contributing to his ever expanding waistline. If he doesn't watch it, he won't meet his weight requirements," Michaels said.

"He is looking a little soft around the middle there, isn't he? So, how have you been? I haven't seen you around here much lately."

"I know," Michaels said. "I've been so busy working on the Peachtree case that I haven't seen anyone. We're not making much headway, but the Director wants this to be top priority in light of Agent Jenson's death. I'm going to have to assign more members to the team."

Tyler couldn't believe his luck. "Oh yeah? Well, my workload has lightened up a little. You can count me in if you need me."

Michaels looked pleased. "That's good to hear. We could use all the help we can get. Hey, isn't your friend Charles Morgan Jr. suing Peachtree Consulting? I saw it on the news."

Tyler groaned inwardly. He knew that Michaels would try to get him to enlist Charles' help. Charles was a lone wolf. He wouldn't have any interest in assisting the Bureau in its investigation. He certainly would have no interest in playing by the Bureau's rules. "Yeah, he is." He walked over to the coffee dispenser and filled his cup.

Michaels followed. "How's the lawsuit going?"

"I don't know. I haven't spoken to Charles since he filed it." He had to buy himself some time to figure out what to do. He picked up his coffee mug. "I'd better go and clear my desk since I'm about to be assigned to the Peachtree case. From what you've said, it sounds like a hot one. See you later." He turned and walked toward the door of the break room as quickly as he could without spilling his coffee. He'd almost made it out the door when Michaels called out after him.

"Wait up, Tyler." Michaels hustled over. "I need to talk to you. Did you know that three other wrongful death cases were filed against Peachtree? We interviewed the plaintiffs who filed those cases but Peachtree's got them so scared and so bound up by confidentiality agreements that we haven't been able to get much from them. And when we threatened them with prosecution for withholding information, they lawyered up. We need to talk to your buddy Charles and see if he knows something that might help us."

Damn. Tyler nodded. "All right, I'll see what I can do."

"You do that Tyler. I know you can do it. I have faith in you, bro," Michaels said.

Tyler pumped his fist in the air in a mock salute, rolled his eyes and left the break room. He heard Michaels laughing as he left.

***

Kathy sat on a bar stool at the Cuban coffee shop across the street from the Miami-Dade County courthouse waiting for Weisman. She'd asked to meet him there on the pretense of discussing the documents Peachtree produced. In reality, the meeting was part of her plan to get the government to back off her law firm. She ordered a *cortadito* – a sugar-laden Cuban style espresso cut with cream – and knocked it back. She put the cup back onto the counter and watched the comings and goings on Flagler Street as she waited.

Lawyers, male and female, wearing suits and carrying briefcases mixed with hapless beggars, haggard looking parties, court reporters, court personnel and shopkeepers on the busy street. Cars moved slowly by to accommodate the throng of people crossing the street.

Stewart Weisman strolled toward her looking as distinguished as ever. He arrived at the stool next to her and set his briefcase upon it. "Counselor." He extended a hand.

Kathy shook it. "Stewart. Thanks for agreeing to meet with me."

"No problem. It's always a pleasure to enjoy coffee with a colleague. Can I order anything for you?" he asked.

Kathy shook her head. "No thanks." She put a hand over her heart. "I just had a *cortadito* and I think I'm having heart palpitations."

Stewart laughed. "Yes, they do make them strong here. They're not for the faint of heart."

She chuckled. "I think I can handle it."

He looked at her. "Yes, I'm sure you can." He ordered an espresso. It came quickly. He knocked it back in a single gulp. "So, what are we discussing today?"

"I asked you here to talk about Peachtree's discovery responses and objections. You objected to almost every interrogatory – even some of the standard ones - on grounds of relevance and national security. Is your client willing to drop some of its objections and provide amended interrogatory answers?"

He grimaced. "Did you really ask me to come all the way down here to talk about discovery issues? We could have done that over the telephone. I must confess that, when you asked to meet me here in person, I was hoping your client had finally come to his senses and was willing to enter into settlement negotiations."

Kathy smiled ruefully and shook her head. "No such luck, I'm afraid. And believe me, I wish he would consider settlement. This case is getting more costly to the firm by the minute. Would you believe that some of our clients have threatened to fire the firm if he doesn't settle this case? The nerve of those people!"

Stewart raised his eyebrows. "Really?"

Watching him feign innocence when she knew damned well he had engineered the entire thing made her want to punch him. But she had to keep her head in the game. "Yes, really. I had no idea the government would play so dirty in this case. Apparently, certain government agencies are putting pressure on the trustees and receivers we represent to get new counsel in the event this case doesn't go away." She frowned. "Are you sure you're not behind this?"

Stewart shook his head, his face the picture of innocence. "I assure you, Ms. Brooks, we have absolutely nothing to do with this. This is the first I've heard about it. I'll have to have a little chat with my client."

"You do that," Kathy said, "because we're thinking about bringing a lawsuit against the federal government for violation of our constitutional rights. And if we find any proof that your law firm is involved, we will not hesitate to bring a Bar complaint against you and seek sanctions against Peachtree in front of Judge McCarthy."

Stewart scowled. "Now look here, young lady, there's no need to make threats. We didn't have anything to do with this, but I'm not shocked that it's happening. I told you the first time we spoke that the government was likely to take measures to protect against exposure of information vital to national security interests. Your client needs to end this before the government takes even stronger measures and we're blamed for the consequences of his being pig-headed."

Kathy stared at him. No he didn't just threaten them and call Charles pig-headed when his client's actions had destroyed the man's life. She silently counted to ten. It was one thing to feign outrage. It was another thing to lose her cool altogether. She narrowed her eyes. "Stewart, I'm going to do you a big favor and pretend I didn't hear that. You just be sure to give your client the message that if GRH loses a single client over this madness, we fully intend to seek very public legal recourse against the government, your client, you personally and your law firm. The time for games is over."

She picked up her Blackberry and shoved it into her purse. She'd gotten the message across. There was no need to continue this charade for a second longer. She slung her purse over her arm and looked at him. His face was red and his lips were pressed together so tightly they had almost disappeared.

"I'll have my associate call yours to try and work out the discovery issues. You have a nice day now," she said. With that, she walked away.

On her way back to the office, Kathy felt her heart pound in her chest. Her hands clenched the steering wheel. She couldn't tell if it was a rush of adrenaline from the confrontation with Weisman, the Cuban coffee, or both.

CHAPTER IX

Kathy met Charles for dinner at O'Shaughnessy's a few days later. She had called him earlier that day to discuss new developments in the case. He'd cut her off mid-sentence and insisted that they meet in person.

She arrived at the bar early and secured a table in the back where they would have a little privacy. She was sitting there, sipping a glass of pinot noir, when Charles walked in.

"Hello, Counselor," he said.

She raised her eyebrows at the formality of the greeting. "Hello client." She smiled at him.

He leaned over to kiss her on the cheek. They took their seats. She felt a little flustered at the contact. She had other clients who greeted her by kissing her on the cheek. It was especially common with clients of certain cultures; however, never before had she had such a reaction to the simple pleasantry.

"I asked you to meet with me so that I can bring you up to date on recent developments," she said. "I met with Weisman last week and threatened him with a Bar complaint and sanctions," she said. "He didn't take that too kindly."

Charles chuckled. "I bet he didn't."

"He denied any involvement but, in the same breath, had the nerve to say that if we didn't settle this case we could expect the government to take even stronger action. Can you believe that?" she asked.

"Yes," Charles said, his voice quiet. "In fact, while I was in the military, I helped the government take some of those stronger measures. I served in the Special Ops division of the Corps."

"I know that you're an ex-Marine-," she said.

"There's no such thing as ex-Marine."

She rolled her eyes. "Excuse me. I knew that you had served in the Marines, but I didn't know you were in Special Ops. What was that like?"

He shrugged. "That's a broad question. How would you answer if I asked you what it's like to be a civil trial attorney? It was boring at times, exciting at times - sometimes a little too exciting - and always dangerous. I was a sniper. We sometimes teamed up with operatives in other government agencies for missions."

"A sniper?" she asked. "You didn't have a problem with that?"

He took a sip of his beer, swallowed and shook his head. "No."

He'd killed people. She didn't know how she felt about that. It was one thing to be a soldier fighting a war and defending the country. It was another thing to be an operative sent out to target and kill specific individuals. He probably saw both situations the same way.

"When you said you helped the government take some

of those stronger measures," she raised her hands and crooked two fingers on each hand to form quotation marks, "what did you mean?"

"Well, without getting into specifics, because I can't, the C.I.A. guys I worked with did everything from turning people against each other to taking them out," he said.

A chill went down Kathy's spine. "Are you telling me there's a possibility the government might take you or me out just to end this case? That's right out of a Tom Clancy novel."

"More like a Robert Ludlum or Jon Land novel. The government, like any other large organization, is filled with a mix of people - some who are willing to uphold and respect citizens' rights and others who just don't give a damn about those things unless it's a means to an end. But don't worry. Taking you out wouldn't make any sense. I could always find another attorney."

She made a face. "Thanks. That makes me feel so much better."

He smiled. "It should make you feel safe. Peachtree and the government are much more likely to try and take me out."

"And you don't have a problem with that?"

"No." He took another swig of his Heineken.

How could he just sit there drinking his beer and talking about his own demise as if it weren't a big deal?

"And the thought of them trying to take you out doesn't make you the tiniest bit nervous?" she asked.

He shrugged. "We've all got to go sometime."

Kathy stared at him. He returned her stare with a bland look. He had to be pulling her leg. No-one would be that blasé about the possibility of becoming the target of a government hit squad.

"Right," she said. "Well, all this talk of government hit squads almost made me forget the main reason I asked to meet with you tonight. Our research uncovered three other wrongful death suits filed against Peachtree. My associate tracked down a witness from one of those cases who is willing to meet with us."

Charles straightened in his chair. "Really? When can we meet with them?"

"Wait a minute. No-one said anything about you meeting with the witness. She's already scared out of her wits. Erin had to beg her to meet with me."

"Oh no," he said. "If you're going to meet with the witness, I am too. Besides, I know what questions to ask."

"Oh really? And I don't? "

"I didn't mean it like that," he said. "I only meant that I know what questions I want to ask."

"Why don't you just give me a list?" she asked.

He shook his head. "You know it's not the same as being there."

She studied him for a moment. Maybe this trip would give her more insight into him. She sensed there was something he wasn't telling her. If this case was as potentially dangerous as he would have her believe, she needed to learn the truth. All of it.

"Fine," she said. "The witness is in New York. I plan to fly out there on Thursday morning, meet with her in our New York office and then try to meet another witness the next day."

"We can charter a private jet," he said. "I'll pick you up

at your condo at 6:00 a.m."

She raised her eyebrows. "Well excuse me. I guess I'll just tell Annette to cancel my flight reservations."

He laughed. "You do that. Where are we staying?"

"Is the Ritz-Carlton good enough for you? ABA members get good corporate rates there," she said.

He sighed. "It'll have to do."

It was her turn to laugh. "Alright then. That's that. Let's order some food."

"Okay, but only if you're off the clock, Counselor."

"The office is officially closed," she said.

They had dinner and enjoyed pleasant conversation. He had a way of making her laugh. She didn't remember the last time she'd enjoyed a man's company as much.

He dropped her off at her condo and kissed her cheek goodnight. That night, she dreamed of him kissing her in other places.

***

The next day, Charles entered a gun range on Biscayne Boulevard in North Miami carrying a gun case. He headed upstairs to a private soundproof booth. Darryl was already there shooting at a target. Charles watched him empty his .44 Magnum. When he was done, he put the gun down and nodded at Charles. "Hey mon." He pushed the button on the side of the window to bring the target forward.

"Hey yourself." Charles stepped up to take a look. There was a tight grouping of bullets in the center mass of the target. "Nice shooting."

Darryl sucked his teeth. "What you expect? Me come from yard. Me must know how to shoot or die."

Charles laughed. "I know that's right."

He moved to the next stall, took out his weapon, and loaded a clip. He pushed the button next to the window to move the target as far back as it would go then he emptied his clip. He set the weapon down and brought the target back. It had a tight grouping of bullet holes dead smack in the center of the head of the target.

Darryl peeked over his shoulder and let out a low whistle. "Where you come from? Beirut?"

Charles cracked up. Darryl joined him. When the laughter died down, Charles turned to Darryl. "Were you followed here?"

Darryl shook his head. "Nah mon."

"Good," Charles said.

"Did you get what you need from the disk I made for you?" Darryl asked.

"I got some useful information from the disk, but to get the rest, I need another favor. I need to get into Peachtree's system."

Darryl let out a long, low whistle. "You want me to crawl into the belly of the beast. A defense firm like that must have levels of encryption on top of levels of encryption. Why don't we just break into the C.I.A.'s database? It's much easier."

"You've already done that," Charles said.

Darryl smiled. "True dat."

"You can do it, right? Break into Peachtree's system and download some files for me?"

Darryl looked insulted. "Yah mon. Of course."

"Can you do it without having the break-in traced to you?" Charles asked. "This is really dangerous stuff. Peachtree will stop at nothing to keep this information from leaking out. I mean nothing."

Darryl nodded. "It's going to cost you, mon. I'm going to need some special equipment and to get a space they can't trace to me. I'm also going to have to send me mother and children away for a while in case something goes wrong."

"You better hope nothing goes wrong. They'll be scraping you off the walls somewhere. You have to get in and out without them knowing," Charles said.

"Chuh. No problem. What am I searching for?"

"I need all of the files mentioning me and my wife. I need all of the files mentioning the name Wilkes that were edited around the time of their deaths and any files mentioning the name Manning." Charles pulled a piece of paper from his pants pocket and handed it to Darryl. "Here. I wrote down what I'm looking for."

Darryl looked down at the piece of paper and squinted. "Ras-clot! With this chicken scratch, you should have been a doctor."

Charles laughed. "Let's practice shooting for a little bit. We may be glad we did."

***

That afternoon, Charles met Tyler for lunch at a diner on Washington Avenue. He liked the spot because it was small, had limited access points and was heavily frequented by homosexual men. Any operative coming in to listen to their conversation would stick out like a sore thumb. Also, parking was very limited on Washington Avenue which made it difficult for anyone to keep a tail.

Tyler walked into the diner. Charles stood up to greet him. They engaged in an elaborate handshake.

"Hey man. It's good to see you. Thanks for coming," Charles said.

"Good to see you too, my brother. You've been pretty scarce these days," Tyler said.

"I know. It's been a little crazy with this lawsuit and all."

Tyler nodded. "I've been following it on the news. How are you holding up?"

"I'm doing okay. Listen man, I have a favor to ask of you."

"A favor? What? Can't a brother order lunch first?" Tyler asked.

Charles laughed. "Yeah, come to think of it, I'm a little hungry myself."

They checked out the menu and ordered lunch. Charles ordered two cheeseburgers, French fries, a shake and a slice of apple pie. Tyler raised his eyebrows before giving the waitress his order. "Damn bro. You really are hungry. I've never seen you order so much food before. When's the last time you ate?"

Charles raised his eyes toward the ceiling. "Last night at dinner. I guess I had a few things on my mind and a couple of things to do today."

"I'd say. So what kind of favor do you need?"

"I need for you to look up a guy named David Manning. I need to know whether he's the same C.I.A. guy you and I worked with on that mission ten years ago."

"You mean that fool who almost got us all killed?" Tyler asked.

"Yup," Charles said. "That fool."

"Why are we looking him up?"

"I ran across the name Manning in the documents Peachtree produced in my case," Charles said.

Tyler frowned. "Wait a minute. Weren't those documents produced for the attorney's eyes only?"

Charles swore under his breath. He'd never been able to hide anything from Tyler. He looked around the restaurant to make sure their conversation was not being overheard. There were only two other patrons in the diner – a young couple sitting in a booth on the other side of the room. They were giggling and feeling each other up. He turned back to his friend. "Yes. My attorney doesn't know I have them."

"How did you -?" Tyler shook his head. "Never mind. I don't want to know. Did you see anything good in there?"

"No. They were heavily redacted. I haven't gotten through all of them yet, but, so far, the only thing I found is a report of the accident and Manning's name."

Tyler looked down at the table then back up at him. Charles saw the serious look in his friend's eyes and knew something was up. "What?"

"I've got to talk to you about something, man," Tyler said.

"Just spit it out."

"The Bureau is running its own investigation into Peachtree Consulting. We suspect them of conducting rogue operations, but we haven't been able to prove it. They have friends in high places. Every time we get close, some government agency backs them up."

Charles nodded. "The same agency or different ones?"

"Different ones." Tyler took a close look at Charles. "You don't seem to be a bit surprised. Why is that? What do you know?"

"When I looked into the accident, I had the same suspicion about Peachtree. I think they're running ops for the C.I.A. domestically. That's why I need for you to find out if the Manning referred to in the documents is the same guy we know."

Tyler leaned forward in his chair. "I didn't see any reference to the C.I.A. in Peachtree's file. Of course, those secretive jerks never openly claim anything. Peachtree could very well be working for them. I'll look into it."

"Thanks man," Charles said.

"Listen, the Bureau wants me to bring you into the investigation. They want me to get you to cooperate."

Charles shook his head. "No. I don't have time to get wrapped up in some bureaucratic turf war. I have my own agenda."

"And what's that?"

"I'm bringing Peachtree down for what they did to me. If the Bureau wants to help me do that, fine. If not, that's fine too. Just make sure they stay out of my way," Charles said.

Tyler sighed. "You know it doesn't work that way. The Bureau doesn't want some lone cowboy messing up its investigation. If you won't cooperate voluntarily, they'll try to make you cooperate and, as usual, I'll be stuck in the middle."

"All right. I'll come in to meet with the Bureau and make

them think I'm cooperating. That'll make you look good and give me access to the information I need. But the minute they try to put a muzzle on me or do something I don't like, I'm history."

Tyler shrugged. "We'll work it out."

"We always do. Now, tell me what the Bureau knows so far."

CHAPTER X

Early Thursday morning, Charles picked Kathy up at her condo and they took a chartered flight to New York. She had never flown on a chartered flight before. She loved everything about it, from the convenience of going through security and boarding the flight to the delicious breakfast made to order for her by the flight attendant.

"Oh man," she said, after they finished eating. "You're in trouble now. You've spoiled me. I'll never want to take a commercial flight again."

Charles laughed. "Yeah. I know what you mean. You know what they say: once you go private, you never want to go commercial again."

Kathy laughed. "I thought the saying was once you go Black, you never go back."

Charles wiggled his eyebrows. "That too."

A car was waiting for them when they arrived at the airport. They climbed in and were spirited off to the New York offices of Gold, Rome & Harris.

Charles whistled when they stepped off the elevator and

into the sumptuous lobby of the law firm. "Now I know why the rates I'm paying are so high."

Kathy shot him a look and led the way to the reception desk. It was manned by a woman so beautiful she could easily have passed for a fashion model.

The receptionist smiled and fluttered long eyelashes at Charles. He grinned at her.

Kathy cleared her throat. "Hi Brenda. Long time no see. How've you been?"

Brenda aimed her megawatt smile at Kathy. "Kathy, it's so good to see you. I've been great. Jessie and I are expecting our third little one." She rubbed her nonexistent stomach through the thin material of the slinky black dress.

"Really? You'd never tell. Congratulations."

Brenda simpered. "Thank you. So, who is this gorgeous male specimen you've brought with you?"

"Brenda, I'd like you to meet our client, Charles Morgan, Jr. Charles, this is the incorrigible Brenda. If you need anything while you're here in New York, she's the one to ask."

Brenda held out her hand. "Very pleased to meet you."

Charles shook it. "Likewise."

"Do I have the same visitor's office I had last time?" Kathy asked.

Brenda tapped a few keys on her computer. "No. This time, we put you in the visitor's office right next to conference room C on the 27th floor. We reserved conference room C for you for the next two days. There's a coffee set-up in there now."

"Thank you, Brenda." Kathy turned to Charles and grabbed the handle of her suitcase. "Follow me."

He followed her down a long hallway past several closed doors into a small office. Kathy took a seat behind the desk. Charles sat in one of the visitor's chairs. "Are we meeting with the witness in here?"

Kathy shook her head. "No, we're meeting her in the conference room next door."

"Okay. I'll set up in there."

Kathy held up a hand. "Whoa. Wait a minute. We need to go over the ground rules for the interview first."

Charles raised his eyebrows. "There are ground rules?"

"Yes. You let me speak to the witness first. Annette had to practically beg her to meet with us. Apparently, Peachtree has her scared out of her wits. After I've got her calmed down and answering questions, then you can ask yours. Try not to intimidate her."

Charles smiled. "I shouldn't intimidate her? What about you?"

Kathy frowned. "I am not intimidating."

Charles merely grinned at her. Kathy felt her lips twitch. The man had her saying the damndest things. "I mean, I know that I can be intimidating sometimes. When it's appropriate."

Charles cracked up. "I don't know. You look pretty intimidating to me right now." He winced under her bland stare. "I'm just saying."

The intercom buzzed. It was Brenda announcing the arrival of the witness.

"Thanks Brenda. Please escort her into the conference room." Kathy turned to Charles. "It's show time."

***

The witness – Ana Cabal – was the former mistress of a man who was killed by employees of Peachtree Consulting during a shootout in the Village. A statuesque, blonde-haired Puerto Rican woman, she wore a low-cut tawny gold sweater dress that hugged every curve of her body, a pair of high-heeled brown suede boots, too much make-up, and enough baubles and bangles to outfit a jewelry store. She jumped when Kathy and Charles stepped into the room. Her eyes darted back and forth and she looked as though she might flee at any moment.

Kathy made sure to close the door behind her. She then held out her hand and headed toward the witness. "Ms. Cabal?" The witness nodded. "My name is Kathy Brooks and this is my client, Charles Morgan, Jr."

Ms. Cabal shook Kathy's hand and then Charles'. "Hello."

"Thank you so much for agreeing to meet with us today. I can't tell you how much we appreciate it."

Ms. Cabal shifted. "I don't know how much I can tell you. I told that lady who called me that I signed an agreement with Peachtree. My lawyer said that I can't mention anything about the case or they could take back the money they gave me."

"They paid you off?" Charles asked, his voice filled with disgust.

"They made a settlement with me." Ms. Cabal folded her arms across her torso.

Kathy sent Charles a look that clearly told him to shut his mouth. He pursed his lips and looked away. She turned back to the woman. "Do you have a copy of the settlement agreement with you?"

"Yes." Ms. Cabal turned to the oversized purse sitting on the chair next to her, extracted some folded up pieces of paper, and handed them to Kathy.

Kathy unfolded the document and read it. It was a standard confidentiality and settlement agreement. Peachtree Consulting had paid her a hundred thousand dollars. In exchange, she agreed not to speak to anyone about the suit brought by her lover's wife, the incident in which he was killed, or the terms of the agreement. Kathy tapped her pen against her lip as she thought about how to approach the witness. On one hand, she needed whatever information the woman could provide. On the other hand, she would be encouraging her to breach her agreement. If Peachtree found out about it, they could bring a suit against her. The least Kathy could do was make sure the woman was fully aware of the risk she was taking.

"Ms. Cabal – Ana – I'm not your attorney so I can't give you legal advice. You should know though, that this agreement is very clear. Unless you are compelled to testify by Court order, it would be a breach of the agreement for you to tell us anything about the suit or the shooting incident. If you do, Peachtree Consulting can sue you for the one hundred thousand dollars they paid you," Kathy said.

Charles sent Kathy a dirty look. She deliberately ignored him and focused on Ana. "But you know what Ana? You're a smart woman. I think you knew that before you walked in here. You're obviously nervous, but you came to meet us anyway. You took a huge risk. Why?"

"Because I don't care about the stupid money. It's all gone anyway. I just want my Rico back." She burst into tears.

Charles looked horrified. Kathy grabbed a pack of tissues from her purse and walked over to sit in the chair next to the woman. She patted her on the back and put the pack of tissues in front of her.

Ana cried herself out. When her tears finally subsided to hiccups she grabbed a couple of tissues and wiped her face. She then grabbed a few more and blew her nose loudly. "I'm sorry," she said. "I couldn't help it. I never realized how much I loved him until he was gone. At first, he was just another - *como se dice* - sugar daddy to me. He was older than me and married. But he was different than the others. He treated me with respect. He bought me a condo in Long Island. He took me places and bought me anything I asked for. He treated me very well and was always kind. I miss him so much."

"I know," Kathy said, patting her on the shoulder. "Why don't you tell us how it happened?"

"You mean the day they took my Rico away?" Ana asked.

"Yes," Kathy said. "Take us back to the day of the incident."

"Well, Rico and I went into the City to have dinner at a nice little café in the Village. He loved to go to the Village. It made him feel young." She looked sad, as if she would dissolve into tears again. Kathy put her hand over hers and squeezed. Ana swallowed hard. "We had dinner. It was nice. Rico could be so romantic sometimes. After dinner, we left the café and started to walk. Two men ran by. One man jumped on the other man and they started fighting. We stopped to look. I heard this popping sound and then Rico was flying in the air through the window of the restaurant. I screamed and ran over to him." She stopped, touched her forehead and made the sign of the cross. "*Madre de Dios*, there was so much blood - so much blood." Tears spilled down her cheeks. She grabbed another tissue from the box and dabbed at them.

"Did you see anything else?" Charles asked.

"The police got there fast. I talked to them and then I went home. I tried to go to Rico's funeral, but his wife had me thrown out. She called me a whore. Can you believe that?"

Kathy swallowed a smile and avoided looking at Charles. "No, that's terrible."

"We had something special and now it's all gone," Ana said.

"What happened with the case? " Kathy asked.

"I didn't even know Rico's wife had filed a lawsuit until one day they served me with papers. I had to appear at her lawyer's office. They asked me the same questions you did. They made me swear that I would tell the truth. A woman typed everything I said."

"You mean they took your deposition," Charles said.

Ana nodded. "Yes, my deposition."

"How did you enter into the settlement?" Charles asked.

"A couple of days after my deposition, a man approached me. He bought me a cup of coffee at Starbucks and we walked around the mall. He said he worked for Peachtree Consulting and that the company was going to settle with the wife. He said they were willing to enter into a settlement agreement with me too. He offered me fifty thousand dollars. I told him that I wanted a hundred thousand or I would tell my story to the newspapers. He told me that I had a deal, but if I ever told anyone about what happened I would be sorry." She shuddered. "He was really scary. I'll never forget his eyes. They had this look in them. Like he had no soul." She shrugged. "It was the most money I ever had, so I took it. What can I say?"

"What did the man look like?" Charles asked.

Ana raised her eyes toward the ceiling. "He was white,

shorter than you, with brown hair and brown eyes."

"Did he have a small tattoo on the back of his right hand?" Charles asked.

Ana's eyes widened. "Yes! I saw it when he handed me my coffee. It was a small American flag. Why? Do you know him?"

Kathy looked at Charles and wondered the same thing. From his questions, it was quite obvious he had failed to share some vital information with her. Information she would probably need for the case. She was tired of it. She was going to have a little chat with him later. But first things first. She turned back to Ana. "Ana, did you order a copy of your deposition transcript?"

"No." Ana shook her head. "It was too expensive. I went to review it at the Court reporter's office for mistakes and I signed it."

"Do you remember the name of the court reporter?" Charles asked.

"Mudrick something," Ana said, waving a hand. "Their office is on 38th and Broadway. The name is on the subpoena they served me."

"Do you still have a copy of the subpoena?" Kathy asked.

Ana nodded. "I brought a copy with me. I also have a copy of the police report. My lawyer got me a copy to help me prepare for the deposition." She opened her purse, rummaged around, and extracted a sheaf of papers. She handed them to Charles.

Charles laid the sheaf of papers down onto the table and separated them. There was a copy of the subpoena, a copy of the police report, and a copy of a court reporter's card with handwritten directions. He and Kathy looked at each other and smiled.

Kathy turned to Ana. "Ana, is it okay if I make copies of these papers and the settlement agreement?"

Ana nodded.

Kathy left the room to make arrangements to have the copies made. She then rejoined Charles and the witness at the conference table. "Ana, thank you so much for coming here and agreeing to talk with us. In a perfect world that would be enough. But the only way we're going to be able to use the information you've given us is if we subpoena you to testify in our case and you agree to do it. Will you do that for us?"

Ana shook her head slowly from side to side. "I don't know."

"One of Peachtree's employees killed my wife and kid," Charles said. His voice was quiet. "He rammed his car into my wife's car on the highway while conducting a high speed chase. He hit her car so hard it slammed into a concrete median and burst into flames. She was six months pregnant with our baby girl when she died. Our baby didn't make it either."

Ana covered her mouth with her hand, her face containing expressions of both horror and sympathy. "Oh my God. That is terrible. Terrible."

"We believe that Peachtree was conducting a rogue operation on behalf of the C.I.A. at the time of the accident," Charles said.

Kathy stared at him. This was the first time she had heard him refer to a rogue operation. That would explain the government's recent actions. If Peachtree was, in fact, involved in an unauthorized or unsanctioned operation at the time of the accident, the government would want to handle that situation quietly. It would certainly want to keep that information out of the public domain.

"We tried to get proof of Peachtree's involvement in illegal activities," Charles said, "but the company does everything possible to keep us from doing that. They settle any lawsuits brought against them early and tie witnesses up with confidentiality agreements and threats. They tried to buy me off too. But no amount of money can replace my wife and my baby girl. It's time someone stopped them from hurting people. Don't let them get away with it any longer."

Ana stared at Charles, clearly affected by what he had said. The war between her fear and her desire to help played out on her face.

He reached across the table and put his hand over hers. "If you won't do it for me then do it for Rico. Those bastards killed him and then tried to buy you off. Do it for him."

A resolute gleam appeared in Ana's eyes. She banged a heavily ringed fist on the table and nodded her head. "Yes. I'll do it for Rico."

A happy smile spread across Charles' face. He aimed a triumphant look at Kathy. Kathy gave him a weak smile and then turned to Ana. "Ana, thank you so much for agreeing to help. Peachtree is going to try to put a lot of pressure on you not to testify. You should get an attorney to represent you. Do you want to use the same lawyer you used before?"

Ana shook her head. "I can't. He's dead, just like my Rico. He was killed not long after I entered into the settlement agreement. They said it was a mugging. Can you recommend an attorney to represent me?"

"Sure," Kathy said. She picked up her Blackberry,

scrolled through her electronic directory, scribbled a name and number onto a piece of paper, and handed it to Ana. "Give her a call. She and I went to law school together. She's an excellent attorney. She'll take good care of you."

"Thank you," Ana said.

"No. Thank you," Kathy said.

She called Brenda to escort Ana Cabal out.

***

Charles wanted to cheer as he watched the receptionist lead Ana Cabal from the conference room. The interview couldn't have gone better. Her description of the man who had offered her a settlement matched Manning to a tee. Now, if they could just confirm that Manning still worked for the C.I.A., they could establish a clear link between the agency and the incident that killed Ana Cabal's boyfriend. That would be enough to fuel the F.B.I.'s investigation into Peachtree and the C.I.A.'s unauthorized domestic activities.

Charles turned to look at Kathy and did a double take when he saw the expression on her face. Her eyes were narrowed and her mouth was set into a grim line. She raised a hand and stabbed an index finger in his direction. "You're going to come clean right now or I will terminate this representation and file a motion to withdraw from this case so fast your head will spin."

"What are you talking about?" he asked.

"Don't play dumb with me, Charles, because I am not in the mood. I heard you tell that woman we believe Peachtree was involved in a rogue C.I.A. operation at the time of the accident. That was the first time I heard about this rogue operation. Where did you get that information? I'd be very careful with my next statement if I were you. If you lie to me one more time, I'm out of here."

Charles looked at Kathy and saw that she meant business. There was a fire in her eye he had never seen before. He knew he had to tell her something or she was going to walk. He couldn't let her do that. He needed her. "Okay. I'll tell you." He gestured for her to take a seat and then sat down himself.

Kathy sat and crossed her arms over her well-endowed chest. He wished she hadn't done that. It caused his mind to wander places it shouldn't when he needed to focus. "When I read the police report of the accident and found out that Wilkes was employed by Peachtree, I began to suspect he was engaged in unauthorized activity at the time of the accident. Defense firms like Peachtree aren't supposed to be chasing people down on highways. They usually provide security or investigate things. There are a whole host of domestic law enforcement agencies authorized to track down criminals and suspected terrorists in the U.S., ranging from local law enforcement officers to the F.B.I., the D.E.A, the U.S. Marshals and Homeland Security. You get the picture. I was hoping to find proof that Peachtree was involved in a rogue operation in their discovery responses. But that turned out to be a dead end."

"We don't know that. We haven't finished reviewing all of the documents yet. Plus, since you didn't tell me about your suspicions, we didn't know to look for that sort of thing. If you had been upfront with me from the beginning, we could have worked together on this. It also explains why the government's so interested in getting rid of this case. Why didn't you tell me?"

"I was afraid that if you knew what I suspected, you wouldn't continue to represent me. You might think the case was too dangerous," he said.

"So you thought withholding this information while putting me and my law firm in danger was a better idea?" She shook her head. "I can't believe you. What other information have you withheld?"

"I have a friend who's an F.B.I. agent. He told me the other day that the F.B.I. was conducting an investigation into Peachtree. They tried to send an agent in to infiltrate the company, but he turned up dead. They can't prove that Peachtree was responsible."

"But they suspect it."

Charles nodded. "Yes. And now that one of their own has been killed, they're more determined than ever to bring Peachtree down. They want me to cooperate with the investigation and provide them with any information we obtain in our lawsuit."

"I don't see how we can do that. The documents Peachtree produced to us are protected by the confidentiality order. We can't give copies of them to the F.B.I. Any facts we obtain from interviewing witnesses are protected from discovery by the work-product privilege – at least until the witnesses testify at trial or in deposition. We waive that privilege if we disclose the results of the interviews with the F.B.I. If we waive the privilege, then Peachtree would have the right to discover our interview notes. They could find a way to stop us from taking Ana Cabal's deposition or, worse yet, take measures to stop her from testifying - permanently. And remember - the F.B.I. is an agency of the federal government. We don't know which agencies use Peachtree or who their contacts are. There could be all kinds of leaks at the F.B.I."

Charles was impressed. She'd raised some very valid points – some he hadn't thought of. As a sniper and the head of a military unit, he was used to calling all the shots when it came to strategy. But sometimes, two heads were better than one. That was especially true when the other head contained a mind as sharp as Kathy's. "You're right. I'm going to need your help with the F.B.I. If I don't cooperate with them, they're going to subpoena me."

Kathy nodded. "Understood. Do you see now why it's best to tell me these things? Here you are facing a possible subpoena from the F.B.I. while I, your counsel, am completely clueless. I can't help you if you keep things from me. We have to work on our lines of communication."

"Okay," he said. "I'll be up front with you from now on." He kept his fingers crossed behind his back.

"Good," she said.

***

McAllister arrived in New York a few hours after Charles and Kathy. He took a cab to the Ritz-Carlton and checked in. He then left the building, crossed the street and climbed into a waiting sedan. The driver, a middle-aged East Indian operative, turned to look at him.

"Report," McAllister said.

"We picked them up at the airport. They took a town car to 455 East Fifth Street. They got off on the 25th floor which belongs to the Gold Rome & Harris law firm. They stayed there for approximately four hours and then came here and checked in. They asked the concierge for dinner recommendations. He made them a reservation at Buddakan's. They took a cab to the restaurant and are having dinner there as we speak."

"Who's watching them now?" McAllister asked.

"Ravi and Sam," he said.

"Good. I'm going to relieve Ravi. Get yourself a replacement. Charles Morgan, Jr. used to be a player. I want a large team assigned to him while he's here and I want frequent rotation. I don't want him seeing any familiar faces."

The operative nodded. "That's a good disguise you're wearing. I didn't recognize you when you first got into the car. It's a good thing you said something. I was two seconds away from pulling the trigger."

McAllister smiled. "Why thank you." He patted his white goatee. "Now, let's go have dinner."

CHAPTER XI

Charles and Kathy arrived at Buddakan, a popular downtown Asian-fusion restaurant. They checked in with the hostess and were led through the airy bar and lounge area down one of the two wide curved staircases leading into the main dining room. Housed in a former cookie factory, the restaurant was huge. The main dining room was a beautifully decorated space with large chandeliers and high ceilings.

The sheer size of the place and the multiple points of entry into the main dining room made Charles a little uneasy. He would have preferred a smaller more intimate environment where he could keep an eye on the other restaurant patrons. He had no doubt Peachtree would try to find a way to stop the progress they were making on his case. They probably knew by now that he and Kathy were in New York. He thought he had detected a tail on the way to the airport in Miami. They might have gotten the charter company to give them information about their intended destination.

On the way to the table, Charles got the lay of the land and took a good look at the restaurant's clientele. Most of the tables were filled with everything from girlfriends giggling their way through dinner to couples enjoying a romantic evening. A large party appeared to be having a celebration at the communal dining table dominating one section of the dining room.

The waitress led them to a table for two in the center of the room. He made sure to take the seat with the best view of both staircases.

"I've always wanted to try this place," Kathy said.

Charles turned to look at her. "Oh yeah?"

"Yeah. Some friends of mine ate here and told me how good the food is."

Kathy kept talking. Charles listened to her with one ear as he continued his surveillance of the restaurant.

A man dressed in a very expensive suit, carrying a black cane with a silver metal tip followed the hostess down one of the staircases into the dining room. He had salt and pepper hair, a mustache and a small white goatee. There was something familiar about him. Charles couldn't put his finger on it though. He watched as the hostess led the man to a table on the other side of the room. He seemed content to dine alone and didn't so much as glance in their direction.

He realized that Kathy had gone silent and turned to look at her. She was sitting back in her seat with her arms crossed looking at him.

"What?" he asked.

"You tell me what. I got tired of talking to myself. Have you heard a word I said in the past five minutes?"

"Yeah, you were talking about clothing trends over the past few decades and how some of the trends that were prevalent in the seventies and eighties have come back recently, like halter tops, short shorts and wedge heels."

She raised her eyebrows. "Wow, I must confess that I'm impressed. How did you manage to hear all that while staring at the man who just walked in? What's going on?"

"He looks familiar to me," Charles said. "Something about the way he walks. I can't put my finger on it though."

Kathy looked over at the man. "You think you might have seen him before?"

"Don't stare at him," Charles said.

She turned back to Charles. "Where did you see him? Here in New York or back in Miami?

Charles shook his head. "I don't know. I'd have remembered the hair, the mustache, the goatee and the cane. Those are all distinguishing characteristics. But I don't."

A small frown appeared between Kathy's brows. He decided to lighten the mood a little. "He's probably just a businessman enjoying a nice dinner and I'm being paranoid. Too many spy movies."

She smiled. He was happy to see it. "You know what they say. Just because you're paranoid doesn't mean they're not out to get you."

Charles chuckled. "Who says that?"

Kathy shrugged. "I heard the line in a movie trailer or something and have used it ever since."

She took a sip of the specialty cocktail she had ordered. It was called "Fate" and, according to the drink menu, was made of elderflower, pineapple and Prosecco. He had ordered a Heineken and nursed it. He needed to be sharp. There were too many excuses for "accidents" to happen to them in New York – a botched mugging, a reckless driver, a stray bullet. New York was a dangerous place. "So, what's on the agenda for tomorrow?"

"Tomorrow morning we're going to drive out to Queens and try to see Rico's widow - Mrs. Eva Roberts," she said. "Erin couldn't get her to agree to meet with us. I was hoping we might have better luck in person."

He nodded. "Sounds like a plan. I made arrangements for the charter to take us back to Miami tomorrow afternoon."

"Good. I have a ton of work I need to do when we get back."

The waitress delivered their food. They shared the dishes, family-style, and feasted on everything from Shanghai soup dumplings to lobster. The food was delicious. They ended the meal with the restaurant's most popular dessert – "Crying Chocolate" – a molten chocolate cake topped with white chocolate ganache, coffee ice cream and caramel. He watched Kathy's eyes roll up into her head.

"Mmmm," she moaned. She licked her spoon and then her lips.

Charles' gaze was riveted to the tip of her tongue. He found himself wanting a taste of her. "Good huh?"

"Positively orgasmic."

Damn. Why did she have to say that? Erotic images of the two of them, together, flashed into his mind. He imagined giving her a real orgasm. Feeling his body respond, he shifted in his seat.

"I'm going to have to work out like a maniac tomorrow to work off these calories, but right now, I don't care," she said.

"Well, don't they say that lovemaking is the best exercise?" he asked.

She pointed her spoon at him. "Yes, that's true. So, in a sense, I'm working out right now."

Charles laughed. "Only an attorney could come up with that logic."

"I can rationalize anything. Even as a child. My mother had a hard time with me. I could argue myself into or out of anything. She always said that I was destined to either become a lawyer or a con woman."

"Well, I, for one, am glad you decided on the former and not the latter."

She smiled. "Me too."

She had a pretty smile that could light up a room. He realized that he was getting distracted by it – by her in general. He needed to get his head back into the game for both their sakes. "We should get back to the hotel. We have an early start tomorrow."

She glanced at her watch and nodded. "You're right. I didn't realize how late it was."

He paid the tab and asked the hostess to call a taxi for them. It was waiting outside when they exited the restaurant. He opened the door for Kathy. As she climbed in, he scanned the street. It was quiet, except for a bum lying on a heat grate. There were several parked cars on the opposite side of the street, but no vans. The cars appeared to be empty. He climbed into the vehicle.

***

Kathy gazed out of the windows of the taxi as they drove back to the hotel. She loved New York. The city always seemed so alive to her. She missed it sometimes – especially in the fall when the trees turned pretty colors and there was a slight nip in the air. She definitely missed New York pizza, bagels and Chinese food. For some reason, those things were better in New York than anywhere else in the world.

She looked over at Charles. He seemed to be lost in his own thoughts. There were times that evening when they really seemed to connect and others when he had seemed so distant. He was staring out the window so she took the opportunity to study his profile. The dimple in his right cheek held her attention. She felt an almost undeniable urge to slide across the seat and kiss him there. He turned to look at her. She looked away and stared out the window.

They arrived at the hotel and rode the elevator up to their floor in silence. Their rooms were right across the hall from each other. When she got to her door, she turned to him, looked up into his eyes and smiled. "Thank you for dinner Charles. I had a nice time."

"I did too," he said.

They stood there for a moment, staring into each other's eyes. Mesmerized by his gaze, Kathy was unable to move. Some emotion passed behind his eyes and they grew darker. His gaze drop to her lips. She really wanted him to kiss her - to see whether it would live up to all those nights of dreaming about what it would feel like.

Suddenly, she felt herself jammed up against the wall, his hard body pressed against hers while he almost devoured her lips. Sensation shot through her body. She groaned. Her hands roamed over his back and then slid lower, until she was gripping and squeezing his taut behind. It was his turn to groan. He ground his pelvis into hers.

The kiss seemed to go on endlessly. Finally, he lifted his head and took a small step back. She sagged against the door of her room, panting slightly through parted lips. She opened her eyes to find him looking at her, a half smile on his lips. He quirked an eyebrow.

She smiled and nodded in response to the unspoken question. She reached into her purse, extracted the room key and opened the door. They had barely gotten inside the room and closed the door before she found herself pressed up against his hard body again. This time, he banded an arm around her back and molded her against him as he kissed her. His hands roamed over her back and then lower, over her buttocks.

He squeezed her there. Heat travelled down her belly and straight to her groin. He pulled back a little and threw her jacket over her shoulders. She dropped her arms so that it slid off her shoulders and onto the floor. He reached behind her and unzipped her dress in one smooth motion. It fell to the floor, revealing her lacy white slip. She stepped out of the dress and kicked it to one side. He stepped back and stood there, drinking her in with his eyes from head to toe as if she were an oasis in the middle of a desert and he was dying of thirst.

He stepped forward hooked his fingers into the thin straps of her lacy slip and slid them down over her shoulders. The slip fell to the floor in a film of white. She stepped out it and stood there, in her white lace demi-bra, bikini underwear and pumps. He licked his lips like a hungry wolf. She put her hand on her hip and posed a little for him. Then she stepped forward and kissed him, her tongue exploring the inside of his mouth. He put his hands on her hips and molded her pelvis against his. She groaned and squeezed his biceps with her hands. She then bit him gently on his bottom lip. He groaned and held her tighter.

She pulled away, yanked his shirt out of his pants, and began to unbutton it. When she had gotten it unbuttoned, she pushed it over his shoulders. He put his arms down to let it slide to the floor. She trailed kisses down his neck over the hard muscles of his chest and teased his nipples with her teeth and tongue. He groaned again. His response to her touch made her feel powerfully feminine.

He pulled back a little, slid his right arm under her knees, picked her up and carried her over to the bed. Laying her down gently, he trailed kisses down her neck and then teased the flesh just over the cups of her bra. He reached for the clip in between her breasts and released it setting them free. Her nipples were as hard as rocks.

He bent down and took one in his mouth, allowing his tongue to circle it. He then teased her nipple with his teeth and his tongue the way she done his. Little shocks tingled from her nipples straight down to her sex. She moaned and arched her back, thinking for sure that she would go mad. He released the nipple and then moved on to the other.

When she was unable to take any more sensual torment, she pushed him back onto the bed and climbed on top. She trailed kisses down his chest and then grabbed his belt buckle. She undid it, opened his fly, grabbed the top of his pants at the waistband and tugged. He lifted his hips to oblige her and she backed away, pulling his pants down over his hips. She kissed his belly just above the waistband of his black boxer briefs, sliding her tongue over his belly button. He groaned.

She gripped the waistband of his boxers, tugged and set him free. His engorged member sprang out. He was very well-endowed. She licked him from the base to the top like a lollipop a few times before taking him deep inside her mouth and applying suction. He moaned and gripped the back of her head. She ringed the base with her thumb and forefinger and worked him over until she knew he was on the verge of releasing. Then she stopped and smiled at him.

He opened one eye and squinted at her before flipping her onto her back and grinding his hips into hers. She moaned. He left a trail of kisses and nips in between her breasts, over her stomach and then right above the waistband of her bikini underwear. He reached down and ripped them right off of her. She gasped, but had no time to recover before he buried his face into her honey pot and proceeded to feast on her most sensitive areas. All rational thought fled her brain as he licked, suckled and penetrated her with his tongue. She writhed against him, threw her head from side to side and cried out as wave after wave of multiple orgasms shook her. At one point, she became too sensitive. She pushed at him and tried to get away, but he pulled her back, pinned her legs to the bed with his elbows and continued his delicious torment.

When sheer exhaustion stopped her from moving, he rose to his knees and pulled her toward him by her legs. Spreading them wide, he plunged himself deep into her wetness. She gasped in shock and pleasure. He pulled out, almost to the end and then plunged into her again before beginning a slow and building rhythm. She cried out and gripped his hips as he plunged in and out of her. After a while, he pulled out, and flipped her onto her belly. He slid backwards off the bed, pulled her back toward him and slapped her across the butt.

"Get on your knees," he growled. She obliged him. He positioned her on the edge of the bed, entered her from behind and began to move in long slow strokes. She took him in all the way and threw her hips back to match him stroke for stroke. Her cries of pleasure intensified as his strokes grew stronger and stronger until he was pounding into her. She used her inner muscles to grip him tighter. He cried out and ground himself against her just as she fell over the edge into a mind-shattering orgasm of her own. When it ended, he fell onto the bed next to her. They lay there, on their backs, both gasping for air.

As the blood returned to her brain, she reflected on what had just occurred. They'd attacked each other like rabid animals in heat. At thirty-five years old, she was not inexperienced. She'd had her share of lovers - some might say more than her fair share. She'd experienced good sex, bad sex, and everything in between. But she'd never had a reaction like that to anyone – not even her ex-husband. Charles had made her reach multiple orgasms. It was as if their bodies were made for each other. He'd played her like a violin and her body had made the most beautiful music.

It scared her that anyone had the ability to make her feel that way. Couple that with the fact that he was her client and she had a recipe for disaster. She didn't know what she was going to do, but she knew she had better find the right way to play this or she might find herself not only out of a client, but also a career.

Charles got up and headed to the restroom. She heard water running in the sink. He came back to the bed carrying a wet washcloth and a towel. He put the towel down onto the bed, then reached down and opened her legs. He gently began to clean her up. The washcloth was warm and comforting. She didn't know what to think. She found the experience oddly sweet. He dried her off with the towel and then took the towel and the wash cloth back into the bathroom.

He came back to the bed, lay down next to her and pulled her close, cradling her head in the crook between his neck and his shoulder. She threw her arm over him and lay there quietly for a while, her face on his chest. It felt so good to be held. No-one had cuddled her like that in years. She hadn't allowed anyone else to get that close.

"That was wild," she said.

"I'll say."

"I want you to know that I don't usually go jumping into bed with clients like that."

"Oh, so it only happens on the rare occasion?"

She chuckled. "No. Silly. I mean that I've never slept with a client before. I don't know what possessed me to do it tonight."

"Well, it's not like I'm in a position to judge here. We pretty much ravaged each other," he said.

She covered her eyes with her hand. "Oh God. Is that what we did?"

He grinned. "Yup. I'd say you gave as good as you got, Counselor."

Kathy lay there with her hand over her eyes. If only the bed could have swallowed her whole. She was mortified at his description of the event. She didn't know how she was ever going to recover a shred of dignity in this relationship. He reached over and pulled her hand from her eyes. "It's no use trying to hide now, Counselor. I've already seen and tasted almost every part of you. And may I say it was a very tasty treat indeed."

She pushed away from him and sat up, pulling the sheet up over her breasts. "Listen, we need to talk."

He closed his eyes and groaned. "Oh no. Right now?"

"Yes. Right now."

"Okay." He sat up and leaned back against the headboard next to her.

"We're two adults who enjoyed each other's company and had a good time."

He smiled. "I'm glad to hear you had a good time,

Counselor. I know I certainly did." He leaned over and kissed her shoulder.

She pushed his head away. "But we can't continue to have a good time."

"Why not?" His voice sounded perilously close to a whine.

"Because if anyone ever found out, I could lose my job and even my license for this," she said.

"Aren't you exaggerating just a little bit, Counselor?"

"No. I'm not exaggerating," she said. "My law firm has a strict anti-fraternization policy."

"You mentioned that once before," he said. "I thought you were just saying that to keep me from getting ideas. Not that it worked."

She smiled. "It's a real policy. Think about it from the firm's perspective. There's a high potential for conflict between attorneys and the clients they're sleeping with. What if they get into an argument and the client decides to leave the firm? It's much easier and safer for the firm to strictly forbid these types of relationships."

He nodded. "I can see how that would be easier for the firm. But what about feelings? The firm can't really expect to regulate those. I mean, we are human beings and being attracted to the opposite sex is natural."

She rolled her eyes. He sounded like a typical man. "We're supposed to be able to control our base urges."

He grew quiet for a moment. "I haven't felt anything like this for anyone else but my wife. I haven't even wanted to be with anyone else."

His words struck a chord in her. She could relate. She hadn't let anyone get this close to her since her divorce. "That's really sweet. Unfortunately, though, this can't continue. I'm not interested in getting fired or disbarred and you can't afford for me to be distracted from your case. We need to put all of our efforts into winning this thing."

"And afterwards?" he asked. "What happens then? I will no longer be a client of your law firm. Will the stupid policy allow you to live your life then?"

She wondered. Never having been in this situation before, she had never looked up the ethical rule or the policy and read it. She'd have to do that when she got back to the office. "I don't know. We'll cross that road when we come to it. If we still want to."

She rubbed her hand down his arm. He put his hand over hers and kept it there. It was such a simple gesture, but for some reason, she felt tears clogging her throat. She blinked them back. "Listen. We need to get some sleep. We have a big day tomorrow. Why don't you go back to your room? I'll see you in the morning. Say eight o'clock in the lobby?"

He stared at her for a moment. Then he nodded. "Okay."

He got up and picked his clothes up off the floor. She watched him. He was a hell of a male specimen. Part of her was tempted to pull him back into bed. She had to be crazy to let that leave.

He put on his jeans, wadded his shirt and his underwear into a ball and turned to her. "Goodnight, Counselor."

"Goodnight."

He walked out and closed the door behind him. She sat there for a long while, somehow saddened by what had just occurred - as if she'd lost something important by letting him go. This time, she let the tears flow down her face. She got up, walked into the bathroom, grabbed some tissues and blew her nose.

What the hell was wrong with her? First, she'd slept with a client acting like a teenager with raging hormones and now she was sobbing for opportunities lost like a heroine in some sappy romance novel. She needed to get a grip on herself. She glanced at the clock and saw that it was 2:00a.m. What she needed was some sleep. She walked out of bathroom, turned out all the lights, crawled into bed and pulled the covers over her head.

***

Charles climbed out of bed the next morning feeling groggy and irritable. He had hardly slept a wink. Instead, he'd tossed and turned all night long thinking about that damned woman. He couldn't get the way they fit together out of his mind. He hadn't experienced anything like that with anyone else besides Patti.

Here he was, risking everything to avenge Patti's death and this woman somehow managed to get under his skin. He tried to think about it rationally. She was a very attractive woman. They'd spent a lot of time together. It was only natural for them to be attracted to each other. And it had been more than a year since he'd been with a woman. Hell, his buddies would say it was about time he got his rocks off.

But he knew this was different. He'd slept with many beautiful women. They were attracted to him – had been ever since high school. They liked his personality, the way he treated them, the way he made them feel. It was a mutual love affair. He enjoyed women and they enjoyed him. He was careful not to make promises he didn't intend to keep. Even so, there was the occasional misunderstanding when a woman hoped for more than he was willing to give.

Patti had changed all that. They met while he was in the Corps. He'd been shot in the chest during an operation in Germany and she was a nurse in the naval hospital there. The first thing he saw when he woke up from the surgery was her smile. She'd looked like an angel to him. During his time at the hospital, she took great care of him. Even when he was grouchy from the pain or from being stuck with needles all the time - he hated needles – she would joke around or soothe him. She would come to his room during her breaks and between rounds and they would talk about everything and nothing.

When he was discharged from the hospital, he missed her. He used his clearance to look up her service record and to keep track of her whereabouts. When she ended her tour of duty in Germany and returned to the States, she moved to Miami. He took a vacation there and engineered an opportunity to run into her. He took her out to dinner that night on Ocean Drive and then he took her dancing at Mango's. Afterwards, they sat on the beach, talked for hours and watched the sun rise. He knew then that he had met his soul mate.

When Patti died, he just shut down. He lost interest in anything other than getting revenge. He didn't think he'd ever find another woman who could make him feel a fraction of what he felt for Patti. But now, he couldn't get Kathy out of his head. He wanted more and more of her - and not just her body. He wanted all of her – mind, body and soul. It was much more than simple lust.

He swore. This was the last thing he needed. He had no business having feelings for his attorney. It would only get in the way. What kind of man got feelings for another woman while in the process of avenging his wife's death? The whole situation made him feel guilty and frustrated. But no matter how inconvenient or inappropriate his feelings were, he had them. There was no denying that.

He would have to deal with his feelings at some point, but that time was not now. Kathy was right. Until this situation with Peachtree was resolved, they couldn't afford to be distracted. One false move could get them both killed. Plus, he needed her focused on winning the lawsuit. So, for now, Kathy would get her wish. Until he succeeded in destroying Peachtree, he wouldn't pursue a personal relationship with her. After he accomplished his mission, however, all bets would be off.

***

The next morning, McAllister and Peachtree watched the video footage taken from Kathy Brook's hotel room. A broad grin spread across Peachtree's face. "Well, looky here. I had no idea the counselor could let her hair down that much. She acts so high and mighty in the courtroom with her hair pulled back into a bun and wearing them fancy glasses. I wonder how she'd feel if some of this footage found its way to the Internet or, worse yet, the 10:00 o'clock news. That ought to give her incentive to get her client to settle this damned case."

McAllister smiled. "Here I was just hoping to see if they met with anybody or discussed trial strategy in each other's rooms. Instead, we hit the jackpot. It just goes to show that it always pays to be prepared."

"I know that I can always count on you for that," Peachtree said. He looked back at the video screen as Kathy's cries and Charles' moans reached a crescendo. "That sure is one fine looking woman."

"Yeah," McAllister said. "I wouldn't kick that out of bed."

Peachtree laughed. McAllister pushed a button on the remote to fast forward the video. "Keep watching. It gets even more interesting afterwards." He fast forwarded to the part where Charles and Kathy were sitting up and talking in bed.

An evil grin spread over Peachtree's face as he listened to Kathy talk about the possible consequences of their illicit activities. "This is better than I even imagined. It's one thing to blackmail a woman with the threat of exposing all of her intimate secrets to the public. But the counselor just gave me an even better idea of how best to utilize this little home movie. If what she says is true, the little filly risked her job and her law license by jumping her client's bones. Greed and pride are very powerful motivators and lawyers are notoriously greedy and arrogant. She's not going to want to risk her license or her standing at the firm to keep this case going. Well now, since she's obviously got the means to make Mr. Morgan forget all about his dead wife, she can put her skills and her cute little behind to work for us if she wants to save her reputation and her livelihood." He pushed the intercom button. "Giada, get Weisman on the line. I need to talk to him."

CHAPTER XII

Kathy met Charles in the lobby the next morning. He looked tired. She'd barely slept a wink herself. She'd tossed and turned all night thinking about him, and, when she finally drifted off, she'd dreamed about him.

"Morning," she said.

"Morning."

They stood there for an awkward moment. He rolled his eyes and took her suitcase from her. "Look, I'll put this in the car. Why don't you meet me in the coffee shop next door and order us up some breakfast?"

She nodded. "Sounds good. I could use some green tea. What do you want?"

"I'll have some coffee, eggs over easy and rye toast," he said.

"You got it," she said.

She gripped the strap of her handbag and headed toward the exit. She could feel Charles' eyes on her as she walked away. When she got to the door, she turned back to look at him and caught him in the act. He grinned. She smiled and exited the hotel.

Her smile faded as she headed toward the café. Okay, so they were attracted to each other. That was fine – even normal. But she shouldn't be encouraging him. There was too much at stake here. The best thing for them both would be to keep it strictly business.

She marched into the café, secured a table and ordered breakfast for herself and her client. When the waitress finished taking her order, Kathy pulled out her Blackberry and began scrolling through her e-mails. She winced. It seemed as if all of her other cases were blowing up at the same time. Charles' case had taken so much of her time that she kept putting things off. Now she had three hearings, two briefs and a deposition scheduled for the following week. She needed some help. She sent an e-mail to Erin requesting that she get started on the briefs.

The little bells above the restaurant door jingled. Kathy looked up to see Charles walking in. Damn. Just the sight of him was enough to make her mouth water. She stared at him, a silly smile across her face, as he walked up to their table. Realizing that she was staring at him, she dropped her gaze and noticed, for the first time, the two steaming mugs on the table. The waitress must have brought their drinks while she was reading her e-mails. She cleared her throat and gestured toward them.

"I ordered the food and there's your coffee," she said.

"Thanks." He sat down, picked up his coffee and took a sip.

She dug into her purse, pulled out one of her green stevia packets, ripped it open and poured its contents into her cup. "I hope Mrs. Roberts will agree to talk to us."

"I hope so too," he said.

***

The Lincoln town car pulled up in front of a large Colonial style house in a nice residential neighborhood in Queens. There were no cars parked in the driveway.

Charles and Kathy looked at each other.

"Maybe her car is parked in the garage," she said.

"Let's go see," he said.

Kathy gathered her purse and briefcase. The driver came around to open her car door and she began to climb out. Just as her feet hit the sidewalk, however, a loud blast erupted. The ground shook. Windows blew out of the second floor of the two story house showering glass onto the sidewalk below. The driver put his hand over his head and hunched his shoulders.

Kathy screamed and pulled her feet back into the town car. Charles, who had already gotten out, opened his car door, reached in, grabbed Kathy under her arms and dragged her backwards out of the car on his side. Kathy, Charles and the driver ran across the street and ducked for cover behind some parked cars just as a second explosion shook the block. Charles pulled Kathy close and covered her body with his as more debris came crashing down onto the street. After a moment, when it appeared the explosions were over, he eased off Kathy.

She pushed at her hair to get it out of her face, adjusted her glasses and sat up slowly, feeling dazed and confused. Charles grabbed her by the chin and turned her head to face him. That's when she realized he was talking to her. Her ears were ringing so much from the explosion that she could barely hear him. She shook her head, hoping to clear them.

Looking worried, he propped her eyelids open with his fingers and peered into her eyes. Annoyed, she pulled her head away from his grasp.

"Are you alright?" he asked

She heard him this time and nodded. "What the hell?"

She turned to look at the house across the street. It was still standing though it looked as if it might collapse any second. Flames licked at the window openings on the second floor and smoke billowed out into the street.

People came out of their houses and milled about watching the fire. Occasionally, someone would point at the town car. The neighbors stared at them curiously. Kathy heard the sound of sirens in the background. They were getting closer. She turned to Charles. "Do you think Mrs. Roberts was in there?"

Charles nodded, his mouth set into a grim line. "Yes, I do."

Kathy swallowed. Was it an accident? A coincidence? It had to be, because if not, then that meant Peachtree would stop at nothing to win this case. Although that was par for the course in high stakes litigation, this took it to a whole other level – one she wasn't sure she could handle.

***

Peachtree sat back in his chair across from his attorney's desk with one ankle propped casually over the knee of his other leg. "I have a little gift for you."

Weisman perked up and inclined his head to the side. "Really? What sort of gift?"

Peachtree smiled. The greedy jerk probably thought he was going to get an extra bonus or something. That was the problem with his type – the Harvard Law stuffed suits who thought they were smarter than everyone else. They had no idea what needed to be done to make sure a company like his stayed at the top of the heap. "The kind of gift that's going to help you settle this case," he said. He handed Weisman a flash drive.

"What's this?" Weisman asked, holding the flash drive up.

Peachtree just smiled and gestured toward the computer monitor sitting on top of the desk with a wide open hand. "Play it."

He watched Weisman insert the flash drive into the computer and boot it up. The attorney's eyes widened then narrowed. He fumbled for the volume control on his computer speaker as the sound of Kathy's moans began to fill the office. He knocked the speaker over. It clattered onto the desk. He righted it without taking his eyes off the screen. He then hit the pause button and turned sharp, speculative eyes upon Peachtree. "Where did you get this?"

"You don't want to know," Peachtree said. "Let's just say I got it from an anonymous source. Is it helpful to you?"

Weisman was silent for a moment. He stroked a hand over his chin a few times. Then he nodded. "Yes. It's helpful on a number of levels. There are ethical rules against sleeping with one's clients. There are also other consequences to this tape going public such as a loss of credibility and the general distaste inherent in having one's most intimate moments publicly displayed. The question is: What is the best way to utilize this information without ramifications to you or my law firm?"

Rage coursed through Peachtree. Ramifications? The bastard had yet to learn of the ramifications of disobeying his orders. He clenched his hands into fists and leaned forward in his chair, boring his eyes into the attorney's. "For what I'm paying you, I don't give a rat's ass about ramifications to your law firm. You just make sure you use that video to my best advantage in this case. Are we clear?"

The attorney simply stared at him - his face

expressionless. Peachtree never could read or rattle him. It made him uncomfortable.

Finally, Weisman nodded. "As crystal."

"Good."

CHAPTER XIII

Darryl Thomas sat behind an old wooden desk in a small office space he had rented under the name of a dummy corporation. The desk was scarred and nicked in several places and paired nicely with the ancient office chair with its cracked faux leather. Wires, tools, discarded computer parts, empty boxes and packing materials littered the moldy threadbare carpet.

He had just completed the setup of a computer system that looked more as if it belonged on the helm of a spaceship rather than in a second rate office space. He rubbed his hands together and booted it up. The sound of the powerful equipment coming to life music to his ears.

When a prompt blinked on one of the two twenty-inch monitors on the desk, he typed in a few commands. Soon, he was at Peachtree's website. His fingers flew over the keys for several minutes then stopped. This was going to be just as hard as he had imagined - maybe even harder.

A special computer program he uploaded caused the computer to send out an alarm signaling that Peachtree's system was making progress in tracking his location. He snarled. "Ras clot!"

He closed his Internet browser quickly and stared at the monitor. He couldn't afford to let Peachtree trace him or he wouldn't live long enough to get the information he needed from its system. How were they able to penetrate his defenses so quickly? He had bounced the signal off a few satellites and set up dummy locations in various locations around the world. He whistled. They must have next level defense technology that even the C.I.A. and the F.B.I. didn't have.

He sat back in his chair, put his arms behind his head, rested his head against them, and pondered what new defenses and red herrings he could set up to give himself more time. That's when it came to him. He smiled, picked up one of his burn phones and dialed a number. It was the first of several calls he planned to make. If he was going to break into Peachtree's system, he was going to need a little help from his friends.

***

Kathy walked into Christie's steakhouse in Coral Gables and looked for Stewart Weisman. She was a bit frazzled. A mountain of work and a ton of unanswered e-mails had stacked up during her trip to New York. With all of the work she had to do on Charles' case and her other cases, the last thing she needed to do was to leave her office and head down to Coral Gables for a lunch meeting. He probably wanted to discuss settlement again and figured that if he wined and dined her, the talks might be more successful.

She had started to politely but firmly decline Weisman's invitation; however, he hinted that they had very important things to discuss. Curiosity won out in the end, together with a hint of nervousness and a strange sense of foreboding that she couldn't explain.

She spotted him sitting at the bar enjoying what looked like brandy. He drained the snifter, threw a few bills onto the bar, picked up a laptop case from the stool next to him and headed over to her. She shook his hand and raised her eyebrows. "A little early in the day for cocktails, isn't it Weisman?"

He laughed. "No. It's noon and we're adults. It's one of the benefits of being your own boss – no-one tells you what you can and can't do."

She chuckled. "Sometimes we're better off having someone keep us on the straight and narrow."

He didn't comment.

The waitress came and led them to a secluded table at the back of the restaurant – away from the other diners. They sat down, perused the menu and gave their orders to the waitress. She left to fill them.

"So, what's so important we had to meet in person on one of my busiest days ever?" Kathy asked.

Weisman cleared his throat and glanced around. "Well, there's something I have to show you."

Kathy stared at him. "There's something you have to show me? In person? You couldn't just fax or e-mail it? What is it?"

He placed a laptop onto the table and turned it in her direction. "This."

Kathy looked at the computer expecting to see a document Weisman would claim to be a smoking gun. Instead, a video played on the screen. She frowned. What was this? A second later, her jaw dropped open. There was a couple in the video having sex. She glanced up at Weisman. Had he asked her all this way just to show her pornography? Was this a new type of sexual harassment? But, wait a minute, something was wrong. The expression on Weisman's face was not one of excitement; instead, he looked triumphant – as if he were holding all the cards and had her every which way from Sunday.

She looked back at the screen and took a closer look. All the breath rushed from her body when she recognized the New York hotel room and realized that the couple having sex on the video was her and Charles. A myriad of emotions ran through her – horror, shame, fear, despair and, finally, anger. How dare he do this to her? Whatever happened, she'd make him pay for this moment - dearly. She glared at him. The triumphant smile faded from his lips and a small frown appeared between his brows. Good, she'd at least wiped the smile off his face. Remembering her mentor's motto that the best defense was a good offense, she went on the attack. She slammed the laptop shut. She wanted to throw it onto the floor and watch it break into a million pieces, but she didn't want to create a scene. Plus, she was sure he had additional copies of the video stowed away somewhere.

"Where did you get this? We both know it's illegal to videotape or record someone against their will. This is a clear invasion of privacy. If you even try to use this video in any way, I'll have you slapped with criminal charges and a civil lawsuit so fast your head will spin," she said. The more she spoke, the more convinced she became that she could turn this situation around to her advantage. She sat back in her chair and sent him a look full of scorn.

"What? Are you so hard up that you have to tape other people having sex to get your rocks off? What are you - some sort of sick voyeur freak? Did you think I would whither into a shrinking violet because you taped me having sex with a consenting adult? Did you think you could blackmail me with it? Get with it – it's the 21st century," she said. Stewart just sat there staring at her impassively.

She frowned. "How did you plan on using the video anyway? You'll never be able to use it in court. First, it's an illegal recording and second, it's not relevant to any issue in the case."

Stewart grinned. "You just don't get it do you? I don't plan to use it in court. I plan to use it to get you disbarred, Counselor," he said. "I can't even take credit for the idea. I wouldn't have thought about it myself until I watched the end of this touching little movie and heard you discussing the ethical implications of your sordid little affair with your client. And, by the way, if it's any consolation to you, I didn't make or arrange for this recording to be made. A little birdie dropped it into my lap."

Kathy's mind reeled. She should have known. Stewart Weisman wasn't known to be the most ethical attorney out there, but he wasn't known as the scum of the Earth either. It had to be his client. She should have known that a government defense contractor like Peachtree would know how to put the squeeze on them to get what it wanted. A wave of despair washed over her. How could she have been so stupid as to play right into their hands?

The waitress brought their entrees and placed them onto the table. It made Kathy realize that she was still there, in Christie's, sitting across the table from Weisman, who watched her face as if he were reading her thoughts. She had to pull herself together. Whatever happened she was still the face of this legal team. She needed time to think and consider their options. She looked directly into Weisman's eyes. "What do you want?"

He smiled. It reminded her of an expression she'd once

seen on a feral cat in a dark alley one night in Brooklyn. She forced herself not to shudder.

"It's not what I want, Counselor. It's what my client wants. He wants this case to go away – for the parties to enter into a settlement agreement with a confidentiality clause. He's willing to pay your client two million dollars and all of the attorneys' fees and costs incurred to date," he said. He picked up his knife and fork and cut off a piece of the rare steak he had ordered. Blood oozed out onto the plate. "It's the best way, really. You and your client get paid and you get to keep your law license and live to fight me another day." He shoved the meat into his mouth and chewed.

Kathy, who had completely lost her appetite, pushed her plate aside. "If we give you what you want, what assurances do I have that you won't keep a copy of that video to use against me in another lawsuit?'

Weisman shrugged. "I can be made a party to the settlement agreement. Both Peachtree and I could agree to destroy any and all copies of the video and to not use it for any purposes whatsoever. That should take care of the issue."

Kathy thought about it. In theory that would probably take care of the issue; however, she'd never know if Peachtree or Weisman or one of their underlings kept a copy of the video for their sick enjoyment. She pushed back her chair, stood up and threw her napkin onto the table. "Well, I've had all of your company that I can stomach for the day. I'll communicate your settlement offer to my client and get back to you."

He looked at her untouched plate. "You're not going to take that with you?"

"No. You can have it," she said.

"Well, don't wait too long to get back to me, Counselor.

I've been ordered to file the Bar complaint by the end of the week. Oh and you can take the laptop with you so you can watch the entire video at your leisure," he said. He waved his fork in the direction of the laptop.

Kathy debated with herself for a moment. She wanted nothing more than to tell Weisman to go screw himself with his laptop. On the other hand, she needed to view the entire video to be able to accurately assess the damage it could do. The attorney in her won out. She picked up the laptop and held her other hand out.

Weisman looked puzzled.

"Give me the case," Kathy said.

"Oh," Weisman said.

He put down his cutlery and wiped his hands on his napkin. Then he reached down, lifted the case off the chair next to him and handed it to her.

She stuffed the laptop into the case, grabbed her pocketbook and strode out of the restaurant.

***

Kathy opened the door to her condominium the moment she heard the knock. Charles walked in. "You don't ask who it is before you open the door?"

She locked the door. "Please, have a seat." She gestured toward the living room.

Charles walked into the living room and took a seat on the couch. "You have a nice place."

"Thank you." She clasped her hands together in front of her. "Can I get you anything to drink?"

"I'll have a glass of wine if you'll join me," he said.

"Okay," she said. "Do you prefer red or white?"

"Red."

So, they had that in common. It's funny the things you learn about a man after you sleep with him and get videotaped in the process of doing it. She poured two glasses of red wine and brought them into the living room. She set the drinks down onto the cocktail table and elected to sit on the loveseat instead of joining him on the couch. She didn't want to give him any ideas.

Charles frowned. He'd probably gotten the message.

"The reason I asked you to come here tonight is because I didn't think this was a conversation we could have at the office," she said. "I needed to speak to you about a meeting I had with Stewart Weisman yesterday."

Charles' frown deepened. "The opposing counsel? Why did you meet with him? This had better not be about settlement again. I already told you that I'm not interested."

"Would you please just shut up for a minute? This is not just about you. There are other people in this world who matter." She regretted the words the moment they left her lips. She took a deep breath and let it out slowly. "Look, I'm sorry. I shouldn't have snapped at you."

He looked at her warily. "No problem. So, why are we here? What did you want to discuss?"

"I have to show you something." She picked the laptop up off the coffee table and opened it up. She then set it on the TV tray between them, clicked on the video and pressed the "Play" button. The sound of moans filled the living room.

Charles stared at the screen. At first, a smile began to spread across his face. Then it disappeared. His gaze sharpened.

He looked up at her. "Where did you get this?"

"I got it from Weisman. He gave it to me yesterday during our lunch meeting at Christie's. I asked him where he got it. He told me that a little birdie dropped it into his lap."

Charles stood up and began to pace the living room. "It had to be Peachtree." He swore. "I should have known they'd be following us. It all makes sense now."

"What are you talking about?"

He whirled to face her. His face livid with emotion. "I'm talking about the murder of Mrs. Roberts and now this video recording of us in your hotel room. These people will stop at nothing to keep their secrets safe. I bet he tried to blackmail you into getting me to settle this case with that video."

"As a matter of fact, he did. And it was a very effective threat too. They didn't just tape the two of us having sex. They also taped our conversation afterwards. You know - the part where I announce that I've committed an ethical violation by sleeping with you. That little statement could be considered an admission on my part in any Bar proceedings. This is serious, Charles. They could take my license for this. I could lose my job. I don't have anyone to take care of me. I'm it." She put her head into her hands and bent over resting her elbows onto her knees. "What the hell did I get myself into?"

Charles walked over and sat next to her on the loveseat. He put an arm around her and pulled her close until her face rested against his chest. She didn't resist.

"Look," he said. "I don't want you to lose your law license because of what we did. I'll settle the case before that happens."

She sat up and shook her head. "No. I'm not going to let those bastards win by blackmailing me. What we're going to do is get you new counsel and bring them up to speed as quickly as possible. I'm going to withdraw from your case. Once I'm no longer your counsel, Peachtree will lose all interest in me and any leverage they think they have over you."

"But I don't want new counsel. No-one else knows this case like you do," Charles said. "If I don't settle the suit, I want you to try it."

"I can't try your case if I'm disbarred," Kathy said.

"There's got to be a way around this," Charles said. He got up from the loveseat, walked over to the balcony doors and stared out at the bay. After a moment, he turned to face her. "What's our deadline for responding to the settlement offer?"

"Friday," she said. "You should know that they've increased the offer to two million dollars, plus attorney's fees. I bet you could negotiate a higher amount if you wanted to."

"Why don't you give me until Thursday to come up with a way to deal with this?"

She shrugged. "I've been over this a million times since yesterday and I can't see a way out other than you settling the case or me withdrawing as your counsel of record. It's not in your best interests to settle the case. If you won, you could recover much more than two million dollars – especially if we proved gross negligence on Peachtree's part. This is precisely the sort of ethical quandary the Bar rules seek to prevent."

"Just give me until Thursday," he said. "If I can't find a way to break Peachtree's hold over you by then, you can file the motion to withdraw."

He walked over to her, pulled her to her feet and put his arms around her. "Don't worry. This will all work out. I promise."

Despite her better judgment, she believed him.

CHAPTER XIV

Darryl sent a coded message to his hacker buddies on Twitter. They'd set up a time and a date to bombard Peachtree Consulting's computer system with simultaneous cyber-attacks from sources all over the globe to give him the chance he needed to infiltrate the system. His message was the signal to begin.

While his friends kept Peachtree's computer defenses busy, Darryl put the finishing touches on his own computer's defenses. He bounced his signal off of four satellites, rerouted it and hid it in a nest of patterns so dense it would take the fastest computer known to man at least an hour to track down. He checked the program he had set up to monitor the attacks on Peachtree's system and its defenses thereto. No less than ten assaults were occurring to Peachtree's system at any given time. He raised his eyebrows. Peachtree's system appeared to be holding its own against the multiple attacks. He shrugged. No computer could withstand sustained simultaneous attacks from multiple hackers forever. He rubbed his hands together and began his assault.

His fingers were a blur over the keys. After fifteen minutes, sweat poured down his brow. He swore when an alarm sounded signaling that Peachtree had already burrowed through the second level of his defenses.

He had five levels of security on his system. At this rate, he wouldn't get the full hour he had hoped for. He checked the program monitoring the hackers' united assault on Peachtree's system. There were now only seven simultaneous attacks taking place. He briefly wondered what happened to the other hackers then shrugged and got back to work on his own attack. He needed to get into that system fast.

***

McAllister walked up to the door of Donald Peachtree's office, knocked once, and entered. He then turned around and left quickly. Peachtree was a little busy. He had his sexy assistant, Giada, bent over the desk facing the door while he rammed himself into her from behind. From the pained expression on her face and the little yelps she had let out with each thrust, she didn't appear to be having a good time.

McAllister waited outside the office for the two of them to finish. Eventually, the door to the office opened and Giada rushed out. Her hair was mussed, her skirt a little askew. She wiped tears from her face with the back of her hand and passed McAllister without so much as a backward glance. He watched her leave then entered the office.

Peachtree finished lighting a cigar before looking at him. "What is it?"

"Sir, we've been experiencing a series of cyber-attacks in the past half hour. The geeks in the tech department say that it's unprecedented. The attacks appear to be coming simultaneously from places all over the world. They traced one of them to a place in New York, another to an address in London and a third to an address in Chicago. Since we have tactical units in all three places, I recommend we deploy and see if we can ascertain who's behind the attacks," McAllister said.

Peachtree grunted. "That's a good strategy, McAllister. Make it happen."

McAllister nodded. "Yes Sir."

***

Darryl cursed steadily as he continued to work the keyboard. He sensed that Peachtree's system was about to let him in and he was determined to get there. So far, no computer system linked to the Internet had been able to elude him. He was what is known in the hacker world as "elite".

He watched as his computer screen finally went blue. A blinking white prompt appeared inviting him to search Peachtree's system. He beamed at the monitor and pumped a fist into the air. "Yes!"

He pulled up a directory of files, found one that was labeled "Charles Morgan" and pulled it up. He slid a flash drive into a USB slot and downloaded the information. Next, he searched for the other information Charles had requested. He implemented a program he had put together to randomly search for files and downloaded those to another flash drive. A high pitched beep sounded causing him to jolt. It was an alarm he had set up to warn him when Peachtree penetrated his fourth level of defenses. Heart beating furiously, he cursed and quickly closed his Internet browser.

He sat there for a moment, staring at the computer screen. He then made three copies of the flash drives. He put one copy in a prepaid stamped envelope addressed to Charles and another in a prepaid stamped envelope addressed to Kathy Brooks. He hid one set of the flash drives in a space created by a loose floor board under the desk and slipped the original flash drives into his pocket. You couldn't be too careful.

He pulled out his I-Phone and sent coded messages to Charles and his hacker buddies. He then slipped the phone into his pocket and left the office.

***

Charles checked his Blackberry and smiled. Darryl had come through. He'd sent a coded message telling Charles to meet him at the Starbucks on Lincoln Road.

He'd noticed on the way back from the airport after his trip to New York that he had picked up a tail. He wasn't surprised Peachtree was keeping an eye on him given recent events. He left his condo early to give himself time to lose the tail before meeting Darryl. As he pulled out of the driveway of his condominium building and turned onto Rickenbacker Causeway, he noticed a blue sedan pull out and head in the same direction. The sedan never got too close and stayed a couple of cars behind him but, no matter what direction he took, it continued to follow him. That was a mistake. It was so sloppy and so obvious that it made him wonder if Peachtree wanted him to know he was being tailed.

An hour later, having lost the tail, Charles entered the Starbucks on Lincoln Road. He spotted Darryl sitting at a table in the back of the store. Even though it was close to midnight on a weekday, the place was packed with patrons. Charles took his time walking through the store looking for anyone who seemed out of place. The patrons were busily sipping on lattes, typing on their laptops, I-pads and I-Phones and/or chatting amongst themselves. It was a typical South Beach crowd – a mix of tourists and locals. No-one looked the least bit out of place. He ordered a tall black coffee and joined Darryl at the table. Darryl was sipping on a soy chai latte and tapping the keys on his laptop. He nodded at Charles.

"What's up?" Charles asked.

Darryl removed two flash drives from his pocket and slid them across the table. Charles picked them up and slipped then into his pocket.

"What's on these?" Charles asked.

Darryl sucked his teeth. "Ras clot! What do you think, mon?"

A smile spread slowly across Charles' face. "All of it? You were able to get all the information I wanted? The files on Manning too?"

Darryl sneered. "Isn't that what you pay me for? Speaking of dat . . ."

Charles pulled a thick envelope from his back pocket and slid it across the table. The Rasta scooped it up and tucked it away. He didn't bother counting it.

"Hell," Charles said, "I got the best of that bargain."

"Remind me to charge you extra next time," Darryl said. "Listen, you are dealing with some very dangerous people. I had to get ten of my buddies to attack their computer system at the same time to get access." He paused for a moment and stared down at the table then he looked up at Charles, his eyes bleak.

"Peachtree tracked three of them down and killed them dead - but not before torturing them. I'm going to have to disappear for a while to make sure they don't get me too," he said.

Charles stared at him. He knew that Peachtree was dangerous and that they'd stop at nothing to keep their secrets. He also knew that he was putting Darryl in danger by hiring him for this job. But now that three of Darryl's friends were dead, witnesses were being picked off, and Kathy's career was on the line, he was beginning to wonder if his single-minded quest for revenge was worth the price others had already paid for it.

"Look man, just let me know if you need more funds to lay low for a while or a passport or anything," he said.

Darryl shook his head. "I'm just going home for a little bit." He patted his pocket. "This should tide me over for a little while. If I need more, I'll let you know."

"Okay," Charles said. He rose from his seat and extended his hand to Darryl. "Safe travels, man. Call me if you need anything. And thanks for everything."

Darryl stood up, clasped Charles' hand and pulled him forward for a shoulder bump. "My pleasure. I hope you find what you need."

"I hope so too."

Charles walked out of the store and headed into the parking garage across the street. He rode the elevator up to the third floor where his car was parked. He took his time peeking into the other cars on the floor. No-one was sitting in any of them. In fact, with the exception of a young couple who, judging from the way they staggered, appeared to have imbibed a few too many drinks, there was no-one else on that floor of the parking garage. He waited until the young couple got into their car and drove away, then he extracted a laptop from the trunk and climbed behind the wheel. He booted it up and inserted the flash drive Darryl had given him.

He scanned the files until he came across an incident report dated the day Patti was killed. The report was written by Wilkes and copied to McAllister and Donald Peachtree. A notation on the report indicated that a copy was sent to a fax number. He'd have to get someone to trace the number for him.

In the report, Wilkes wrote that, as a result of the

accident, he'd lost the "target" he was assigned to follow. He referred to the target as "Viper." He stated that Patricia Morgan - the occupant of the car with which he had collided – was killed on impact. That was consistent with what the police told Charles when they investigated the crash.

His hands balled into fists. Willing himself calm, he searched the other reports authored by Wilkes on the flash drive. He learned that Wilkes and others had been conducting surveillance on "Viper" for ten days prior to the accident. They had picked up his tail outside of a cheap airport motel and documented his whereabouts during that time period. He was described as being a tall male of Middle-Eastern descent in his early twenties. There were references to his meeting other men of Middle-Eastern and African descent in restaurants, parks, malls and other venues. The report mentioned a meeting that took place at a warehouse near the airport and stated that a raid of the warehouse was conducted by someone named Manning. There was that name again.

The Manning he knew was a C.I.A. operative. Since when did the C.I.A. conduct raids of private warehouses on U.S. soil? If this Viper was thought to be a potential threat to national security, why wasn't the raid conducted by Homeland Security or the F.B.I.? The reference to Manning didn't make sense unless the C.I.A. was operating on U.S. soil.

He searched the flash drive for other references to Manning and found several. They were contained in reports prepared by Peachtree employees pertaining to assignments going as far back as three years. The reports referred to surveillance and security operations taking place all over the U.S. and in Europe. Three of the reports were written by Wilkes.

Charles exited the files on the flash drive. He then pulled up his copy of the documents produced by Peachtree from the hard drive. Armed with his newfound knowledge, he conducted searches for Wilkes' report on the incident. He found the report, but it was so heavily redacted as to be almost unintelligible. All references to Viper were gone. He next searched Wilkes' employment file and located his expense reports. A smile spread across his face when he saw that Wilkes' travel records lined up with the reports he had filed on the assignments involving Manning. He had them. With this proof, he had Peachtree right where he wanted it - by the balls.

He sat there for a moment thinking how to best utilize the information. With the confidentiality order in place, no-one except the Judge, the jury, the attorneys and a few Court clerks would ever see the documents or learn the truth. To destroy Peachtree, he needed to expose the documents to the public and make them available to Homeland Security, the F.B.I. and a congressional oversight committee. The government agencies would start a turf war with the C.I.A. and shut Peachtree down as a defense contractor once and for all.

He thought about handing the documents over to the F.B.I., but quickly dismissed the idea. They'd want to keep the information quiet pending their investigation while they played everything by the book. No. The best way to get this information out to the public would be to give it to a reporter. He knew just the one. He pulled out a burn phone and made a call.

***

An hour later, he knocked on the front door of the Miami Shores home of Judith Bailey - a reporter for the Miami Herald. A tall, thin, attractive African-American woman with a short Afro, dressed in a pair of sweat pants, an old t-shirt and a pair of flip flops opened the door. She yawned and gave him the beady eye. "This had better not be a booty call. I've been working on a big story for weeks and I just turned it in. I was just about to shower and hit my bed with a sledgehammer when I got your call. I almost didn't pick up the phone."

Charles smiled and lifted his right hand. "I swear this is not a booty call." He then looked her up and down. "But could you really blame a brother for trying if it were? You're looking mighty good there girl."

Judith shook her head and twisted her lips in an unsuccessful effort to mask a smile. She stepped back and pulled the door open further to let him in. "Come on in here before my neighbors hear you talking that foolishness."

Charles stepped inside and gave her a kiss on the cheek. They were really good friends who had known each other for years. He knew her from high school back in New York when they worked together on the school newspaper. They were New York transplants who had come to Miami for the sun, the fun and the job. She was a good reporter with lots of good sources, a knack for getting to the heart of a story and a keen sense of ethics. He knew he could trust her. He also knew that she wouldn't submit the story unless she had reliable sources and corroboration. He'd have to convince her.

Judith locked the door behind him. He took a seat at her dining room table and set the laptop down on top. She took a seat at the head of the table next to him. "So, what's up?"

He told her everything. Well, almost everything. He left out the part about how he had obtained the computer files and the fact that Kathy may have to face disciplinary proceedings from the Florida Bar because they'd decided to get involved. Judy would find that out soon enough.

He showed her the documents to back up his story. When he finished, she slid her chair back, stood up and started pacing the dining room. He could see the wheels turning in her head as she figured out the angles.

"So," she said, "let me get this straight. You want me to publish a story accusing one of the largest defense contractors in the country of assisting the C.I.A. with operating illegally in the United States and link that to Patti's death."

"Right," he said. "The proof is right here."

Judy scratched delicately at a spot on her scalp just above her right temple with a perfectly manicured fingernail. She shook her head. "Sorry. My editor will never let me run the story based on what you've shown me so far. I need more proof."

Charles sat back in his chair and threw his hands up. "More proof? What more could you possibly need? The proof's right there." He pointed a hand toward his laptop.

"No. It's not all there," she said. "For example, we don't have proof that Manning is a C.I.A. operative."

When Charles opened his mouth to speak, Judy gave him the look she used to give him when she was the editor of the high school newspaper and he used to argue with her over a story. He closed his mouth.

"You know that Manning used to be C.I.A. because you worked with him on joint missions when you were in the military. But that was more than ten years ago. For all you know, Manning could have left the C.I.A. and joined the F.B.I., the N.S.A. or any other government agency authorized to operate in the U.S.," she said.

Charles sat there for a moment considering her point. He hated to admit it, but she was right. They needed more proof that Peachtree was acting on orders from the C.I.A. He rested his elbows onto the dining room table, put his head into his hands and racked his brain trying to figure out how they could acquire the proof they needed. He ran a hand over his face and noticed the stubble on his chin. It had been a long day and it promised to be an even longer week. Then it came to him. He looked up at her. "I've got a buddy in the F.B.I. who should be able to confirm that Manning is not an F.B.I. agent. He may be able to find out whether Manning is C.I.A., but he's not going to be able to confirm or deny that publicly."

Judy smiled and joined him at the table. "All I need is a reliable source telling me that Manning is still a C.I.A. operative. That source could be you once you confirm with your F.B.I. buddy that Manning is still working with the C.I.A."

"We also have the fax number that Wilkes and the other Peachtree operatives sent their reports to. There's got to be a way to look up who owns that number," he said.

"Leave that to me," she said. "I've got a friend at the telephone company."

It was Charles' turn to smile. "Why am I not surprised? You always had lots of helpful friends."

She laughed. "How else is a girl supposed to get what she needs in this world?"

"I can't thank you enough for agreeing to help me," he said.

She waved a hand at him. "Anything for a friend. Besides, I should be thanking you. This is a big story. I need something like this to put me on the map. Who knows? After this, maybe the New York Times will offer me a job."

"Just be careful," Charles said. "These people are dangerous. They've already taken out four people to cover this up. I don't want you to be next."

"Don't worry about me. I know how to take care of myself. Besides, once the story's out, the cat will be out of the bag. Peachtree won't dare touch you or me then for fear of giving it credence.

"I hope you're right," he said.

"I know I am," she said.

***

Giada sat in an unmarked sedan parked across the street from the entrance of a Publix parking lot. She watched Charles stroll down the street and enter the lot. A minute later she saw his car exit. Peachtree's operatives tailed him.

She pursed her lips. Manning had warned her that Charles was good. He had obviously lost Peachtree's operatives. So, where had he been and what was he up to? It was her job to find out. She called Manning to report that Peachtree's operatives were back on the job. Her next call was to her unit's resident geek – Gus Lambda.

"Yo," he said.

"Gus, I need you to pull all the surveillance footage in a one mile radius around the Publix supermarket on Coral Way off of Brickell. We're looking to track the footprints of the Purple Ghost from 8:30p.m. until just now. I'll contact you tomorrow for the information.

"Got it," Gus said.

Giada hung up. They would see what they could see.

***

The next day, Annette escorted Charles into Kathy's office. The more he thought about it, the more he realized he needed to warn her to keep her safe – at least until the article came out and Peachtree and the C.I.A. were exposed. He decided not to tell her about the article. He didn't know much about the

Florida Bar's ethical rules, but he suspected that if Kathy knew he had divulged confidential information to a reporter, she'd be duty bound to report it. He didn't want to put her in that position. He'd already put her in quite a few tight positions – both literally and metaphorically. He grinned at the thought.

His grin disappeared when she looked up at him and he saw the evidence of strain in her face. Her skin lacked its usual healthy glow. Her eyes contained none of the sparkle they normally did. Dark circles appeared under them. She looked as if she hadn't slept in a week and tried to cover it up with makeup. Guilt welled up within him.

She stood up to greet him. "Hello Charles. Please have a seat."

Charles sat in one of the visitor's chairs. Kathy sat behind her desk.

"Can I get you something to drink?" Annette asked.

When both Kathy and Charles declined, Annette left the office, closing the door behind her.

"You look like hell," Charles said. He regretted the words the instant they left his lips. Kathy recoiled in her seat as if she'd been slapped. He caught a brief glimpse of hurt in her eyes.

"Why thank you very much. That's just what a girl needs to hear." She sat back in her chair and breathed out a long sigh. "Did you come here this morning to tell me something useful?"

She looked so tired, so worried, so defeated, that he wanted to get up, pull her into his arms and just hold her. But he knew he couldn't. Annette or someone else could come through the door any moment and catch them. He sighed. He wished he had some magic words to give her comfort. But instead, he had to give her more to worry about.

"As a matter of fact, yes."

"What?" she asked.

"I picked up a tail yesterday while I was running around doing some errands. It was an unmarked sedan."

"You picked up a tail? What is this? Some sort of spy novel?" She waved a hand at him. "Charles, we've got a real problem on our hands. You need to find another counsel to represent you and I need to bring them up to speed as quickly as possible."

"You're not listening to me woman," he said. "I can't say too much in here, because, for all I know, your office is bugged." He watched her eyes widen. Good. He had her attention.

"I thought I spotted a tail in New York. I definitely spotted one when we got back to Miami. And when I got home, I discovered listening devices – bugs – in my apartment."

Kathy's jaw went slack. She stared at him for a moment before closing her mouth. A frown appeared between her brows. Her eyes narrowed and she leaned forward in her seat. "And you think they might have bugged my office and my condo too?"

He nodded. "Yes."

"You mean to tell me that Peachtree's operatives and God only knows who else could have been listening to every conversation, every telephone call, hell every sound I've made for days both here and at home? Why didn't you tell me this when you first discovered the bugs in your place?"

He shrugged. "At first, I thought they were only keeping tabs on me. After the blackmail business, I began to suspect that they may be keeping tabs on you too." He sighed and rubbed a hand over his face. He had handled this – her – wrong from the very beginning. He should have trusted her. "You're right. I should have told you immediately."

"Yes, you should have. This is very serious business. It's not only a complete invasion of my privacy, but also a violation of the attorney-client privilege. It's my duty to protect the sanctity of communications between the firm and its clients. I need to know when the privacy of those communications could be compromised."

She turned away from him, picked up the telephone handset and dialed a few digits. "Listen," she said into the receiver, "we may have a security breach at the firm. Send Kevin to my office right away. Thanks." She dropped the receiver back into its cradle.

"Look," he said. "I'm sorry about this."

He searched her face. It unsettled him a little that he couldn't read it. Was she scared? Upset? Hurt? Angry?

"I know," she said. "But right now I have to report and deal with this possible breach of security."

He nodded. He felt terrible. He had brought nothing but trouble to Kathy since the day he met her. "I understand. Here, take this." He handed her a burn phone that had the number of his burn phone coded into it.

"What is this?"

He shook his head and held his right index finger to his lips. "In case you need to reach me."

"Okay." She put the burn phone into her right top desk drawer and stood up. "Let me walk you out."

They left her office together. After they had walked down the hall a little ways, she pulled him into an alcove occupied by a copy machine and a couple of printers. She kept her voice low to mask it under the mechanical sound of the printers spitting out pieces of paper. "How extensively would they have bugged the firm? Would they plant bugs in here?" She glanced around as if half expecting to see them.

The cozy surroundings and the worried look on her face made Charles want to put his arms around her. He shook his head. "No. It's probably just your office, your paralegal's, your associate's and maybe the conference rooms on this floor. Otherwise, there'd be too many feeds to follow."

She nodded. "I'm going to have a security firm brought in to sweep the office, my car and my apartment every day until this issue is resolved."

"That's a good idea. Try the McKinley firm. They're very reliable," he said.

"I'm glad you think it's a good idea since you'll be footing the bill for this expense," she said.

Charles winced. Ouch. The woman knew how to hit where it hurt. He wanted to protest, but thought better of it when he saw the glint in her eye. He swallowed. "Understood. "Let me know what McKinley finds."

"I will," she said.

CHAPTER XV

On Thursday at noon, Peachtree sat on a park bench pretending to read a newspaper. Sweat rolled into his eyes. He cursed under his breath. It was 92 degrees with 80 percent humidity and here he was, outside, waiting for Manning. He was tired of waiting for the man and, although he hated to admit it, nervous about the meeting. Manning probably didn't think they were moving fast enough to contain the problem. Or maybe he knew about the security breach caused by the hackers the other day. Peachtree hadn't reported it.

He pulled out a handkerchief and wiped at his brow. How did Manning get his information? He probably had informants inside the company. He put the handkerchief away and looked up to see Manning sitting on the bench next to him. He forced himself not to jump. The man gave him the creeps.

"I'm very disappointed in you Peachtree. You've been keeping secrets from me," Manning said.

The saliva dried up in Peachtree's mouth. It was just as he'd feared. He was silent a moment as he tried to figure out how to handle the situation. Finally, anger took over. Manning had talked to him as if he were a little boy about to be spanked. It reminded him of how his father used to talk to him before meting out some severe punishment. Well, he wasn't a little boy any longer. He decided to brazen it out.

"Excuse me?" Peachtree said. "I have no idea what you're talking about. Why did you call this meeting and why are we meeting outside when it's ninety two degrees with eighty percent humidity?"

Manning looked him dead in the eye for a long moment. Peachtree fidgeted and was the first to break eye contact. Manning's voice was soft when he spoke.

"We're meeting here today because I deemed it necessary to get my point across in person. I also wanted to make sure that no-one else overheard our conversation. The situation with Morgan has spiraled out of control. We no longer trust your company to handle it. You failed to report a very serious breach in your data security earlier this week and your operatives lost the tail on Morgan for several hours," Manning said.

"It was only for a couple of hours, after which we picked up his tail again," Peachtree said. "As far as the data breach is concerned, there was nothing to report. We handled the situation."

Manning simply stared at him. Peachtree caught himself fidgeting again. He forced himself to stop. This time, he didn't break eye contact. Manning's eyes narrowed.

"That sort of bullshit is precisely the reason we no longer deem your company capable of handling this. Do you know where Mr. Morgan went during those hours you deem so insignificant? He went to see a reporter for the Miami Herald named Judith Bailey."

The color drained from Peachtree's face. Judith Bailey was known for exposing government corruption and cover-ups. She was also known for having reliable sources. Charles Morgan had gone to see the reporter the day after the security breach. He put two and two together and didn't like what he came up with.

"Want to know how we found out about Bailey? One of her contacts at the telephone company accessed information on the fax number we use for your operatives' reports. When we paid him a visit, we found out he had acquired the information for her," Manning said.

"She's going to have to be dissuaded from going forward with any story about Peachtree," he said. "I'll-."

"It's already been handled," Manning said, cutting him off. "I took care of it personally."

Something in Manning's voice sent a chill down Peachtree's spine.

"Thank you," he said.

"You're welcome. Just see to it there are no more reporting lapses or data breaches on your end. Otherwise, we'll have to tie up all our loose ends."

***

On Friday morning, Kathy sat in her office and stared at the telephone. She had to do something about Weisman's threat to file a Bar complaint against her before it was too late. She needed to inform the powers that be at the firm and find an attorney to represent her.

Just thinking about the firm's possible reaction to the situation filled her with dread. She had no idea what would happen. Would they fire her? Would they keep her but never trust her to lead another case again? Which scenario was worse?

She put her throbbing head into her hands and groaned. How the hell had she gotten herself into this mess? The better question was: Why? She knew better than to sleep with a client.

She'd represented good-looking clients in the past and never felt the attraction for them she had for Charles. What was it about him that had made her throw all caution to the wind?

She thought of the time they'd spent together in New York. Truth be told, she'd thought of little else over the past few days. The video of their lovemaking, while humiliating in the sense that it had been watched by Weisman, Peachtree and God only knew who else, was also a poignant reminder of the way she had responded to Charles - of the level of passion they had shared. She'd watched it several times and each time, it never ceased to arouse her. She bit her lip. There was no use thinking about that. With all that had happened since that night, there was no going back. She sighed.

A knock sounded at the door.

"Come in."

Erin walked in. She must have stopped by Kathy's office on the way in since her purse and briefcase dangled from her right shoulder, a newspaper was tucked under her left arm and she carried a Starbucks coffee cup. She looked a little excited - as if she had some juicy gossip to share.

"Hey." She closed the door with her hip and plopped down on one of the visitor's chairs in front of Kathy's desk. She set her coffee cup down on the desk and her bags on the chair next to her.

"Hey yourself," Kathy said, happy for the distraction.

"Have you seen this morning's paper yet?"

Kathy made a face. "You know I don't read the newspaper on weekdays."

Erin smirked. "Well maybe you should."

"Why?"

"There's an article in here about Peachtree Consulting. It basically accuses the company of illegally conducting operations for the C.I.A. in the U.S."

Kathy felt her eyes bulge open. "What? Give me that." She held out a hand and reached across the desk for the newspaper.

Erin grinned, holding it out of reach. "And that's not all. According to the article, Peachtree was engaged in one of these illegal operations when its employee - Wilkes - got into the car accident that killed Charles Morgan's wife. Isn't that great? If they were involved in illegal activities at the time of the accident, we should be able to get them on negligence *per se*." Erin looked as though she'd just solved world hunger.

Kathy stared at her, a sinking feeling in the pit of her stomach. *Please Lord, tell me he didn't do what I think he did.* She prayed silently. *Because if he did, I'm going to kill him.* Some of her emotions must have shown on her face because the smirk disappeared.

"What?" Erin asked.

Kathy silently held out a hand for the newspaper. This time, Erin handed it over. Kathy unfolded it.

The story had made the front page. As Kathy read it, her worst fears were confirmed. The reporter referred to documents that were covered by the confidentiality order such as Wilkes' employment records and expense reports. The article also mentioned other records she was not sure Peachtree had produced. She assumed Charles provided the reporter with the documents. But how had he gotten hold of them? She hadn't given them to him.

She looked up at Erin. "Did you give the client copies of any of the documents produced by Peachtree?"

Erin's brow furrowed. "No. Of course not. They were designated "AEO." I would never have done that. Why would you ask me such a thing?" After a moment, her jaw went slack. She stood up, grabbed the newspaper, plopped back down into her chair and scanned the article. She then looked up at Kathy, surprise and disbelief all over her face. "He didn't. But how?"

"That's what I want to know. Get MIS to check the document database and account for every person who accessed it. I want a list of names, dates, times and methods. And I want it yesterday," Kathy said.

Erin nodded, her lips pursed into a grim line. "I'm all over it." She grabbed her bags and her coffee cup and left.

Kathy sat there for a moment staring out of her office window. She didn't see the view of Biscayne Bay. All she saw was her career and her case going down the drain. Charles only cared about destroying Peachtree. He didn't give a damn who else got hurt in the process.

A single tear slid down her cheek. She dashed it away. She didn't have time to cry. She'd deal with the hurt feelings later. It was time to act. She turned back to her desk, picked up the telephone and made two calls. The first was to a friend who happened to be one of the best employment lawyers in the state of Florida. The second call she made was to Steve. She didn't bother to call Charles. She'd deal with that bastard later. In person.

***

Charles entered his condo carrying a copy of the Miami Herald and a cup of coffee he had picked up from Starbucks on the way home from his morning run. He plopped down on one of the stools at his breakfast nook, unfolded the paper and smiled. Judy had come through. The story had made front page headlines: "Peachtree Consulting Complicit in Illegal Government Operations." He read the entire story with a grin on his face. Let Peachtree and the C.I.A. try to weasel their way out of this. They certainly had some explaining to do.

His grin faded when he thought of Kathy's likely reaction to the story. Peachtree and the C.I.A. were not the only ones who had explaining to do. Kathy was bound to realize that someone had leaked confidential documents to the media. She'd eventually trace that leak to him. He felt a little guilty about using her to exact his revenge, but he didn't see any other way he could have achieved it. He didn't know when he made this plan that he would develop feelings for the woman. And after Peachtree killed a witness and three hackers and then tried to blackmail Kathy, the only way he could think of to protect her was to expose Peachtree and the C.I.A.'s illegal activities. He could only hope he could get her to understand that.

He thought of how right she had felt in his arms that night in New York and how much he had needed to protect her when the bomb exploded at Mrs. Robert's house. He'd make her understand. He had to.

He glanced back at the newspaper and scanned the headline of the next story. His blood froze. It read: "Herald Reporter Found Slain in Miami Shores." A picture of Judy appeared next to it. The article reported that Judy's body had been found in her home the previous afternoon by her cleaning lady. She'd been severely beaten, her throat was slit and there were signs of a struggle. The Miami Herald offered a $10,000 reward to anyone who provided information leading to the arrest of the person or persons responsible for the crime.

Oh my God. What did I do? Judy.

Despair rose over him like a fog. *It all my fault*. If he hadn't been so hell-bent on revenge this would never have happened and Judy would be alive. He thought of the terror she must have felt in those final moments. According to the article, they beat her nearly to death before slitting her throat. Despair turned quickly into rage.

He slammed a fist down onto the counter. They would pay for this. He would make sure of it.

***

Charles walked into the 11th Street diner where he had agreed to meet Tyler for lunch. Due to the late mid-afternoon hour, the place was relatively empty.

Tyler sat in a booth at the back of the diner. Next to him was a stuffed shirt dressed in a suit. He was a clean-shaven Caucasian man in his mid-forties, of average height and average build, with dark hair. Charles walked up to the booth.

"Hey Man," Tyler said.

Charles nodded. "I see you've brought company. What? We can't have lunch together without you bringing backup?" It was an old joke – one Charles made whenever Tyler showed up to the party with an uninvited guest. He knew it wasn't a good sign when Tyler didn't chuckle.

"Charles, this is Agent Michaels. We wanted to talk to you today about Peachtree Consulting – specifically, the article that came out in today's newspaper," Tyler said.

Charles forced himself to grin. "Yeah. I read that. Peachtree's dirty laundry aired all over the front page of the newspaper."

"Were you the source of the documents the reporter referred to in her article?" Michaels asked.

Charles weighed his options. If he told the truth, the F.B.I. would haul him in for questioning and try to force him to cooperate with its investigation by threatening him with prosecution for hacking into Peachtree's files. They'd want him to settle or otherwise put his lawsuit on the back burner pending the investigation. Although having the F.B.I. investigate Peachtree was an integral part of his overall plan to destroy the company, putting his case on the back burner was not. He shrugged. "I have no idea where she got her information from."

"The reporter referred to documents she could have only gotten from an insider at Peachtree or you if they were produced by Peachtree in your case. We can't ask the reporter about her sources because she's dead. She was murdered yesterday. We suspect Peachtree had a hand in that as well, but we can't prove it yet. I understand you and she went to the same high school together," Michaels said.

Charles looked at Tyler, who remained impassive. "Yes. We were friends. What information did you say you had regarding Peachtree having her killed?"

A ghost of a smile played around Michaels' thin lips. "I didn't say we had information on that subject. I just said we suspect Peachtree had her killed. Listen, the F.B.I. needs your help on this. We need to know what you know about Peachtree and what documents you've received from them in discovery. Surely, you want to help us bring Peachtree down. I know I would if I were in your shoes."

Charles shrugged again. "I'd like to help you. I really would. But the documents produced by Peachtree are subject to a confidentiality order.

Michaels' lips got even thinner. His cheeks reddened slightly. He leaned forward. "I could subpoena your documents and haul you in for questioning."

Charles smiled at the agent. "Good luck with that."

He sat back in his chair in a relaxed pose that appeared to infuriate the F.B.I. agent even more. He picked up a menu from the table. "I'm going to order some lunch. Anybody else hungry?"

He imagined steam coming from Agent Michaels' ears and saw Tyler try to smother a grin. Agent Michaels slid out from the booth and stood up. "I am shocked and dismayed at your lack of cooperation. I'd think you'd want to help us investigate the company that killed your wife and your friend. But apparently, you're only interested in getting as much money as possible from your lawsuit. You are playing a very dangerous game, sir. Take care that you don't end up being just another one of Peachtree's victims." He looked at Tyler. "Are you coming?"

Tyler shook his head. "No, I'm going to grab some lunch and see if I can't talk some sense into Charles here. I'll see you back at the office."

"Okay," Michaels said. He stalked out of the diner.

Charles and Tyler burst into laughter as soon as the diner doors closed behind him. Charles was the first to catch his breath. "Man, that cat sure was pissed."

"He certainly was," Tyler said. "I can't say I blame him though. You played him like a damned violin." He paused for a moment. "Listen man, I know you and Judith were close. I'm sorry about that."

Charles' hands balled into fists. "They're going to pay for that, Tyler. They're going to pay for Patti and Judy and all of the other people whose lives they destroyed."

Tyler looked worried. "Hey man. Don't do anything stupid. Let us handle this before you get into something you can't get out of. Speaking of which, why the resistance to assisting us with the investigation? I mean, I know you're not holding out for more money. So what's up?"

Charles briefly debated how much to tell him. In the end, he decided to play it straight. He knew he could trust Tyler with his life. "Okay. I'm talking to you now as a friend – not as an F.B.I. agent."

Tyler twisted his lips, balled up a napkin and threw it at him.

Charles laughed. "I was Judy's source for the article. Some of the documents I gave her were subject to the confidentiality order. The others, well . . . ." He let the sentence trail off.

"The others what?" Tyler asked. His eyes widened as realization dawned. "You didn't. Tell me you didn't go see our friend Darryl and ask for his assistance in this matter."

Charles couldn't quite cover the smile that came to his face. Tyler knew him too well. "Ask me no secrets and I'll tell you no lies, my brother. So, you see, I can't have the F.B.I. all up in my business right now. Besides, between the hacking and the confidentiality order, the F.B.I. won't be able to use the documents even if I did hand them over. But if I can get Peachtree to produce clean copies of the documents in my case and get the jury to find that Peachtree was engaged in illegal activities at the time of the accident, then that finding will be public. The F.B.I. would have all the probable cause it needs to get access to both Peachtree's files and the documents Peachtree produced in my case."

Tyler stared at him in admiration and chuckled. "Now I see why you were the big dog in the Corps. As usual, you've thought of everything."

Charles thought of the people who had died as a result of his plan and the situation with Kathy. He grimaced. "Not everything. I didn't figure on them killing Judy or some of Darryl's hacker buddies who helped him out. I also didn't anticipate them trying to blackmail my attorney into getting me to settle the case." He told Tyler about the video.

Tyler shook his head. "Michaels is right about one thing. You are playing a very dangerous game, Bro. You have feelings for this woman?"

Charles nodded. "I do, but I don't see them going anywhere. Too much has happened. She's going to be pissed when she reads the article. She'll never trust me again if she ever did."

"You were just trying to protect her the best way you knew how. Maybe she'll see that."

Charles shook his head. "I don't think so."

After Charles finished his lunch with Tyler, he headed back home. He kept an eye out for surveillance, but didn't notice anyone tailing him this time. Maybe, now that the cat was out of the bag, Peachtree didn't see a need to keep tabs on him. They probably thought he'd done all the damage he could. They were wrong.

CHAPTER XVI

After meeting a friend and retaining her services as an employment law attorney, Kathy headed over to Charles' condominium. She'd gotten the address off the bills that were sent out by the firm's accounting department for his legal work. She needed to speak to him and this conversation could not take place in the office. When she got to his building, however, the guard called upstairs and determined that he wasn't at home. She told the guard she'd wait in the lobby until he returned.

By the time he walked through the automated lobby doors, she'd paced the tastefully decorated seating area for twenty minutes. He spotted her immediately and stopped short. She could see guilt and some other emotion she couldn't define all over his face. It just made her more angry. She stalked across the lobby toward him at warp speed, her pumps clicking a staccato beat on the marble floor. She got a little satisfaction from the wary look he gave her as she approached. She wanted to deck him or at least curse him out right there in the lobby with the security guard as an audience, but instead, she summoned up all the control she could muster and spoke through clenched teeth.

"We need to talk," she said. "Have you done the necessary exterminating in your apartment or do we need to go elsewhere?"

"We can go upstairs," he said. "I'll make sure it's clean."

She nodded. Good. She'd be able to kill him in the privacy of his own home without witnesses.

He pressed the elevator call button and they rode upstairs in silence. They got out on the Penthouse floor and headed left. It was a beautiful building located on the water in Key Biscayne. There appeared to be only two apartments on the Penthouse floor. Kathy could see the Atlantic Ocean from the windows they passed in the hallway. It was overcast. Dark storm clouds loomed on the horizon.

Charles extracted a set of keys from his pocket and let them into his apartment. He closed the door behind her, put an index finger to his lips and signaled for her to wait there. He took out what appeared to be a miniature version of one of the scanners she'd seen McKinley Consulting use to scan her office and made a thorough sweep of the apartment.

Kathy stood there, seething, and waited for what seemed like an eternity. Finally, he came back into the foyer, dropped his keys and the scanner onto a small table by the door, and turned to her.

"It's safe to talk. The apartment's clean," he said. "Please, come in and have a seat." He gestured toward the breakfast nook. "Can I get you something to drink?"

He moved into the kitchen. She remained on the outer side of the breakfast nook. She didn't trust herself to get too close to the chef's knives set in a rack on the kitchen counter next to the large stainless steel gas range.

"I saw the article on Peachtree in the paper this morning," she said. When he started to speak, she held up a hand, palm facing outward, and shook her head. "No, don't even bother to deny that you leaked confidential information to that reporter because I know you did. My MIS department found that our network had been accessed by an outsider through the web shortly after you and I met to prepare you for your deposition."

Pain flooded through her as she thought about how much she had trusted him and how he had violated that trust. She paused for a moment, struggling to get enough of a grip on her emotions to get out what she had to say. "I trusted you. I trusted you, you bastard and what did you do? You put this case and my career in jeopardy by leaking confidential information to a reporter. That was your plan all along wasn't it? You wanted to expose Peachtree and the C.I.A.'s illegal activities to the public. You never gave a damn about the case. You certainly didn't give a damn about me. What was that in New York – a little dessert on the side to go with your revenge? A little tension release?"

"No," he said quietly. "That night was real. I never meant for it to happen, but it was real." He took a step toward the breakfast counter - toward her. She took a step back.

He sighed. "Yes. You're right. Publicly exposing Peachtree's illegal activities was my agenda from the start. In fact, destroying Peachtree altogether is still my agenda. I was so hell-bent on revenge that I didn't think about or care who got hurt in the process. I never meant to hurt you, but after Weisman threatened to release the video and file a Bar complaint against you, the only way I could think of to protect you was to take away their need to carry through with the threat. I knew that if Peachtree and the C.I.A.'s secrets were publicly exposed, they wouldn't resort to extortion and more killings to keep those secrets."

Kathy stared at him. "Trying to protect me? How convenient. You get to further your revenge agenda by leaking confidential information to a reporter and protect me at the same time." She crooked two fingers on each side of her head to simulate quotation marks when she said the word "protect." She shook her head, slowly. "I don't understand. If you really think I'm so stupid as to believe that bullshit, why did you hire me to represent you?" When he opened up his mouth to answer her, she held up her hand again. "Don't answer that. I've had all the bullshit I can stand for one day."

She took a step forward and slapped her hands down onto the breakfast counter. He took a step back.

"This is the deal," she said. "First, if you were harboring any fantasies of ever touching me again - in life - you can forget them. I don't trust you and I damn sure don't like you very much right now. I don't care whether you fire the firm or not. In fact, it would be better for me, and for you, if you did. The firm will probably insist we file a motion to withdraw from your case anyway when Weisman files the Bar complaint."

"Second, your little stunt did more harm to your case than you realize. If I were Weisman, I'd file a motion to have the case dismissed as a sanction for violating the confidentiality order. While the Judge probably won't throw the case out, she is likely to impose a lesser sanction."

"Like what?" he asked.

"Like barring you from being able to use any of the leaked information in proving your case. She'll probably hold this against you when making other rulings in the case too. So, you have to decide whether you want to proceed with this case or not. If you do, then you have an uphill battle. And I doubt, very seriously, that Peachtree's last settlement offer is still on the table."

Charles was quiet for a moment. He looked down at the floor and appeared to be, well, sad. There was no other way to describe it. She wondered what he was sad about – that he'd probably messed up his case? That Peachtree's settlement offer was probably off the table? That he'd never get to touch her again? Or was he only sad that he had gotten caught? Who knew? And why did she care?

He looked up at her, his eyes filled with pain. "More has gone wrong with my plan to bring Peachtree down than you know. The reporter who ran that story was a good friend of mine. She was killed last night. The F.B.I. thinks it was Peachtree, but they can't prove it."

Kathy slumped against the breakfast nook and stared at him. "Oh my God." What had he done? She hadn't expected to feel anything but anger toward him. But now, she couldn't help but feel a twinge of sympathy for the guilt and loss he must feel over the death of his friend.

"I was hoping to be able to assist the F.B.I. in its investigation of Peachtree by getting the documents into evidence and getting the jury to make a special finding on the verdict form that Peachtree was involved in illegal activities at the time of the accident. But, from what you just said, that's not very likely to happen," he said. He lowered his elbows onto the breakfast counter and put his face into his hands.

He looked so tired, so utterly defeated, that, despite her anger, the fighter in Kathy kicked in. She hated bullies – especially corporate ones – and she'd be damned if she'd let Peachtree win this lawsuit using murder and blackmail as its legal strategy.

"It's not very likely the Court will let the documents in, but it's not impossible," she said.

Charles looked up at her. "What?"

She backed away from the breakfast nook and began to pace as she thought it out. "Even if we can't get the documents that were leaked into evidence, we may be able to get the Court to compel Peachtree to produce clean copies of other documents we could use to prove they were conducting operations for the C.I.A. on U.S. soil at the time of the incident. Yeah, we could file a motion to compel." She waved a hand. "That is, unless I get disbarred first, then your new attorney could file the motion."

She looked at him and thought she saw a glimmer of hope in his eyes. Why did that make her feel better?

***

Kathy went back to her office and assigned Erin to work on the motion. Erin tried to get details about Kathy's confrontation with Charles, but Kathy evaded since Erin only knew half the story. She'd learn the rest of it soon enough when and if a Bar complaint was filed and the news of her affair with Charles became public.

In her e-mail in-box was a copy of Peachtree's motion requesting to have the Court dismiss the lawsuit. Weisman had wasted no time. According to Annette, the papers had been hand-delivered to her office just before noon. As she read through them, she got a sinking feeling in the pit of her stomach. The motion was pretty sound. Despite all the assurances she had given Charles, she wasn't sure how Judge McCarthy would rule on it. If the Court granted Peachtree's motion, the lawsuit would be over. Peachtree would win.

She sighed, put the cap back on the yellow highlighter she held in her right hand and tapped it on her desk. She sat back in her chair. There were too many issues she had to deal with at once. She didn't even know whether the firm would allow her to remain on Charles' case after Weisman filed the Bar complaint. Had he filed it yet?

She turned to her computer and accessed the Web to check the Florida Bar website. Once there, she typed in her password and entered the "Members Only" section. She then pulled up her record. Even though she had half expected to see it, the breath whooshed from her body and her right hand rose to cover her heart when she saw a notation on her previously spotless record that a Bar complaint had been made.

That was it. She had to talk to Steve and she had to inform the firm before the Bar complaint became public knowledge. Steve defended lawyers against Bar complaints all the time. He was usually successful. As a past President of the Florida Bar, he still commanded the respect of the organization. She wanted to die with shame at the thought of having to tell her mentor about the videotape and the complaint. She'd put this moment off for as long as possible because she knew he was going to be so disappointed in her. She hated to disappoint him. In some ways, he was like a father to her.

The telephone rang. It was Patti, the receptionist. "There's a process server here to see you."

***

"What the hell were you thinking?" Steve Perdue rose from his chair to pace the space behind it, the Bar complaint in his hand.

Kathy hung her head in shame. "I don't know. I wasn't thinking."

"That's for damned sure." He threw his hands up and waved the Bar complaint in the air. "Damn it Kathy. How could you get into this mess? You of all people?" He took his seat. He then turned away from her and stared out into space for a moment.

Kathy sat there feeling like a miserable child who had just terribly disappointed her parents by doing something uncharacteristically bad. She was going to have to shake this feeling if she was going to be of any use in her defense.

He turned back to her. "First, we're going to have to tell the firm about this," he said. "Then, we're going to have to respond to the allegations in the complaint. I'm afraid it's going to get very personal."

She looked up at him. Having known her for ten years, he knew how much she liked to keep her love life private and how much of a violation this whole business would be to her psyche.

"Uh yeah. There's a videotape of me having sex with a client in the hands of the Florida Bar Grievance Commission. It doesn't get any more personal than that. And now the whole world's going to learn about it." She put her burning face into her hands. "Just shoot me. Put me out of my misery."

"The complaint alleges that, at the end of the videotape, you made an admission to the effect that, by engaging in a sexual relationship with a client, you violated the Florida Bar's ethical rules. Did you actually say that?" he asked.

"No. Yes. I mean – I explained to Charles why we couldn't see each other anymore. I mentioned that there were ethical rules about this sort of thing and that I could lose my license."

She looked up to see Steve shaking his head, a look of utter disgust on his face. She got defensive. "I didn't know I was being videotaped at the time."

Steve stopped shaking his head and cleared his throat. "Are you sure you want me to represent you in this matter? If so, I'm going to have to see the video." Two red spots appeared in his cheeks. Was he blushing? Wow. He was as embarrassed as she was by the whole business.

She nodded. "I know. You might as well. The rest of the world will have seen it by the time this is all over. Besides, there's no-one else I'd trust to represent me in this case. You're the best and I know you have my back."

"I always will, Kathy. You know that." He hit the speaker button on his telephone and dialed the number of the firm's general counsel.

CHAPTER XVII

Kathy stood behind the counsel's table on the right hand side of Judge McCarthy's courtroom and tried to organize her thoughts. Erin sat next to her. Charles sat next to Erin.

The courtroom was packed – standing room only. Reporters and attorneys filled the gallery and the jury box and lined the back of the courtroom. The noise level was so high the bailiff threatened to clear the courtroom twice even though Judge McCarthy had not yet taken the bench. Kathy felt curious eyes staring at her. She tried to ignore them. Someone, presumably Weisman's office or Peachtree, had leaked information to the press concerning the Bar complaint. The story had run in that morning's newspapers.

Kathy was used to public speaking; however, she was not used to having her sins displayed for all the world to see. She was what her sisters described as "under cover." She took a deep breath and ordered herself to focus. She could only fight one battle at a time.

The meeting with the general counsel of the firm had not gone well. He had insisted that the only viable course of action was for the firm to withdraw from the case. He was known for being ultra-conservative when it came to taking risks and patronizing toward female attorneys. It galled Kathy to no end that, by getting herself into this mess, she'd given his attitude even an ounce of validation.

Judge McCarthy entered the courtroom, moved swiftly to the bench and took her seat.

"All rise," called the bailiff.

The chattering in the courtroom ceased.

Judge McCarthy waved a hand. "Please be seated."

Those who had seats sat down. Kathy and Weisman remained standing. The Judge looked at them. "Please state your appearances."

"Kathy Brooks and Erin Carter from Gold Rome & Harris on behalf of the plaintiff, Charles Morgan," Kathy said. She gestured with an outstretched arm toward Charles.

"Stewart Weisman on behalf of the defendants," Weisman said.

"We're here today on three motions – a motion for sanctions, a motion to compel and a motion to withdraw," Judge McCarthy said.

"Yes, your honor," Kathy said.

"Alright, let's deal with the motion to withdraw first," the judge said. "What's the basis for the motion?"

"Your honor," Kathy said, "as we state in the motion papers, an ethical complaint has been filed against me, personally, in connection with my law firm's representation of

Mr. Morgan. Under these circumstances, we think it best, for all parties involved, that Gold Rome & Harris withdraw as counsel of record for the plaintiff and that he be given thirty days in which to obtain new counsel and bring them up to speed in this case."

Judge McCarthy turned to Weisman. "Do Defendants have any objection to the motion?"

"Yes we do, your honor," Weisman said. "We object most strenuously to the motion and request that it be denied. This case is set for trial which is scheduled to take place in three months. The parties have already identified witnesses, set up a schedule for taking depositions and developed their strategies for the case. In his motion, Mr. Morgan seeks a stay of the proceedings for thirty days to hire new counsel and bring them up to speed. New counsel will mean new strategies, new theories, and, most likely, a need to postpone the trial to explore and implement them. My clients need to have this case behind them so that they can get on with the very important work of national security. They shouldn't have to suffer delay just because Ms. Brooks had a lapse in judgment and decided to hop into the sack with her client."

The courtroom erupted. Spectators chattered amongst themselves. Reporters frantically scribbled notes. As the voices rose to a crescendo, Kathy realized that her jaw had gone slack. She glanced over at Erin and saw that she wore a similar expression.

Judge McCarthy banged her gavel. "Order! Order in the Court! If I don't have silence right now, I will clear this courtroom!"

The courtroom grew silent.

Kathy, who was now in full battle mode, ignored the

stares of the spectators and got down to business. "This is precisely the sort of hoopla and negative attention the plaintiff seeks to avoid. It will only serve to act to his detriment."

Judge McCarthy sat there for a moment considering their arguments. "The motion to withdraw is denied. Trial of this case is set to take place in twelve weeks and I will not entertain any motions to postpone it. My docket is quite full already. The remainder of the courtroom proceedings in this case will, however, be held in a closed courtroom. That should address the plaintiff's concerns with respect to hoopla and negative attention."

Kathy glanced over at Charles and noticed that he was glaring at Weisman. She caught Erin's eye and inclined her head toward Charles. Erin got the message. She tapped Charles on the shoulder and said something to him when he turned to look at her. He turned his chair slightly toward her and away from Weisman.

Kathy looked at Weisman. She wanted so badly to wipe that smug expression off his face. She turned her attention back to the judge who was already moving on to the next motion.

"Next, I'll hear the motion for sanctions," she said.

"Yes," Weisman said. "Your honor entered a confidentiality order in this case forbidding the parties from disclosing confidential documents produced in discovery to third parties. In reliance upon that order, Peachtree Consulting produced tens of thousands of confidential documents – fifty boxes in fact – to counsel for the plaintiff. Yesterday, an article appeared in the Miami Herald specifically referring to some of the confidential documents Peachtree Consulting produced in this case. Those documents include Defendant Thomas Wilkes' employment records, travel records, expense reports and other reports authored by him. The reporter who wrote the article attended the same high school as the plaintiff. They even served as reporters on the high school newspaper together. It's clear that Mr. Morgan was the source of the documents referred to in the article and that he violated this Court's confidentiality order."

Judge McCarthy aimed stern looks at Kathy and Charles. "The plaintiff's response?"

"Your honor, there are a number of problems with Defendants' motion for sanctions. First," Kathy said, using her right index finger to count the arguments off on the fingers of her left hand, "the defendants have not met their burden of proof with respect to the motion. It is based solely upon conjecture. No affidavits have been submitted in which a single witness testifies that my client is the reporter's source for the article or that he provided her with any documents whatsoever, much less documents covered by the confidentiality order in this case. Moreover, the article doesn't contain a single quote from Mr. Morgan. The fact that he and the reporter knew each other in high school, twenty years ago, is not probative of anything."

Kathy moved on to her next finger. "Second, the newspaper article refers to documents Peachtree never produced in this case – specifically, the incident reports authored by Defendant Wilkes which contain the fax number traced by the reporter to the Central Intelligence Agency. Defendants' failure to produce these documents, which are clearly responsive to Plaintiff's document requests, is one of the grounds for Plaintiff's motion to compel which is also before the Court this morning. Under these circumstances, Defendants' motion for sanctions should be denied."

Kathy stepped back and glanced at Erin to see if she had left anything out of her argument. Both Erin and Charles smiled at her. Erin gave her a thumbs-up sign.

Weisman stepped forward. "Your honor, if I may make

a very brief response."

Judge McCarthy nodded. "You may, Counselor."

"Although Ms. Brooks made a very eloquent argument in defense of the motion for sanctions, I notice that she never affirmatively represented to the Court that her client did not, in fact, provide the reporter with the confidential information. Moreover, she did not submit any affidavits or other testimony from her client to that effect in opposition to the motion. She merely argued that Defendants failed to provide any direct proof that he had leaked the documents," Weisman said. "Under these circumstances, we ask the Court to make a factual finding, based on the circumstantial evidence, that he did disclose confidential information, and to grant our motion for sanctions."

Damn. She had hoped to skirt around that issue. She didn't want to subject herself, her law firm, or Charles to sanctions by falsely representing that he didn't leak the confidential documents to the reporter when she knew that he had. She also couldn't allow him to lie under oath on the issue. Her solution was to point out that the defendants had not met their burden of proof. She was legally correct. After all, it was their burden to prove the factual allegations of their motion for sanctions.

But being right on the law didn't always translate into winning. Judge McCarthy was a human being and an ethical one at that. She would take a dim view of what she perceived of as legal shenanigans. She could rule against them and then they'd have to wait until the end of the lawsuit to appeal her ruling.

Judge McCarthy sent a suspicious look over at Charles. Then, she turned to Kathy. "Any response, Counselor?"

"Yes, your honor. By making the argument they just did, the defendants are attempting to improperly shift the burden of proof on the motion upon the plaintiff. The law is clear that they bear the burden of proof with respect to proving the factual allegations of their motion. As a result, no representations or testimony on my client's behalf are warranted, necessary or appropriate," Kathy said.

Judge McCarthy glared at Kathy for a moment then banged her gavel. "I find that there is adequate circumstantial evidence to support a finding that the plaintiff did, in fact, violate the confidentiality order in this case by leaking confidential documents to the Miami Herald reporter. Therefore, I grant the motion for sanctions and hold that the plaintiff may not use any of the documents referred to in the article for any purpose in this case."

The judge leaned forward in her seat and peered at Charles over the rims of her glasses. "Mr. Morgan, if I even suspect that you've leaked any additional confidential documents in this case in violation of my order, I will dismiss this lawsuit so fast your head will spin and you will spend time as a guest of the federal prison system for being in contempt. Have I made myself clear?"

Charles stood up to address the judge. "Yes, your honor."

"Good. Next, we have the motion to compel the defendants to provide clean copies of the documents responsive to the plaintiff's document requests."

Charles took his seat as Kathy stepped forward.

"Yes, your honor," she said. "As I mentioned earlier, one of the grounds for the motion to compel is that the defendants never produced some of the documents referred to in the newspaper article in response to our document requests. Specifically, the defendants never produced any incident reports authored by Defendant Wilkes. We specifically requested those documents."

"Your honor," Weisman said, "that is simply not true. We did, in fact, produce the incident report pertaining to the accident that is the subject of this case. We objected, however, to the production of all incident reports authored by Mr. Wilkes in the three year period preceding the incident on grounds of national security. Such documents are not relevant to this case."

"Your honor," Kathy said, "we have searched the fifty boxes of documents they provided to us high and low and did not find a copy of the incident report pertaining to the death of Patricia Morgan. To the extent they did produce the incident report, it was so heavily redacted as to be unrecognizable. That leads us to the second ground of our motion to compel. All of the documents produced by Peachtree in this case were so heavily redacted - with most of the words crossed out in thick black ink - as to be indecipherable. We can't even tell what the documents are in some instances."

"Your honor, we redacted the documents we produced in the interests of national security. You just made a finding that, despite the confidentiality order you entered in this case, Mr. Morgan leaked some of the documents to the press. Redacting the documents appears to be the only safeguard we have for protecting national security interests in this case," Weisman said.

"Your honor, we believe that Peachtree is using the claim of national security as a smokescreen to avoid having to provide any meaningful discovery. The only way to clear this up, once and for all, is to order the defendants to produce clean copies of the documents to the Court. The Court can then inspect the documents and determine whether redaction is necessary to protect national security interests. There is quite a bit of authority supporting this type of procedure. We cited the cases in our motion," Kathy said.

Judge McCarthy was silent for a moment then she banged her gavel. "I'll take the motion to compel under advisement for now and inform the parties of my ruling on the motion in writing. In the interim, I hereby order the defendants to produce clean copies of the documents to the Court for inspection. And that includes any reports authored by Defendant Wilkes in the one year period preceding the incident giving rise to this lawsuit as well as any reports pertaining to the incident."

Weisman stepped forward. "But your honor -."

Judge McCarthy banged her gavel again, cutting him off. "I've made my ruling." She rose from her seat.

"All rise," the bailiff called.

Everyone in the courtroom rose from their seats. The judge left the courtroom. Reporters raced outside to make phone calls. Spectators began talking amongst themselves.

Kathy turned to look at Erin and Charles. They looked like they wanted to get into a discussion of the afternoon's events. She shook her head. "Not here. Wait until we get back to the office. First, we have to deal with the press. No comment all the way. I don't care what they ask you. There will be no getting angry or defensive or indignant on camera – no gratuitous comments. Do I make myself clear?"

Charles and Erin nodded. They packed up their stuff and left the courtroom.

***

An hour later, Kathy met with Charles in a conference room at GRH. She was exhausted and wanted nothing more than to leave the office for the day, sort out everything she was feeling and figure out her next move in privacy. Unfortunately, privacy was a luxury she could no longer afford. She sat back in her chair, tipped her head back and gazed at the ceiling for a moment. Then she brought her chin down and looked at Charles.

He was watching her. He did that a lot when they were together. It was difficult to mask your emotions when someone was always watching you. She gave him what she hoped was a reassuring smile. He smiled back at her, bringing out those dimples and that cleft in his chin that she loved so much. She shook her head. She must be more tired than she realized. It was that sort of thinking that had gotten her in this mess to begin with.

"What a hearing," Charles said. "After that epic battle, you must be tired."

Kathy tilted her head. Considering how the hearing had gone, she had half expected him to gripe and complain. Instead, he thought about her. "Yes. I must confess that I am a little tired. But, as one writer put it, I have 'miles to go before I sleep.'"

He leaned over and touched her arm. "Listen, I didn't fully appreciate how difficult our relationship would make life for you - both personally and professionally - until I saw what happened in that courtroom today. I just wanted to say that I'm sorry for my part in all this."

She stared at him with mixed emotions. Part of her wanted to crawl into his arms and be comforted. Part of her wanted to run from the room to avoid feeling anything more for him. Part of her knew it was already too late.

She decided to mask her emotions with humor and to keep it light. She shrugged, which had the added effect of dislodging his hand from her arm. "I'm a big girl. It takes two to tango and I knew better. I really can't blame anyone but myself for this mess."

He sat back in his seat, his eyes searching her face. "So, where do today's rulings leave us in terms of the case?"

"Not in great shape, I'm afraid." She got up and began to pace the conference room. "We'll discover more about the full ramifications of the Court's ruling on the motion for sanctions later on as we prepare for trial. But, as it stands now, we can't use any of the documents mentioned in the reporter's article to prove your claims. That includes the travel records you used to track Wilkes' movements and the incident reports with Manning's name and fax number on them."

"But that's crazy. The incident report produced by Peachtree in this case redacted out the fax number and any references to Manning. In fact, all of the documents were so heavily black-lined that the only useful ones were the travel records. It wasn't until I got clean copies of Peachtree's records that I was able to put two and two together. And even then, Judy wouldn't go to print until she got corroborating evidence that the fax number belonged to the C.I.A."

"How did she do that?" Kathy took her seat.

"I don't know. She said she had a friend at the telephone company."

Kathy was quiet for a moment as she formulated strategies in her mind. She got up to pace again. "On one hand, we don't need those documents to prepare your case for trial. We already have Peachtree's admission that Wilkes was driving the company car that hit your wife's and that he was engaged in company business at the time. We have our expert's testimony about the rate of speed at which he must have been driving to cause the damage he did. All we need to do is to take the deposition of Peachtree's corporate representative, Wilkes and any expert they designate to avoid any surprises. With that, we'll probably get a verdict in our favor. The question then will be one of damages."

"But I don't just want damages," he said, "I want a finding that Peachtree was involved in illegal activities at the time of the accident."

Kathy stopped pacing and turned to him. "I know. The Court's ruling stops us from being able to use the leaked documents. But the ruling is wrong. Peachtree never produced clean copies of those documents in our case so they were never subject to the confidentiality order in the first place. You may have violated a dozen laws getting the documents and giving them to your reporter friend, but not the confidentiality order."

When he opened his mouth to speak, she raised a hand and shook her head. "I don't want to know."

He closed his mouth and grinned at her.

"So," she said, "our next move is to file a motion asking the Court to reconsider its ruling on the motion for sanctions. We have strong grounds for getting the order reversed on appeal but we can't appeal it until after the trial. Judge McCarthy has a good record. She doesn't like being overturned. If that happens, she'd have to try this case all over again."

"That sounds like a plan," he said. "Who knows, after inspecting the documents, she may decide they were never confidential to begin with. That might get her to change her mind too. And if she orders Peachtree to produce clean copies of its records, we might find other documents linking Peachtree to the C.I.A."

Kathy shrugged. The odds were not in favor of that happening. But having beaten the odds on numerous occasions, she knew that getting lucky wasn't impossible. "We can only hope."

***

Peachtree ground his teeth as he listened to Weisman's report. He glared at his counsel.

"So what you're saying is that the Court could order us to produce clean copies of the documents we already produced some of which this Morgan fellow has already leaked to the press? What's to stop him from leaking additional documents to the press or even the F.B.I.?" he asked.

"Well, the confidentiality order prohibits him from disclosing the records to third parties --."

"So far, the only thing that confidentiality order's proven to be good for is wiping my ass," Peachtree said. "It didn't stop that boy from disclosing those documents to that reporter. Do you have any idea what problems I'll have with the C.I.A. if I have to produce those records? What good is a defense contractor that can't keep secrets? You need to do something about this."

"It may not be possible for us to change the judge's mind –."

"Then what the hell am I paying you all this money for?" Peachtree asked.

"However," Weisman said, as if he had not been interrupted, "we could file an emergency appeal and try to get the order reversed."

Peachtree stroked his chin with his fingers. The lawsuit had become a train wreck. If he couldn't find a way to get it under control, Manning would make good on his threat to clean house. Peachtree didn't need a dictionary to figure out what that meant. He didn't plan to stick around for the fallout. He had some money stashed away and a little hideaway on an island off the coast of South America for just this sort of contingency. Maybe he'd take Giada with him. His mind drifted a little at the thought. He realized that Weisman had stopped speaking and was staring at him. He pointed a finger at his attorney. "File an appeal, bribe somebody, hell, bump off a witness, I don't care. You just do whatever it takes to get rid of this case. Do you hear me?"

Weisman nodded.

"Good," Peachtree said.

CHAPTER XVIII

A week later, Kathy read the Court's order granting their motion to compel and smiled. She picked up her telephone headset, put it on her ear and dialed Charles' number. He picked up on the second ring.

"Hello?"

"Hey, it's Kathy. I have great news."

"Good. I could use some of that right now," he said.

"The Court granted our motion to compel," she said.

"What? Oh that's great! What does it say?"

She could hear the smile in his voice. It was good to hear. "I'm e-mailing a copy to you as we speak." She clicked her mouse on the "send" button. She could hear Charles walking, presumably to his computer. Soon, she heard the click of computer keys. "Basically, she ordered Peachtree to turn over clean copies of all the documents they produced to us. She found that the documents did not merit protection from discovery under national security interests."

"I can see that," Charles said. "This is fantastic. But the

documents are still designated 'Attorney's Eyes Only' which means that I can't see them. So, what's our next step?"

"We file a motion challenging Peachtree's designation of the documents as highly confidential and a motion for rehearing of their motion for sanctions. If the Judge decides that the documents aren't highly confidential, she might be willing to rethink the harsh sanctions she imposed on us."

"Alright then, that's what we'll do. You're a damned good lawyer Kathy. Don't let this business with the Bar complaint make you believe otherwise."

She smiled. It was nice to have his support. "I was going to say that compliments will get you everywhere but that's how we got into this mess to begin with."

He laughed. "It's nice to hear you joke about it."

"It's either that or cry and I'm not big on tears."

"Me either."

The conversation was getting a little personal. It was probably time to end it.

"Okay then, I'll get right on those motions. In the meantime, I'll have Erin make arrangements for us to get the documents."

"Sounds like a plan."

"Yes. Well okay. Take care." It was awkward. She didn't really want to hang up. She got the distinct feeling he didn't either.

"You too," he said.

"Bye." She ended the call and sighed. She was tired of analyzing her feelings for him and wishing things weren't so complicated. What she needed was a distraction. She decided to call her sister and invite her out to dinner. She needed to get out and clear her mind of this madness for a little while and Ivy always made her laugh. She picked up the telephone and dialed Ivy's number.

***

Across town, Peachtree slammed the telephone receiver down. He took a deep breath and struggled to regain his composure. Weisman had just called to tell him about the Court's order. He knew his almost violent reaction to the bad news was due to fear - of Manning. He couldn't figure out why he was so afraid of the man, but he was. It bothered him. In all his years as a soldier, he'd never succumbed to fear and he wasn't about to now. He had a problem and he'd fix it. Right now, that problem was getting rid of this damned lawsuit. The best way to do that was to get rid of Morgan. It was high time he did what needed to be done.

He hit the intercom button.

"Yes?" Giada asked.

"Get McAllister in here," he barked.

"Right away," she said.

Moments later, McAllister walked in. "You wanted to see me, Sir?"

Peachtree waved him in. "Yes. Come in and close the door behind you."

McAllister did as instructed. He sat in one of the visitor's chairs and looked up at his employer.

"We just got some very bad news. That bitch of a judge ordered us to turn over clean copies of the documents we produced." Peachtree grimaced. He was getting upset all over again when he needed to be calm. He rose from his chair, pushed it toward his desk and began to pace back and forth behind it. He glared at McAllister when he saw him raise his eyebrows. "You think this is funny soldier?"

McAllister snapped to attention in his chair. "No Sir. It's just that, as long as we've been working together, I've never seen you so agitated."

"I am agitated - agitated as hell. I should have handled this my way from the very beginning. Instead, I relied on the lawyers and look where that's gotten us – out of the frying pan and into the fire. It reminds me of something my father used to say: 'If you want something done right, do it your damned self.' He was a bastard, but a very wise man." Peachtree placed his hands on the back of his desk chair, leaned over it and glowered at McAllister. "Listen to me. I want Morgan gone. I don't care how you do it or how much money it takes. I want that bastard eliminated. I want that bitch of a lawyer taken out too. Since they were sleeping together, there's no telling how much he revealed to her over pillow talk. And we all know how much whores love to run their mouths. Are we clear?"

McAllister nodded. "Yes Sir."

"Good. Get to it then."

After McAllister left, Peachtree pulled out his desk chair and sat down to think. He didn't have any illusions. The deaths of Charles Morgan, Jr. and his attorney would be viewed as suspicious by the powers that be. Even if the F.B.I didn't have enough proof to pin their deaths on his company, it was likely Manning would still see him as a liability. It was time to put his contingency plan into place. He pushed the intercom button again.

"Yes?" said Giada.

"Giada, please come to my office."

"Right away."

***

That evening, Kathy walked into Sushi Samba on Lincoln Road. It was her favorite restaurant. She was meeting her baby sister for cocktails, dinner, laughs and some much needed recreation. Since Ivy was twenty-five years old, she probably needed to stop thinking of her as her baby sister; but that was easier said than done. Kathy was the oldest of four sisters, Ivy was the youngest and their mother lived in New York. Despite the ten year age difference between them, they were very close.

Kathy spotted her immediately. She was hard to miss since her tall, busty frame was encased in a bright red dress with a plunging neckline. Her hair was dyed a honey blonde color, braided and done up in an elaborate up do that must have cost a fortune. She was seated at the bar next to a Caucasian man who stared at her chest and nodded occasionally as she talked. Kathy smiled and shook her head as she walked up to the bar. "Hey baby sis."

Ivy turned to look at her, a big smile on her face. "Kathy!" She hopped off the bar stool, teetered over on ridiculously high heels, wrapped her arms around Kathy and gave her a kiss on the cheek.

When Ivy released her, Kathy stepped back to take a good look at her sister and raised her eyebrows. "So, where's the rest of your dress?" The frock was so short it barely concealed Ivy's private parts.

Ivy giggled and waved a hand at her. "Silly woman. This is South Beach. I'm supposed to be half naked. You're the one about to be arrested by the fashion police. What? Did you come here straight from work?"

Kathy glanced down at her sleeveless top, black slacks and sandals. "What's wrong with what I'm wearing? I didn't think I needed to change into a hoochie mama outfit to hang out with you."

Ivy laughed. "Like you even own a hoochie mama outfit."

"I've got a couple of sexy dresses in my closet," Kathy said. "I seem to recall you trying to take some of them the last time you came over."

Ivy's eyes widened. "What are sisters for if not to borrow the occasional outfit?"

Kathy laughed. "Mmmhmmm. And the occasional pocketbook, necklace, earrings, shoes . . ."

Ivy rolled her eyes. She opened her mouth to retort, but closed it when the hostess came to tell them that their table was ready.

After they were seated and had ordered cocktails and appetizers, Kathy turned to Ivy. "So, what have you been up to lately?"

"No good of course."

Kathy laughed and kept laughing while Ivy regaled her with highly entertaining stories of her very active dating and club life throughout dinner. It was good to forget about her problems for a little while.

Kathy picked up her spoon and dove into the chocolate dessert they had ordered to share. "Thanks for coming out tonight, baby sis. I needed this."

"Thanks for inviting me. You know I like to hang out with you. You looked a little down earlier. What's going on with you? And don't tell me it's nothing because I know better."

Kathy grimaced. "You wouldn't believe me if I told you."

Ivy smiled. "If you told me what? You always think the world will end if you step one foot out of line. I bet it's nothing."

Kathy sighed. "I wish it were nothing. I messed up big time and now I'm paying the price."

Ivy's brow furrowed. She leaned forward. "What did you do?"

"I slept with a client."

Ivy's mouth fell open. She covered it with her hand. "You did what? Not you. See – all anyone can talk about is me and my exploits. I always tell them you're the one they should watch out for. But they never believe me. So, you slept with a client. Why is that the end of the world?"

Kathy shook her head. "No Sweetie. You don't understand. There are ethical rules prohibiting attorneys from sleeping with their clients. I could lose my license over this."

Ivy's eyes widened. "Oh no," she said. "You mean like the rules preventing psychiatrists from sleeping with their patients?"

"Yeah. Something like that."

Ivy nodded slowly. "Okay, but you only have to worry about losing your license if someone finds out you slept with him. All you have to do is stop seeing him."

Kathy grimaced. "If only it were that easy." She picked up her glass and drained the rest of her Lemon Samurai cocktail.

"What do you mean? It is that easy. I've had some good sex in my lifetime, but none worth losing a law license over." Ivy picked up her martini glass.

"I mean the cat's already out of the bag. You know that big case I've been working on? The Peachtree case? Well they've got me and the client on video doing the nasty and they filed a Bar complaint against me."

Ivy choked on her drink. She set her martini glass down with a thud, covered her mouth and coughed repeatedly.

"Are you okay?" Kathy started to slide out of the booth to help her sister, but stopped when Ivy nodded her head and gulped in air.

"A video? What the hell? You better start at the beginning."

Kathy told her everything that was not privileged. When she was done, Ivy shook her head. "It sounds like you're going up against some very dangerous dudes who will stop at nothing to win this case. You must really like this guy to risk your law license and your life to help him. Are you sure he's worth all that? I mean, I saw him on the news and he is fine and everything, but still, I've never had any worth dying for." She leaned toward Kathy and lowered her voice. "What did that man do to you in that hotel room?"

Kathy laughed. "You are a fool. This isn't just about Charles, although, I do seem to have strong feelings for the man. It's about getting justice for a client. It's about winning and not backing down to a bully. If I let every powerful company I went up against scare me into backing off a case, what kind of lawyer would I be? How could I effectively represent my clients and protect their interests?"

"Well, won't it be a little difficult for you to effectively represent your clients if you get killed?" Ivy asked.

Kathy twisted her lips. "Peachtree wouldn't kill me. I'm replaceable. Another litigator at GRH would step right over my cold lifeless body and finish prosecuting the lawsuit. Or, Charles could hire another law firm. No, if they want to end the case, they need to take him out, not me."

A light bulb went off in her head as soon as the words came out of her mouth. Her heart lurched. Peachtree could very well send its agents after Charles. Now that the Court had ordered the company to turn over its documents, he was probably in more danger than ever. She wondered if Charles had already figured that out. She grabbed her purse, rummaged inside and pulled out her cell phone.

CHAPTER XIX

Charles shifted the bag of groceries he held from his right arm to his left and fished his keys out of his pants pocket. He found his apartment key and inserted it into the lock. That's when he noticed that the piece of thread he had taped across the door jamb before he left was no longer there. He removed his hand from the key and quietly set the grocery bag down onto the hallway floor. He then bent over, pulled up his left pants leg and retrieved a Glock .9 millimeter pistol from his ankle holster. He released the safety.

He looked up and down the hall to make sure no-one was waiting for him there. He then put his ear to the door and listened. He could hear the telephone ringing. It rang five times then went to voicemail. He listened for a moment more. There was only silence. He turned the key in the lock, pushed the door open and went in low and fast.

The apartment was dark save for the light spilling in from the hallway. He scanned the living room and the kitchen area. They were empty. So far, so good. Maybe Peachtree's people had broken into the apartment to plant more bugs. He'd check out the hidden surveillance camera footage later to see what they were up to. First, he had to check out the rest of the apartment and make sure he didn't have company.

Adrenaline pumped through his veins. His heart pounding loudly in his chest, he headed silently down the hall. When he got to his office, he flattened himself against the wall and then peeked inside. The room appeared to be empty. He stepped inside and checked behind the desk and in the closet. They were clear. He left the office and headed down the hall toward his bedroom, leading with the gun. As he got to the bedroom door, he caught a glimpse of movement out of corner of his eye and instinctively dropped into a crouch. The move saved his life. A silenced bullet with his name on it embedded itself into the wall above his head. Before the shooter could recover, Charles aimed the Glock at him and fired with deadly accuracy. The bullet landed in the middle of the assailant's forehead, dropping him instantly.

Taking no time to pause, Charles stood up, flattened himself against the wall and continued to inch his way down the hall to his bedroom. If Peachtree had decided to take him out, they would most likely send more than one shooter to handle it. He continued inching his way down the hall until he stood next to his bedroom door. He was just about to peek inside when a man rolled quickly out of the room into the hallway. Charles tracked the man with his Glock and fired just as the man started to bring up his gun. The bullet hit the assailant center mast. He fell to the floor, landing on his back. Blood leaked from the corner of his mouth. His breathing was labored.

Charles walked over to the assassin and kicked the gun out of his hand.

"Who sent you?"

The man was gravely injured and in obvious pain. Still, he refused to answer Charles' question. "I can't tell you that."

"Look, man, your partner's dead and you're hurt bad. You need medical attention. I can get that for you. All you have to do is tell me who sent you," Charles said.

The man remained silent save for his labored breathing. Charles would have to apply some pressure. He raised his foot and pressed it down hard onto the wound in the man's chest. The man cried out.

"Who sent you?" he asked.

The man struggled to breathe, making loud gasping noises. His eyes bulged. Charles took some of the weight off his foot.

"McAllister," the man said. His voice was weak. "He said . . . take you and your girlfriend out. One team here . . . . the other to South Beach."

His girlfriend? South Beach? *Kathy!* Charles heart leapt into his throat. He took his foot off the man's chest. He then leaned down and grabbed the man by the front of his shirt. "Where on South Beach? Are you talking about my attorney, Kathy Brooks?"

The man's eyes closed.

"No, No. Wake up." Charles shook the man, but it was no use. The would-be assassin was out for the count. He released his grip and the man's head dropped to the floor with a thud.

He raced to the front door. On his way out, he snatched his keys out of the lock where he had left them. He didn't bother to close the door behind him or lock up. His neighbors would have heard the gunshots. The police would be there any minute. He didn't have time to give them a statement. He had to get to Kathy. He prayed he'd get there in time.

***

After dinner, Ivy drove Kathy back to her condo.

"I need to ask you something," Ivy said.

"What?" Kathy asked.

"You know that emerald necklace you bought last year in Maui? I want to borrow it. It would go perfect with the outfit I'm wearing tomorrow. Oh and those green heels you have too."

Kathy laughed. "You don't ask for much, do you?"

Ivy smiled and shrugged her shoulders. "Hey. Closed mouths don't get fed."

"Alright. But I better get them back. And soon. That's one of my favorite necklaces and I bought those shoes to go perfectly with my green party dress."

Ivy grinned. "You will."

They arrived at Kathy's building. Ruben, the valet, came out to greet them. "Hello Mrs. Brooks. Ms. Ivy." He always insisted upon calling Kathy "Mrs. Brooks" no matter how many times she told him that she wasn't married. For some reason, he never called Ivy "Mrs. Brooks." That was probably because she was younger and usually half naked.

"Hi Ruben," Kathy said. "Ivy's only going to be here for a moment. Can you keep her car right here?"

Ruben nodded. "Yes, Mrs. Brooks."

"Thank you Ruben." Ivy smiled at him and handed him her car keys.

A tinge of color rose in his cheeks. "You are welcome, Ms. Ivy."

The women headed into the lobby. Ivy pressed the call button for the elevator. Raul, the guard manning the front desk, greeted them. "Good evening, Ladies."

"Hello," Kathy said.

"Ms. Brooks, some men were here to see you earlier. They had badges and said they were federal agents. I called upstairs but you weren't there."

Kathy frowned. "Federal agents? Which agency were they from? The F.B.I.?"

"Their badges said they were F.B.I. Are you in some sort of trouble?" he asked.

"No," Kathy said. "It probably has to do with a case I'm working on. But they shouldn't be coming to my house at night."

The elevator arrived.

"Good night, Raul," she said.

"Good night," he said.

Kathy and Ivy stepped into the elevator.

"You've got F.B.I. agents coming to your house late at night because of that case?" Ivy asked. "You need to get off that thing."

"We tried. Remember? The judge won't let us out. It's strange though for them to come here instead of going to my office during the day or calling to request an interview of Charles."

"This whole thing sounds strange if you ask me. You sleeping with a client, hidden cameras, videos, blackmail . . . I feel like I'm reading a spy novel or watching a movie or something. It doesn't seem real."

"I know what you mean."

They arrived at Kathy's floor and stepped off the

elevator. As they walked to her unit, Kathy spotted a guy standing at the end of the hall outside of one of the corner units. He looked at her and then knocked on the door. He was probably there to see one of the guys who lived in that apartment.

Kathy fished her keys out of her pocketbook and unlocked the door to her unit. She stepped inside, flipped on the light and, as usual, threw her keys onto the dining room table. She was happy to be home. It had been a long day and she had a lot on her mind. She looked forward to watching some mindless television and settling down with a cup of ginger peach tea. Ivy followed her in.

"So, let's see where I put those shoes and that necklace," Kathy said.

She had started to walk across the dining room when she heard Ivy cry out. She stopped and turned around. The man she had seen down the hall earlier had entered the apartment behind Ivy and grabbed her. He had a knife to her throat.

"I'll cut her if you don't cooperate," he said. He kicked the door shut with his foot.

Kathy's pulse sped into hyperdrive. *Oh my God.* Who was this and what did he intend to do? Her first instinct was to protect Ivy at all costs. She had to get control of the situation somehow. "We'll cooperate. There's no need for the knife. What do you want? Money?"

She reached into her purse, grabbed some cash out of the pocket part and held it out. "Here."

The man shook his head and smiled. "No. You won't be able to buy your way out of this Counselor."

Counselor? He knows who I am.

"Who sent you here? Peachtree? The C.I.A.?"

Although the man didn't respond, she saw a flash of recognition in his eyes. Kathy's heart sank. If Peachtree sent him, then he probably had orders to kill her. She and Ivy would have to fight their way out to survive. Kathy looked at her sister. Despite the circumstances, Ivy looked more pissed off than afraid. Kathy caught her eye and willed her to act. Her message was received because the next thing she knew, all hell had broken loose. Ivy slammed her stiletto heel down onto the man's instep. She then elbowed him in the gut with her left arm while at the same time pushing at his knife hand with her right. The man cried out and briefly loosened his grip allowing Ivy to duck out of his grasp and take a couple of steps away from him. Kathy grabbed one of the heavy wrought iron candlestick holders from her dining room table, raised it over her head, stepped in and slammed it down over the man's head as hard as she could. She grunted with the effort. His eyes rolled up into his head and he toppled forward to the floor as if pole-axed.

Kathy and Ivy stared down at him, breathing heavily.

"Nice work, Sis," Ivy said.

Kathy rushed over to Ivy and hugged her. "Are you alright?" She pulled back, raised Ivy's chin and checked her neck for cuts.

"I'm fine. I'm just glad I took that self-defense class. I never dreamed I'd ever have to actually use it," she said.

"We have to call the police before he wakes up. Check him for weapons and take that knife out of his hand. Use a tissue or something. I don't want your prints on it. And try not to wipe off any of his."

Ivy shook her head. "You've been watching too much C.S.I."

"I don't watch C.S.I. I watch N.C.I.S." Kathy stepped

over to the telephone, picked up the handset and dialed 911. While it rang, she watched Ivy grab a kitchen towel, return to the unconscious man, gingerly remove the knife from his hand and put it onto the dining room table. Next, Ivy patted the man down, pausing when she got to his ankle. She lifted up his pants leg to reveal an ankle holster. Kathy felt a pang of fear as she watched her sister pull the gun from the holster.

"911. What's the emergency?"

"My name is Kathy Brooks. I live at 20 Island Avenue, apartment 2011 on Miami Beach. Please send some units right away. An armed burglar or assassin or whatever broke into my house. My sister and I knocked him unconscious but I need the police here fast before he wakes up."

"Ma'am, did you say the man was a burglar or an assassin? And he's inside your apartment?"

"Look, I don't have time for twenty questions right now. An armed man broke into my apartment intending me some grievous bodily harm. Send the units now. I'll answer their questions when they get here. 20 Island Avenue, Apartment 2011." She hung up and turned to Ivy.

"We need to get downstairs with the security guards and wait for the police," she said. "Put that gun on the table and let's go."

"Let's not rush off so soon," a man's voice said.

Kathy gasped and turned to see Wilkes standing in the hallway leading to her bedroom. He was holding a gun.

She swallowed. It was one thing to disarm a man holding a knife. It was another thing entirely to outrun or outmaneuver a bullet. She'd have to try and talk their way out of this. "Wilkes. What are you doing here? You're only making things worse for your case you know." She wanted to wince as soon as the words came out of her mouth. How lame. If that was the best she could do, she and Ivy were doomed.

"There is no case if there's no you and no Charles Morgan, Jr.," he said.

She felt sick at the thought of Peachtree's goons going after Charles. But there was nothing she could do at the moment to save him. She needed to protect Ivy. "Hey, there's no point in killing me or my sister. I'm replaceable. Look, why don't you just walk out of here. I'll pretend you were never here. I'll just say that your friend here broke in by himself."

Wilkes shook his head. "You were shagging your client, Counselor. There's no telling how many of Peachtree's secrets he shared with you over pillow talk. My orders are to take you out."

"Let my sister go," Kathy said. "Please. She has nothing to do with this."

He shook his head again. "Sorry, can't leave any witnesses." He raised his gun hand. His finger tightened on the trigger.

Kathy turned away and cringed. She heard a loud blast as the gun went off and waited for the pain to hit her. Then she heard Ivy yell.

"Kathy, run!"

She looked at Ivy and watched her kick off her heels and run out into the hall. She turned back to see that Wilkes had thrown himself backwards. There was a hole in the wall above the place where his head had been. She kicked off her shoes and raced down the hallway after her sister.

They couldn't wait for the elevator - it would leave them too exposed - so they headed for the stairwell at the western end of the hall. The cold concrete stairs hurt Kathy's bare feet as she pounded down them. She lived on the twentieth floor. There was no way in hell they would get down to the lobby fast enough to keep Wilkes from catching them. They had to hide somewhere.

"This way," Kathy said when they got to the sixteenth floor. She turned, headed through the doorway and raced down the hall looking for a place to hide. The only places available to them were the stairwell on the eastern side of the hall and the trash/laundry room next to the elevator.

She hadn't heard anyone coming after them on the stairs. But she and Ivy had been running so fast and making so much noise she wouldn't have. Eventually, the killer would figure out that she and Ivy had taken the stairs. She didn't want to take the chance of running into him or his partner in the stairwell, so she ducked behind the door that led to the trash and laundry rooms. Ivy followed her.

They stood behind the door in the small hallway catching their breath and listening for any sign they had been followed.

***

Charles drove like a bat out of hell up the driveway to Kathy's condo building. He screeched to a halt behind a parked police car. Was he too late? Fearing the worst, he hopped out and all but threw his keys at the valet.

"I'm going to see my attorney, Kathy Brooks, in apartment 2011," he said.

"The police are here to see her too," the valet said. "She called 911 and reported a burglar in her apartment."

Charles grabbed the valet by the shoulders. "Is she okay?"

The valet winced. "I don't know. Raul went up there with

the police. He said they found a man knocked out on the floor but that Mrs. Brooks and her sister weren't there. Her neighbors told them they heard gun shots. They found a bullet in one of the walls, but there was no blood. The police are looking for her."

Charles thought for a moment. Either Kathy or her sister carried a gun or they got one off the killer the police found in her apartment. She probably got off a round and was hiding somewhere in the building since she wasn't in the lobby.

"Let me up there. Mrs. Brooks and her sister are in terrible danger. The man they found in her apartment is a hired killer. I'm sure he didn't come alone," Charles said.

Ruben nodded. "Okay. You can go up. Mrs. Brooks and her sister have always been nice to me. Do you need some help?"

"No. It's too dangerous. Here, take this card and call my friend, Tyler. His cell phone number is on the back. He's an F.B.I. agent. Tell him what happened and tell him to get some people over here fast. "

"Okay," Ruben said.

"Tell me about the layout of the building. Where are the stairwells?" Charles asked.

"There are stairs at both ends of the halls," Ruben said.

"Are there any public areas on the apartment floors?" Charles asked.

"Public areas? I don't understand," Ruben said.

Praying for patience, Charles explained.

"Places that aren't locked like the apartments are. Places Kathy and her sister could hide in."

"Oh. Yes," Ruben said. "There are rooms to put the *basura*." He gestured with his hands.

Charles racked his brain to bring back his high school Spanish classes. "*Basura*? Oh, you mean the trash."

"*Si*. I mean, yes" Ruben said. "The room for the trash is next to the elevators on the left."

"Thank you," Charles said. "Are there any other public areas?"

"Yes. There is a solarium on the roof. There's also a gym and a restaurant on the Mezzanine floor," Ruben said.

Damn. With all of those options, Kathy could be hiding anywhere. He had to find her before the killer did.

Since she lived on the twentieth floor, his best bet was to start at the top and work his way down.

CHAPTER XX

Kathy and Ivy hid in the trash/laundry room area for a while in silence.

"You know," Kathy whispered, "this is ridiculous. If he's still here searching the building for us floor by floor, then we're just sitting ducks. We need to move and get to the police so they can protect us. They should be here by now. They're probably still in my place processing the scene."

"I wish I hadn't dropped my purse when that guy grabbed me. I could really use my cell phone right now to call my boyfriend," Ivy said.

"Your boyfriend? What can he do to protect us against armed assassins?" Kathy asked.

"You'd be surprised. He could bring some of his boys. They'd take care of these fools," Ivy said.

"What kind of man are you dating?" Kathy shook her head. "Never mind, we'll deal with that later. That's actually a good idea - getting to a phone I mean. We could call 911 and get the police to come down and get us. We need to knock on some doors and get one of these people to let us in and use their phone."

"But what if he's out there, just waiting for us to come out?"

"That's not likely. If he was on this floor already, he'd have checked in here by now. He can't watch every trash room on every floor to see if we come out. He could check them though. I'll go out first and knock on the doors. It's me they want. If they get me, they might leave you alone. You just be ready to blast anyone who walks through this door."

Ivy grabbed Kathy's arm. "No. I'm not letting you go out there alone. Are you crazy? You always want to be Wonder Woman. This isn't a game. This is for real. There are real killers out there. It took teamwork for us to get this far. It will take more teamwork to get us out of here. I'll go first. I have the gun. Besides, two people can knock on more doors than one."

"Give me the gun," Kathy said.

"Do you know how to shoot?" Ivy asked.

"I've gone to a shooting range a couple of times. I have a clue. Your shot, on the other hand, missed that guy by a mile and put a hole in my wall."

Ivy twisted her lips. "Oh, excuse me for missing the assassin after I just finished fighting off another assassin who had a knife to my throat. Jeez, it's just drywall."

Kathy stared to retort, but the absurdity of their argument hit her and she shook her head. "Come on." She slowly opened the door to the hallway and inched her way along the wall of the elevator bank. When she reached the edge, she peeked up and down the hallway. It was empty. She walked quickly down the hall to the first apartment and knocked on the door. There was no response. Ivy walked to the apartment across the hall and banged on the door. There was no response.

The door to an apartment at the end of the hallway

opened and a little old lady peered out. Kathy recognized the snow white hair. It was the Treasurer of the condo association. "Oh, Mrs. Carmichael. I need your help."

"Kathy, is that you banging on those doors?"

"Yes, Ma'am. I need to use your telephone to call the police. You see, burglars broke into my apartment. My sister and I were able to fight them off and get away, but we're afraid to go back up there." She felt a little guilty lying to Mrs. Carmichael, but she didn't want to scare the woman to death by letting her know that armed killers were after them. She headed down the hallway toward Mrs. Carmichael's apartment.

"Burglars? Oh my. Thank God you girls are safe. Come on in."

Kathy turned to make sure Ivy was following her. What she saw nearly gave her a heart attack. Ivy was following her down the hall; however, she was not the only one. Wilkes stalked down the hall toward them, his gun aimed at Ivy.

"Ivy get down!" Kathy turned and pushed Mrs. Carmichael into her apartment. "Call the police."

Ivy spun around and fired a round at Wilkes. He ducked out of the way, giving Ivy a chance to dive for cover inside a doorway alcove.

At that moment, Charles came running out of the stairwell across from Mrs. Carmichael's apartment. He pushed Kathy into the apartment and pointed a finger at her when she started to run back outside. "Stay in there."

"My sister's out there!"

"I'll get her," he said.

Silenced bullets flew past them and thudded into the wall. Kathy screamed and stepped inside Mrs. Carmichael's apartment. Charles ducked into the stairwell for a second. He then took a deep breath, came out and returned Wilkes' fire. He kept firing as he headed down the hall toward the doorway alcove Ivy hid in. Wilkes backed down the hall and took cover outside the trash room, giving Charles the opportunity to get to Ivy.

"Hi, I'm Charles," he said.

"Nice to meet you," Ivy said. They transferred their weapons to their left hands and shook hands.

"You might want to continue the introductions after we deal with the assassin," Kathy called out.

Ivy shook her head. "She has elephant ears."

Charles grinned. "And a mouth like a razor blade."

"I heard that," Kathy said. "Mrs. Carmichael called the police. They're on their way down from my place."

Charles took Ivy's gun out of her hand and checked the ammo. He motioned for her to get behind him and squeeze into a corner of the alcove. He then dropped into a crouch, pushed out his left hand, aimed one of the weapons in Wilkes' general direction and fired. He got lucky. Wilkes grunted with pain. Charles launched himself out of the alcove, turned and fired both guns at the assassin, who was already clutching his leg. His second shot hit him in the throat. Wilkes dropped his weapon and fell to the ground, clutching at his neck.

At that moment, the elevator bells rang and the doors opened. Police officers rushed into the hallway their weapons drawn. They aimed them at Charles.

"Drop your weapons! Do it now! Get down on the ground! Face down!" they screamed at him.

Charles carefully set his weapons onto the floor. He then

laid face down and laced his hands behind his head.

Kathy rushed out into the hallway.

"Ma'am, get back inside. This is police business," said one of the officers.

Kathy continued walking down the hallway. "I'm Kathy Brooks, the person who called you from apartment 2011. This," she said, pointing at the assassin lying on the floor, "is the man who tried to kill us." This," she said, pointing at Charles, "is my client. He saved our lives."

The police allowed Charles to get up. The first thing he did was walk over to Kathy and take her in his arms. He closed his eyes and held her tightly for a moment. "I thought I'd lost you."

Kathy closed her eyes and held on. It felt so good to be safe in his arms. "I was afraid I'd lost you too." She pulled back a little and looked up at him. "Thank you for saving Ivy's life. Mine too."

"You're welcome," he said.

Kathy broke away from Charles and went to her sister who was still cringing in a corner of the alcove. She gave Ivy a big hug. "Come on out, Sweetie. It's okay. It's over. I'm so glad you're safe."

"So am I," Ivy said. "Hanging out with you is never boring, but this was a little too exciting."

Kathy laughed, as did Charles and the police officers who overheard her comment.

The police took statements from Kathy, Charles, Ivy and Mrs. Carmichael who appeared to be quite excited by the incident. No doubt she'd have a lot to tell her bridge buddies the next day.

After the local police were done with them, Tyler and the other F.B.I. agents took Charles and Kathy into protective custody.

"What about my sister?" Kathy asked.

Ivy shook her head. "No. I don't need to go into protective custody. The only reason they went after me was because I was with you. I'm better off letting Deke and his boys protect me. Trust me when I say that no-one in their right mind would come after me with them around. Don't worry about me. You just make sure you stay safe. Don't take any crazy chances."

"I don't know what I'm worried about more - you being out there without witness protection or you being so tight with that thug and his boys. The only reason I'm letting you go is because you'd probably be in more danger if you stayed with me. You be careful out there," Kathy said.

"I will."

CHAPTER XXI

The agents took Charles and Kathy to a safe house in Coral Gables. It was a luxurious home with a two car garage and a pool in back. Tyler gave them the grand tour.

Kathy looked at the expensive artwork and furnishings and raised her eyebrows. "So, these are my federal tax dollars at work."

"Not really," Tyler said. "The house used to belong to a drug trafficker. We took him down in the 90's and impounded it. The Bureau's been using it ever since."

"Oh." Kathy liked Tyler. He was funny and attentive and she could tell that he and Charles were like brothers.

He showed her one of the bedrooms. "This will be your room. I figured you'd want this one since it has its own bathroom."

Kathy smiled. "Yes. Thank you. It was very considerate of you to think about that."

Tyler shrugged. "I have three sisters."

"Oh, I see. So you're well trained."

Tyler laughed. "Yeah, something like that."

"I'm just going to freshen up a little," she said. "I'll be downstairs soon."

"Okay. See you later."

After he left, Kathy walked over to the bedroom door and closed it. She crossed the room and threw herself facedown onto the bed. She hadn't slept in almost twenty-four hours. In fact, she was still wearing the clothes she'd worn to work and then to dinner the night before. She needed a shower, a bed, and a therapist - in that order. She flipped over onto her back and threw her arm over her eyes. Who was she kidding? She needed Charles. She thought about how safe and warm she had felt in his arms and how he'd risked his life to save Ivy. He'd raced right over to her place after fending off his own would be killers to make sure she was safe.

God help her, she loved the man. How could she not? He'd earned it. She never had a hero before or even a man reliable enough to be there for her when she needed him. In her experience, men weren't the most reliable or trustworthy creatures. Her father had cheated on her mother. Her ex-husband cheated on her completing the vicious cycle.

Charles was certainly no choir boy. He had deceived her with respect to his ultimate agenda; but he seemed to have had a change of heart. She thought about how he had offered to settle his case - even though he really didn't want to - just to keep her from having to go through the Florida Bar proceeding.

That was the least of her problems now. It's funny how near death experiences put everything into perspective. She flopped back onto her stomach and groaned. She had to get up, take a shower, change her clothes and start figuring out what they were going to do strategy wise. She had a case to win, a client to represent and, if she lived long enough, a law license to save. She dragged her tired bones off the bed and into the shower, stripping along the way.

The shower felt great. Having the warm water slide over her skin loosened up the knots she'd been carrying in her neck and shoulders all day. She grabbed some of the pomegranate body wash she had brought from home and lathered up. She rinsed the front side of her body first and then turned to let the warm water cascade over her shoulders and back. The shower curtain opened. She was about to scream bloody murder when she realized that it was Charles. She threw her squeegee at him. It hit him dead in the face. "Charles, you almost gave me a damned heart attack. You know better than to sneak up on me like that after the night we just had. What's the matter with you?"

Charles didn't respond. He absently wiped soap from his face with one hand while staring at her as if he were dying of thirst in a desert and she was an oasis.

His gaze made her body tingle. The bathroom heated up with more than just the steam from the shower. She bit her bottom lip. "Isn't this how we got into trouble in the first place?"

"I don't care. I can't go another day without you." He reached out, grabbed her by the waist, pulled her toward him and kissed her hungrily. The kiss sparked a reaction in the pit of her stomach that traveled lower. She kissed him back with a hunger just as fierce.

Her wet torso soaked his shirt. She could feel the buttons digging into her skin. She pushed back, unbuttoned his shirt and pushed it over his arms. She wanted to feel his skin against hers. She undid his belt and unbuttoned his pants, all the while looking into his eyes. He unzipped them and let them fall to the floor. He took off his briefs and kicked them aside. He climbed into the bathtub and kissed her again. She reached down, grabbed his manhood and ran her hands up and down his length. He was rock hard.

He moaned. Their kisses grew deeper and deeper until they were all but devouring each other. He picked her up by the legs and walked forward until her back fell against the wall. He entered her. She was so wet and he felt so good. She moaned and began to grind her hips against him, wanting more. He pulled back and plunged into her. She gasped and dug her fingers into his shoulders. He plunged into her again and again taking her up and over the line of sanity. She cried out and rode wave after wave of orgasm. He roared and ground himself against her. His knees buckled slightly with his release. He set her down gently and held her. They remained like that for a little while - her face against his chest, his arms wrapped around her, the water pouring down over them like a baptism. She could have stayed in his arms forever, but she knew she couldn't.

She sighed. "We need to clean up and get downstairs. The Feds are probably wondering where we are."

Charles chuckled. "I'm sure they have a pretty good idea."

"Oh, great. That's all I need – a bunch of yahoos thinking about us getting lucky instead of focusing on what we have to do next," she said.

"They're professionals. They know how to multitask," Charles said.

Kathy laughed. She pushed him away, grabbed some of the pomegranate soap and smeared it over his chest. "Clean up."

He eyed her. "That felt nice. Would you mind going a little lower?"

She turned away, grabbed some more soap and began to lather herself again. "No perverted sex games. We have work to do."

"Can we play them later?"

She smiled. "Maybe."

***

Manning sat in a parked utility van outside Morgan Sr.'s house waiting for him to return from his morning run. He couldn't believe Peachtree had sent two teams after Charles Morgan, Jr. and his attorney and both teams had botched the job. They'd either been killed or taken into custody.

He should have handled the operations himself. The men Peachtree sent were good, but Morgan was better. Even though Morgan had caused nothing but grief since the case began, Manning couldn't help but feel a grudging admiration toward the man. His attorney was no slouch either. She and her sister had managed to get the best of some well-trained operatives.

The lawsuit had to go away. It was the only way to protect his team and the agency. In deciding how to best accomplish that goal, he'd considered making Morgan disappear. Although, at first glance, it appeared to be the easiest scenario, it wasn't. The lawsuit was too public and Morgan's disappearance would be highly suspicious.

He'd considered making Peachtree and Wilkes disappear, along with enough funds to throw the company into bankruptcy. That too would look suspicious in light of recent events. Still, he'd keep that option open in the event all else failed.

He decided that the best way to get rid of the lawsuit was to convince Morgan to settle it. Blackmailing his girlfriend with the possible loss of her law license hadn't achieved that goal; neither had the murder of his reporter friend. Apparently, Morgan needed to be threatened with the loss of someone he cared about more - like his father. An evil smile crossed Manning's face. Yes. That was the best way.

He'd watched the old man every day that week. He had a set routine. Every morning, he left the house at 6:00 a.m., jogged for approximately two miles then stopped at a Starbucks on the way back to pick up two coffees. By 10:00 a.m., he was at the golf course playing a few rounds with his buddies.

After lunch, he'd spend the afternoons running errands or performing tasks around the house. He would then either have dinner at home or take his wife out to eat. After dinner, he would watch television or fool around with her. It wasn't a bad life at all. Too bad it was about to be disrupted.

It was almost a shame he was going to have to resort to kidnapping and extortion. He would have liked to have faced Morgan in a fair fight. But he couldn't take any chances. There was too much at stake.

He picked up his cell phone and tried to reach Peachtree. He hadn't been able to reach him since Giada reported the botched assassinations. His calls went directly to voicemail. Giada and Peachtree were probably too busy going at it somewhere to answer the telephone.

He was about to leave a message when he saw the old man enter his house. He disconnected the call and hooked his cell phone to his belt. He then grabbed a meter and a clip board and turned to the two men in the back of the van.

"I'm going in," he said. "Stay on com. I'll call you when I'm ready to bring him out."

He exited the van, walked up to the front door and rang the doorbell. After a moment he heard footsteps. He saw the big man peek through the window in the front door before he opened it.

"Yes?" he asked.

"Good morning, Sir. I'm from Florida Power and Light,"

Manning said. "I'm here to read the meter."

"It's a little early for that, don't you think?" Morgan Sr. asked.

Manning nodded and pretended to stifle a yawn. "Yes Sir, it is. Sorry about that."

The old man smiled. "Oh well, just doing your job. Come on in. The meter is out back."

He opened the door wider and stepped aside to let Manning in. When he turned to close the door, Manning took advantage of the moment to wrap his arms around the old man's neck and squeeze with his forearms. The lack of oxygen to the brain made the old man pass out. He slumped. Manning let him fall to the floor. He stood over him, breathing heavily, listening for any signs of Mrs. Morgan. Hearing none, he grabbed his radio and signaled to his men.

He opened the garage door and the van pulled inside. He and his men lifted the old man and placed him into the back of the van. He went back into the house and used a cloth to wipe off the doorbell, the garage switch and any other surfaces he might have touched. He went back out into the garage, climbed into the van and drove off.

The entire operation took less than five minutes.

CHAPTER XXII

Charles, Kathy, Tyler Fox and Agent Michaels sat at the dining room table in the safe house.

Charles watched Kathy pick up a coffee mug, take a sip and make a face. He smothered a grin and turned to Tyler. "Hey man, can we send someone out to get some green tea and some of that new sweetener, Truvia? That's what she likes." He nodded his head toward Kathy who smiled at him.

Tyler and agent Michaels tried, unsuccessfully, to hide the smirks on their faces. Charles narrowed his eyes at Tyler who cleared his throat and turned to Kathy. "Ah, sure, we could do that. Is there anything else you need while we're at it?

"As a matter of fact, yes," she said. "I don't eat dairy or white carbs. Do you think you could get me some Silk almond milk, agave nectar, whole grain wraps . . ."

Charles could see Tyler's eyes glaze over. He bit the inside of his lip, grabbed a legal pad and a pen from the middle of the table, and slid it over to Kathy. "Here. Why don't you just make a list?"

Kathy's lips twitched. "That's a good idea." She picked up the pen and began making a grocery list.

"So," Charles asked. "Where do we go from here?"

"Well, in terms of the F.B.I.'s investigation of Peachtree, the events of last night may have been a break in the case," Agent Michaels said. "In your statement, you said that one of the assassins said that he was sent by Peachtree to kill you and that Peachtree had dispatched another team to take out Ms. Brooks, right?"

"Yes. That's how I knew I had to get to Kathy's condo. I tried calling her to tell her to get out of there, but she didn't answer her cell or her home phone," he said. He glanced at her.

She grimaced. "My cell phone is usually at the bottom of my pocketbook. I didn't hear it ring. I check it periodically, but not as much when I'm hanging out on the weekend."

"You should have called us or at least the police first instead of heading over there to handle the situation yourself. You might have been killed," Agent Michaels said.

Charles shook his head. "All I could think about was getting to Kathy before the killers did. I couldn't trust you or the police to get there in time. I did arrange to have the valet call Tyler when I got there. And the police were already in the building. As it was, I got to Kathy and her sister first. If I hadn't of done it like I did, they'd be dead."

He looked at Kathy and noticed the stricken look on her face. He reached out under the table, took her hand into his and squeezed it gently.

Agent Michaels frowned. He opened his mouth to speak, but Tyler stepped in before he could utter a word. "Look, it all worked out for the best. Charles, Kathy and her sister are safe and sound. Charles was licensed to carry a gun and he used it to defend himself and them. It's all nice and legal. The question we need to address now is where do we go from here?"

Agent Michaels shrugged. "We get warrants for Donald Peachtree's arrest and to search Peachtree Consulting's records for evidence they paid those assassins and ordered the hits. While we're at it, we see whatever other evidence we can find. In the meantime, we keep Mr. Morgan and Ms. Brooks in protective custody."

"That's not going to work," Kathy said.

"What's not going to work?" Agent Michaels asked.

"For starters, I'm not sure that anything you find in Peachtree's files outside of the scope of the warrant will be admissible in any subsequent proceedings the U.S. Attorney brings against Peachtree. Second, all you've got is Charles' word with respect to what the killer told him. If the assassin denies making that statement, you may or may not have enough to even get the warrant," she said. "Third, I have a case to prep for trial. I can't just stay here."

"Staying here is the best way for us to protect you from Peachtree's assassins. The case has got to be a secondary consideration. It's going to be a little difficult for you to prep your case for trial if you're dead Counselor," Agent Michaels said.

Kathy looked Agent Michaels dead in the eye. "The case may be a secondary consideration for you, but it's not for me and not for Charles. If you had any sense, you'd see that, by prosecuting his case, we're actually trying to make the F.B.I.'s evidence stronger so that when you take Peachtree down, it will be for good."

Agent Michaels frowned. "How do you propose to do that?"

"Our plan is to argue that the documents produced by Peachtree don't rise to the level of attorneys' eyes only confidentiality. Once Charles is able to review them, he should be able to provide us with leads proving Peachtree conducted illegal operations for the C.I.A. If we're allowed to present evidence of that at trial, the F.B.I. will have good cause to investigate Peachtree. I can't see Judge McCarthy keeping F.B.I. agents with high level security clearance out of the courtroom during trial," Kathy said.

Agent Michaels stroked his chin for a moment then turned to Charles. "What makes you so sure you'll be able to use the records to prove that Peachtree is involved in illegal domestic operations on behalf of the C.I.A.?"

"Because I've seen some of the documents already and recognized the name of a C.I.A. operative I had dealings with when I was in the Corps," Charles said.

Agent Michaels leaned forward in his chair, an eager gleam in his eye. "You did what? How? Which documents did you see?"

Kathy shook her head. "Charles, don't say another word." She turned to Agent Michaels. "If you want to continue this conversation, you'll have to get the U.S. Attorney's office to draw up an immunity agreement for my client."

"Your client had better tell us everything he knows right now or we're going to take him down to F.B.I. headquarters and book him for impeding a federal investigation. We may even just drop you off at your condo on the way," Agent Michaels said.

Kathy smiled. "Who are you kidding? You need this information. If you arrest my client, he'll just get a sudden case of amnesia. And if anything happens to me when I'm supposed to be in protective custody, my family will become multimillionaires from the lawsuit they'd bring against the F.B.I. How long do you think you'll be able to keep your job after that?

I strongly suggest you get that immunity agreement drawn up and stop playing games." With that, Kathy got up from the table and left the room. The men watched her go.

"That woman is a piece of work," Agent Michaels said between clenched teeth.

Charles grinned. "Yes she is."

***

Charles and Tyler sat in the living room. A football game played on the television, but neither of the men watched it. Agent Michaels had left to get the immunity agreement drawn up. Other agents patrolled the house and the grounds. For the moment, the two old friends were alone.

"So what's up between you and the counselor?" Tyler asked.

Charles shrugged. "What do you mean? She's my attorney."

Tyler sucked his teeth. "Don't give me that, man. This is me you're talking to. I've known you since you were two years old in nursery school. I saw you two holding hands under the table. And any fool can see the way you two look at each other."

Charles grinned. "Okay, I guess I can't hide it from my boy. I care about her man - a lot." His smile faded as he thought about how close he had come to losing her. He shook his head. "Man, when that killer told me Peachtree had sent a team to her house, all I could think of was getting over there in time. I don't know what I would have done if they'd gotten to her."

Tyler stared at him. "You're in love with her, man. I knew it!" He pointed at Charles, threw his head back and laughed.

"Shh!" Charles said. He glanced toward the stairs.

"Damn man. Do you have to be so loud?"

Tyler lowered his voice. "Man, I knew you were whipped when you asked Agent Michaels to send out for some green tea. Seriously though, I like her. She's nice, smart and fine too. If you don't want her, I'll take her."

Charles punched him on the arm.

"Ow!" Tyler rubbed his arm. "That's assault on a federal peace officer. I could take you in for that."

Charles gave him a one eyed leer. "Yeah, just try it."

They heard a key slide into the lock of the front door. The two men tensed and turned to stare at it. Tyler drew his gun. Charles wished he had one. The police had confiscated his after the shooting at Kathy's building.

Agents Michaels walked in. "We have a situation."

"What sort of situation?" Tyler holstered his weapon.

Agent Michaels held up a flash drive and headed over to the laptop computer set up on the dining room table. Charles and Tyler followed him. He inserted the drive into the U.S.B. slot and hit a few keys. An image flashed onto the screen.

Charles stared at the screen in horror, his mind not wanting to believe what he saw – his father bound, gagged and strapped to a chair in the middle of an otherwise empty room, glaring into the camera as if he wished he could break free from his bonds and throttle the person behind it. Below the image was text: "Elaine Gordon Park at three o'clock by the west playground. Come alone and don't be late or your father dies."

A cold rage replaced the horror. Charles balled his hands into fists and wished he could use them. It had to be either Peachtree's goons or Manning who had kidnapped his father. He suspected it was Manning. It was just his style. He glanced at his watch. It was almost noon. He turned to Agent Michaels. "Where did you get this?"

"We have your cell phone at F.B.I. headquarters. We've been monitoring your incoming messages and rerouting your satellite signal to a specific location in the hopes of catching any additional killers Peachtree sent after you. This came in about an hour ago," Agent Michaels said.

"Were you able to trace the source of the message?" he asked.

"It came from a burn phone that was turned off and probably destroyed after the message was sent," he said.

"What about the picture? Did analysis provide any information regarding the location where it was taken?" Charles asked.

Agent Michaels shook his head. "There's not much to go on in the photo. Whoever sent this picture knew what he was doing. The room and the chair look generic as does the duct tape used to tie your father's ankles and, presumably, his hands. The gag appears to be a simple red bandana. There are no windows in the picture and no mirrors or other objects containing reflective surfaces. I'm afraid that what you see is what you get."

"So you have nothing to go on?" Charles asked.

"I wouldn't say that," Agent Michaels said. "We're doing everything possible to locate your father. We have an A.P.B. out on him and on Donald Peachtree. We have heightened security at the airports and borders –."

"Peachtree's missing?" Charles asked.

"Yes. We got a warrant for his arrest and sent men to his home, his office and his country club to bring him in. He couldn't be located. His wife claims not to know where he is either. She said he didn't come home last night," Agent Michaels said.

If Peachtree was missing in action, it had to be Manning. He was probably cleaning house. The thought sent a sinking feeling through Charles' stomach. Manning was a cold and crazy son-of-a-bitch. If he was cleaning house, he'd never let Charles or his father live to testify against him. He looked at Agent Michaels and wondered how much to tell him. He really didn't have much choice. He needed the F.B.I.'s help to get his father back. They needed to know what he knew in order to do that. "Did you get the immunity agreement drawn up?"

Agent Michaels opened his briefcase and pulled out a document. "I have it right here."

Charles turned to Tyler. "Can you get Kathy down here?"

Tyler nodded and headed toward the stairs.

***

Kathy reviewed the immunity agreement carefully then handed it to Charles. "It's okay. You can sign it."

Charles executed the document and slid it over to Agent Michaels, who added his signature.

"Okay," Agent Michaels said. "Now tell us what you've been holding back. I want everything."

Charles nodded. "The documents Peachtree produced were heavily redacted, so I had a buddy of mine hack into Peachtree's system and download some additional files. I reviewed them –."

Agent Michaels' eyes bulged. "You did what? Peachtree is a defense contractor that handles highly sensitive materials for the U.S. government. What you and your buddy did was tantamount to theft of state secrets. In the wrong hands, information from Peachtree's files could be used to make terrorist attacks. If I'd have known this, I would never have gotten that immunity agreement for you. What's the name of this buddy of yours?"

Charles pointed an index finger at Agent Michaels. "Look. I never had any interest in downloading classified information from Peachtree's system. My only interest was in getting clean copies of the documents the Court ordered Peachtree to produce – specifically any files pertaining to me, my wife and child, the accident and whatever Wilkes was working on at the time of the accident. I'm not going to incriminate the guy who helped me get those files. That's not part of the agreement."

"He's right about that," Kathy said. "The agreement only requires him to cooperate in the investigation of Peachtree – not to incriminate others."

Agent Michaels crossed his arms and glared at Charles. Charles glared back at him. Finally, Agent Michaels sighed, uncrossed his arms and gestured with his hand for Charles to continue. "Go on. What did you find?"

"I found a report from Wilkes and a fax showing that the report had been sent to someone named Manning. I knew a guy named Manning in my days in the Corps. He was a crazy son-of- a- bitch who worked for the C.I.A. at the time. I needed help to determine whether Manning still worked for the C.I.A., so I gave the lead to a friend to follow up. She was a reporter for the Miami Herald."

"You mean the reporter who wrote the story about Peachtree and was killed?"

"Yes," Charles swallowed and stared down at the floor.

An almost overwhelming sense of loss ran through him. He fought his way through it. "She was killed because I got her involved in this. And now my father's in danger."

He felt Kathy put her hand over his under the table. That simple touch provided a measure of comfort.

"We'll get your father back, man," Tyler said.

Charles nodded. They would. He had to believe that.

"So you think this guy Manning is behind your father's kidnapping?"

"I don't believe in coincidences. What are the odds his name would be in Peachtree's documents? You tell me what the C.I.A. wouldn't do to keep its dirty laundry from being exposed," Charles said.

"Huh. Not much," Tyler said.

Agent Michaels was silent for a moment. "Okay, here's what we're going to do. We're going to put undercover agents in the park and outside the park's entrance. They'll tail Manning back to the location where you're father's being held. Once we know the location, we'll plan a rescue operation."

Charles shook his head. "You saw what the video said. If I don't attend the meet, he's going to kill my father. That's not going to happen. I'm going to the meet."

"I can't let you do that. If you go to the meet, he could kill you," Agent Michaels said.

"That's a chance I have to take. Besides, you can't stop me from attending the meet. I'm not under arrest and I have the right to refuse F.B.I. protection. Isn't that right, Counselor?" He looked at Kathy. She looked really worried, but she nodded.

"Yes, that's right. But I would advise against refusing

F.B.I. protection." She turned to Agent Michaels. "Look, your plan could work. All you have to do is factor in Charles attending the meet. You could let him carry a weapon, suit him up with a Kevlar vest or something and surround him with undercover agents."

Agent Michaels frowned. He shook his head.

"I don't like it," he said. "I don't like it at all. He's too valuable a witness to expose like that."

Charles stared at him. "Too valuable a witness? Man, screw you and your investigation. This is my father we're talking about. I'm going to the meet and I don't need F.B.I. permission or assistance to do it."

CHAPTER XXIII

At two forty-five that afternoon, Charles walked into the park. Young children played in the playground while their older siblings were stuck in school. Parents and nannies chased after them, helped them onto slides, pulled them around in wagons or pushed them around in strollers.

It was a hot, sultry South Florida day. Sweat pooled at the base of Charles' spine under the Kevlar vest. Made of the latest technology, the vest was ultra-thin and completely hidden under the sports jersey he wore.

He scanned the park trying to figure out who Manning's operatives were. He knew Manning wouldn't come alone. He could only hope Manning didn't have a sniper lined up somewhere and that he didn't spot the undercover F.B.I. surveillance team. He knew he was hoping for a lot. Oh well. It was too late to change things now.

He walked up to an empty bench and sat down. He sat

there for what seemed like ages when one of the fathers who'd been playing with a little boy handed the kid over to his mother and approached the bench. Charles did a double take. It was Manning.

Wow. He must be slipping. He couldn't believe he hadn't spotted him earlier. As Manning drew closer, Charles realized why. He had lightened his hair until it was almost a dirty blonde. It was longer than he remembered it too.

The years had not been kind to him. Lines that weren't there before had etched themselves into his face further altering his appearance.

"Hello, old chap," Manning said. "Fancy meeting you here."

Charles was not the least bit amused. "Let's get down to it. What do I have to do to get my father back?"

"What? No small talk? You always were all business. I like that about you," Manning said. His grin faded in the face of Charles' continued silence.

"How do you know I want anything from you other than your life?"

Charles, looked away, feigning boredom. "You wouldn't have dragged me all the way here or kidnapped my father if you just wanted to take me out," he said. He turned back to Manning and looked him dead in the eye. "So what do you want?"

"I need for you to file a notice of voluntary dismissal of the lawsuit with prejudice. I also need for you to return all the documents your little hacker friend stole from Peachtree. Don't worry, a large sum will make its way into your bank account for your trouble and your father will be released," Manning said.

"I need proof of life," Charles said.

Manning nodded. He pulled out a cell phone and made a call.

Charles could hear the music used by the Skype program. "I swear, if you have harmed a hair on my father's head, I will kill you."

Manning yawned. "Your father is fine." He turned the phone toward Charles. "See for yourself."

Charles looked at the phone. His father was still strapped to the chair that appeared in the video file. His face wasn't bruised and he didn't appear to have any injuries, but he looked tired. He watched his father blink. "Where is he?"

Manning shook his head. "First things first. Go have your hot little girlfriend file the notice of voluntary dismissal. When we receive notification that it's been filed, you'll get a call from me telling you where you can find him. The money will be in your accounts by close of business tomorrow."

Charles weighed his options. His first impulse was to beat Manning senseless and torture him until he gave up the location. He wanted to put his hands on Manning so badly he could almost taste it. But it wouldn't work. Manning was well trained. He could probably withstand a great deal of torture. By the time he gave up his father's location - assuming he ever did - it would be too late. He had no choice but to rely upon the F.B.I.'s plan to tail Manning in the hopes he led them back to his father's location. He had to make Manning believe he had given up.

"How do I know your operative didn't kill my father the minute you hung up or that you won't send someone after me once the lawsuit is dismissed?" Charles asked.

Manning shrugged. "You don't. I guess you're just going to have to trust me."

"I'll tell you what. I'll trust you to know your life won't be worth living if my father is not returned to me safe and sound." He looked Manning in the eyes. "Tell me I'm lying."

Manning said nothing.

Charles turned and walked out of the park.

**

Two hours later, Kathy watched Charles enter the safe house. Sighing with relief, she walked up and put her arms around him. His arms came around her. She buried her face in his chest for a moment and held on. She didn't give a damn what the agents thought.

"I was watching the surveillance footage. I was so scared it was a trap," she said. She pulled back. "What took you so long to get back here?"

"I had to be sure I lost any tails Manning might have set on me," Charles said.

"Are you sure you did?" she asked.

He shrugged. "I didn't spot any. Either they were damned good or there weren't any. I'm betting on the latter. Since Manning has my father, he doesn't need to know where I am. He knows he can get me to come to him." He turned to Agent Michaels. "How about the tail on Manning? Any luck on getting the location where he's holding my father?"

Agent Michaels shook his head. "No. Manning's as good as you are at slipping surveillance. He lost the teams we put on him an hour ago."

"Damn it." Charles pulled away from Kathy, turned and kicked the nearest piece of furniture. He rubbed his hands over his face. A thought came to him. He removed his hands and looked up. "He made a Skype call from his cell phone when I was with him. Proof of life. Can you isolate his cell phone signal?"

"Maybe." Agent Michaels pulled out his cell phone and made a call to someone at F.B.I. headquarters.

Charles turned to Kathy. "I need for you to prepare a notice of voluntary dismissal and send it over to Stewart Weisman for comment. Can you do that from here?"

Kathy nodded. "Sure. Better yet, I can get Erin to do it. That would be much easier and there would be no way for Peachtree or Manning or anyone else to trace the e-mail back to us here. I guess you've decided to dismiss the lawsuit."

Charles shook his head. "No. I'm just going to make Manning believe I decided to do it to buy us time to find my father. He's not going to leave witnesses around who are able to testify about the kidnapping. He doesn't intend to let my father go and he knows better than to leave me alive if he kills him. He plans to take us both out after I dismiss the lawsuit and return the documents I downloaded from Peachtree's server."

Kathy blanched. "Can he really be that ruthless?"

Charles laughed. The sound was anything but mirthful. "Oh, this is nothing. Manning would take down an entire plane full of people just to get to one target. The man has no scruples whatsoever."

Agent Michaels walked back into the room. "We've got a location."

"Where?" Charles asked.

"The address is a commercial warehouse building near the Miami Airport." Agent Michaels opened up his laptop, pressed a button and a picture of the building came on screen. "There's a security camera installed in the building next door and a traffic cam in the light on the corner that gives us a view of the entrance." He pressed some buttons. "This is footage from yesterday evening."

They watched as a utility van pulled up to the entrance of the warehouse. Two men jumped out the back of the van and carried Mr. Morgan inside. The driver opened his door and stepped out. He wore a Florida Power & Light uniform and carried a clipboard. His face was hidden by his cap for the first few shots, but when he turned his head to address the men, the camera got a clear shot of his face. It was Manning.

Charles' hands curled into fists. "We have to go get my father."

Tyler walked up to Charles and patted him on the back. Although the gesture was meant to soothe, Kathy could see the anger Tyler felt in his eyes and the rigid set of his jaw.

Agent Michaels nodded. "I agree. But first we have to conduct a little recon. We don't want to go off half-cocked and get your father killed."

"Alright, but do it quick. We don't have much time," Charles said.

***

At eight o'clock that night, Charles, the F.B.I. agents, and a S.W.A.T. team met in a commercial warehouse building near the Miami airport. Agent Michaels stood at the head of the table near a screen showing schematics of the warehouse and the surrounding area.

"Gentlemen, we're going to post S.W.A.T. team snipers here and here," he said. He turned to the screen and pointed to the rooftops of two nearby buildings.

"How do we know Manning doesn't already have men

or eyes there?" Charles asked.

"Because my men did recon of the area and those locations were clean. They detected no video surveillance," Agent Michaels said. He brought up a large schematic of the warehouse building. "The only entry points are the front and back entrances to the building. There is a large warehouse space with an office and a bathroom on the right hand side. There are no windows in the warehouse. Heat signatures indicate there is a single person in the middle of the larger room. There is no indication of any other persons in the building."

Something was very wrong. It wasn't like Manning to leave his flank exposed and it certainly wasn't like him to leave a hostage alone. Charles pondered that for a moment and then it came to him. He felt a sinking feeling in his chest. "Oh my God."

All of the men turned to look at him.

"What?" Agent Michaels asked.

"He rigged the place to blow," Charles said, almost under his breath.

"Speak up man, I'm trying to get this operation moving," Agent Michaels said.

"I said Manning rigged the place to blow. That's been his plan all along – to give me the address to the building after I dismissed the lawsuit and then take me and my father out in the explosion. If done right, the explosion could be passed off as a tragic accident," Charles said.

Agent Michaels rubbed a hand over his face and raised weary eyes to Charles. It had been a long day for all of them. "What makes you think that?"

"Why else would Manning leave my father alone in that warehouse? I bet you money that place is rigged to blow and that he's around here somewhere watching and waiting for me to walk into that building. Either that or he has eyes inside the building. He might even have a remote trigger to make sure the bomb doesn't go off prematurely."

"He's right," Tyler said. "Charles and I dealt with that lunatic when we were in the Corps. He's cold-blooded and crazy. This is just his style."

Agent Michaels pulled out his cell phone and called for a bomb squad.

***

Manning sat in a room at the Comfort Inn and Suites near the airport. The hotel wasn't up to his usual standards, but it served its purpose. He watched the surveillance footage from the cameras he had planted in the warehouse. The minute father and son were reunited they'd be blown to hell.

Manning smiled. His plan was virtually foolproof. When Morgan died, his lawsuit would die with him.

He'd worked with Morgan before. Morgan always did the right thing. He was the good guy who couldn't live with what he believed were unnecessary casualties. To Manning, civilian casualties were just collateral damage – a necessary sacrifice to achieve the objective.

Charles would enter that warehouse because he was a dutiful son and he had to believe he could get his father out alive. Charles had a faith Manning could never understand. Whatever faith he once had was lost during his stay in a Chinese prison camp. When he finally escaped after killing a dozen guards, he vowed never to stray from his objective ever again. That's what had gotten him captured to begin with. He shook his head as if to clear his thoughts and focused on the surveillance footage again.

***

"We've got to find Manning," Charles said. "He probably has a remote detonator."

"We're working on that," Agent Michaels said. "But if he's within sight of that building he must be invisible or very well hidden. My men have searched the surrounding area thoroughly. There's no sign of him."

Charles turned to one of the bomb techs. "How close would he have to be remotely detonate the bomb?"

The bomb tech shrugged. "It depends on how he rigged it. If it's rigged to a cell phone, for example, he could phone it in from anywhere. Cell phone signals out here are spotty though. If it were me, I'd want to be close – no more than a mile or two away."

"Gear up! We're going in," Agent Michaels said.

Charles turned to him. "I'm going with you."

"No. You're not," Agent Michaels said. "You're a civilian and a material witness. I'm not going to be responsible for putting you in danger."

The stress and strain of the past forty-eight hours finally got to Charles. He lost it and grabbed Agent Michaels by the lapels of his F.B.I. jacket. "Listen you bloodless, by the book, bastard. That's my father in there. I need to get him out and you can't stop me."

Agent Michaels jerked out of Charles' grasp. "Oh no? I could have your ass arrested right now for assaulting a federal officer."

Tyler walked up and stepped in between the two men. "Gentlemen, there's no reason for this to escalate. Look, we're all on edge right now." He turned to Charles and looked him in the eye. "I will go in there and get Mr. Morgan out. You know how much he means to me. You stay here and help them find Manning."

As much as Charles wanted to protest, he knew Tyler was right. If they didn't find Manning and stop him from using that remote trigger, the chances of getting his father out in one piece were slim to none. He sighed. "Alright, but you better get him out or your life will not be worth living."

"If I don't get him out, it's because I'm no longer living," Tyler said.

Charles nodded. He held out his fist. "*Semper fi*, my brother."

Tyler bumped his fist against Charles'. "*Semper fi.*"

***

After Tyler and the others left for the warehouse, Charles turned to one of the agents left behind. "Agent Peters isn't it?"

The man nodded.

"Do we have any leads at all with respect to Manning's location?" Charles asked.

"Yes. We cross-referenced all calls made to and from the phone he used at the park. One of those calls came from a Comfort Inn on LeJeune. We're sending some agents there to check it out."

"We need to go check that out ourselves. If I know Manning – and unfortunately I do - he's holed up somewhere close where he can pop by and see the results of his handiwork. That airport hotel is the perfect place. It's large enough for him to check in unnoticed and has plenty of exits in case he has to get out of there fast. I don't want your agents to spook him. Let's go." He stood up.

Agent Peters hesitated. "My orders are to stay here with you."

Charles shook his head. "No. Your orders are to protect me. I'm going there. You can come with me or you can stay here by yourself. I'm not a suspect and I'm free to leave." He walked to the door and then turned back to face Agent Peters. "Are you coming or do I need to get a cab to the Comfort Inn?"

Agent Peters looked at his partner, who shrugged his shoulders. They followed Charles out the door.

Ten minutes later, they walked into the lobby of the hotel and approached the front desk. Agent Peters flashed his badge and showed the front desk clerk a photo of Manning. "Is this man staying at your hotel?

The front desk clerk, a grizzly old man, glanced at the photo with bleary eyes then shook his head. "We have a lot of people staying at the hotel. It's season, you know. I can't remember every Tom, Dick and Jorge who walks by."

Charles stepped from behind Agent Peters and leaned against the front desk. "This is very important. Take a good look at the photo and try to remember. Have you seen this man? He's armed and very dangerous – not the type of man you want staying at your hotel."

The old man looked at the photo more closely. Recognition flared in his eyes. He scratched his scalp. "Yeah. Come to think of it, I saw someone who kind of looked like that walk by here yesterday. Except his hair was lighter. I remember wondering where he was going because I didn't remember him checking in. He must be part of that group."

"Part of what group?" Agent Peters asked.

"Most of our rentals are short-term. You know, people on vacation or business trips. They stay for a few days or a couple of weeks max. But there are some companies that rent out rooms for thirty or more days. They get a monthly rate. I remember thinking he must be going to one of those rooms."

Charles heart beat a little faster. "How many rooms are you currently renting out on a monthly basis?"

The old man turned to the computer on his desk and tapped a few keys. "Two. Rooms 408 and 1532."

Two more F.B.I. agents joined them at the front desk. Agent Peters greeted them and brought them up to speed.

"We're going to need keys to those rooms," Charles said.

The old man shook his head. "I can't let you have those. It's against hotel policy. I could lose my job over that. I'll have to send security with you to the rooms."

"Fine, but make it quick. The man we're looking for is responsible for planting a bomb that's about to go off any minute and kill F.B.I. agents and innocent civilians – one of which is my father." Charles looked into the old man's eyes. "Do you have any children? Grandchildren? A wife?"

The old man nodded. He programmed two keys and handed them to Charles. "These master keys will get you into both rooms. I'll send security up after you."

Charles shook his hand. "Thanks man." He turned to Agent Peters and held up the keys. "Let's go."

Agent Peters took one of the keys and handed it to one of the agents. "We'll take 408. You take 1532."

The agents nodded and headed off. Charles, Agent Peters and his partner took the stairs up to the fourth floor.

"You need to stay back while we check this out," Agent Peters said.

Charles' hands curled into fists. It was so frustrating to keep running into these obstacles when they had no time to fool around. "Whatever. We don't have time to argue. Just get in there and separate him from that detonator."

Agent Peters nodded. He walked down the hall to join his partner who had his ear to the door of the hotel room. His partner shook his head, indicating he had heard nothing. Agent Peters pulled out the master key and slid it into the lock. A low buzzer sounded and the light above the door handle flashed from red to green. He turned the knob and pushed the door in. His partner led the way. Agent Peters followed, going in low.

Gunshots erupted. Charles' heart froze.

CHAPTER XXIV

Agent Michaels, Tyler, and the others stood outside the door of the warehouse.

"Scans show just one heat signature in the middle of the warehouse. No-one has been observed entering or leaving the building," one agent said. "We also scanned the front door looking for booby traps and found no signs of any."

Agent Michaels nodded. "How much longer until they take the hinges off the front door?"

"Not long. They have to go slow to make sure the door isn't wired."

"All clear!" called out one of the bomb techs.

The bomb techs went in first, carefully searching the warehouse for explosives. They came out a few minutes later. The head bomb tech walked up to them. "We found the hostage strapped to a chair in the middle of the room. He's alive, but he's sitting on ten blocks of C-4 wired to a pressure switch, a remote detonator and a cell phone. We also found hidden cameras that appear to be transmitting the feed to a remote location."

"So what you're telling me is that the bomb could go off

if he phones it in, detonates it from a remote location or if the hostage gets off that chair," Agent Michaels said.

The bomb tech nodded. "That's right."

"Can we disarm it?" Agent Michaels asked.

"Yes, but it's going to take time. Meanwhile, he could see us working on it through the video feed and set it off. I told the men to evacuate the building on the off chance he hasn't seen us yet. The cameras are trained on the hostage and the bomb. We jammed all cell phone signals around here before going in, so he wasn't able to set off the bomb by phoning it in. He could still have someone set it off by remote though. Maybe the other agents have gotten to him. We're waiting for a report," he said.

"What other agents?" Agent Michaels asked. "Have we found out where he's hiding?"

"We traced the surveillance signal back to a laptop in the Comfort Inn on LeJeune. I reported in and headquarters told me agents had already been dispatched there. We got ahold of two of those agents, but the suspect was not in the room they checked out. We haven't been able to get in touch with Agent Peters or Agent Phillips," he said.

"Manning probably got past them and is on his way here. How close does he have to be to detonate the bomb by remote?" Tyler asked.

"I'd say no more than thirty feet outside the warehouse in any direction," the bomb tech said.

"That's a lot of ground to cover," Agent Michaels said. "We're going to need some more men."

"Is there any way you could do something to delay the detonation long enough for me to get Mr. Morgan out of there?" Tyler asked.

The bomb tech nodded slowly. "We could spray the bomb with liquid nitrogen. That would give you maybe ten seconds' delay. A young healthy man who's a fast runner might be able to get far enough away to survive the blast, but the hostage is an older man who looks tired. He'll never make it."

"Is there any way to fool the pressure switch so that someone could trade places with him?" Tyler asked.

"Theoretically, yes. As long as the right amount of pressure is applied to the seat of the chair, the switch won't know the difference. But we're talking about a very delicate operation here. One wrong move and both men could go boom. I don't know if the hostage is in good enough condition to slide off that chair slowly enough to do the transfer without registering a weight change to the pressure sensor. Who could we get to switch with him anyway? This would be an extremely high risk operation," the bomb tech said.

"I'll make the switch," Tyler said. "Just tell me how to do it."

"Are you sure?" Agent Michaels asked. "We're not ordering you to do this. You heard him. This is extremely dangerous."

Tyler looked at him. "Yes. I'm sure. That man in there is like a father to me. You don't have to order me to do this. You couldn't stop me."

The bomb tech raised his eyebrows. "Well, in that case, let's get started."

***

Charles silently inched down the hall to the door of the hotel room and peered inside. Manning stood in front of the desk staring into the screen of a laptop computer his back to Charles. The two agents sprawled bloody and motionless on the floor.

As Charles crept into the room, he saw Manning pull a cell phone out of his pocket. He sped up, grabbed Manning by the neck with one arm and used the other to knock the cell phone out of his hand. He tightened the choke hold, seeking to cut off Manning's air and render him unconscious. He wanted to break the man's neck.

Manning rammed his right elbow into Charles' midsection. The pain was intense causing Charles to grunt and momentarily loosen his grip on Manning's neck. Manning took the opportunity to spin in Charles' grasp and bring his knee up into Charles' groin. Charles saw stars and doubled over. Manning kicked him in the face. He fell back and then down next to Agent Peters, who was lying on the floor bleeding from a gunshot wound in the chest.

Manning brought his gun hand up and aimed his weapon at Charles. "So, you thought you could beat me at this game old chap? Well, bully for you for trying. Unfortunately, your high opinion of your skills didn't meet up to your expectations." Keeping his weapon trained on Charles, he walked over to where the cell phone had fallen and picked it up.

A gurgling sound from Agent Peters caught Charles' attention. Agent Peters caught his eye then turned his head to look in the direction of his right hand which lay between them. He still held his weapon.

Charles looked up at Manning. He'd taken his eye off of Charles and was hitting buttons on his cell phone with his thumb.

Charles snatched the gun out of Agent Peters' hand, raised it and fired. The bullet hit Manning in the chest and threw him backwards against the desk. He fell to the floor.

Charles got up and ran over to him. He snatched the cell phone from Manning's hand and looked at it. To his horror, he saw that Manning had hit the redial button. Ten digits appeared on the screen.

Charles' eyes flew to the laptop. He expected to see camera snow. Instead, he saw a clear image of Tyler, his father and someone wearing a bomb squad jacket. He breathed a sigh of relief then squinted at the screen. What the hell were they doing?

Tyler appeared to be sliding his weight onto the chair and his father appeared to be sliding off it with the help of the bomb tech. The bomb must have a pressure switch.

Something made him look down at the floor. Maybe it was a slight sound or a movement. Maybe it was just gut instinct. He glanced down just in time to see Manning raise his gun. He kicked the gun out of Manning's hand and then he kicked Manning in the head, rendering him unconscious.

He went over to check on Agent Peters. He was still alive. He checked the other agent's pulse and felt nothing. He returned to Agent Peters and applied pressure to the wound on his chest. He could hear sirens wailing as they approached the hotel.

"Hold on, man," he said. "Help is on the way." Although he was not in the habit of praying, he sent up a silent one for Tyler and his father.

***

Kathy waited in the safe house feeling helpless and growing more frantic as each report came in. So far, all they knew was that shots were fired at the Comfort Inn, men were down, Manning had been arrested, and they were still trying to defuse a bomb at the warehouse where Charles' father was being held hostage. No-one could tell her if Charles was alright or where he was.

"Take me to the warehouse," Kathy said to the agent closest to her. It was Agent Rosaria Santos, a tough looking Latina who wore a dark pants suit, a crisp white button down cotton shirt and her long black hair pulled back into a sleek ponytail.

Agent Santos shook her head. "No can do. My orders are to keep you here until we know you're safe."

"You can't keep me here against my will. I need to know if Charles is alright. If he is, then I know he'll go to the warehouse to make sure his father is safe. Please, no-one can tell me anything here," Kathy said.

"There's a bomb at the warehouse, Ms. Brooks. It's not safe to take you over there. And even though Manning is in custody, there's no telling where the rest of his team is or whether Peachtree has sent any more killers out to look for you. The safest place for you to be is right here," Agent Santos said.

"I don't care," Kathy said. "Charles isn't answering his cell phone. I need to know he's safe. He may even need my help. Are you coming or do I need to call a cab?"

Agent Santos sighed and raised her eyes to the heavens. "Fine. I'll take you over there. Agent Michaels will have my ass for it though."

Kathy smiled. "Don't worry. Just tell him that I forced you to take me there. He'll believe it."

"I'm sure he will," Agent Santos said.

***

Beads of sweat poured down Mr. Morgan's forehead as he slowly transferred the remainder of his weight off the chair and Tyler took his place. His cramped leg muscles tensed with the effort of making sure he didn't move too quickly. The minute his right buttock cleared the chair, the bomb tech raced him out of the warehouse and onto the street. What took only seconds felt like forever as he ran half expecting the bomb to explode.

Once outside, he was taken to an emergency vehicle. They sat him on a stretcher while the EMT's checked him out. An F.B.I. agent walked up to him.

"Mr. Morgan, my name is Agent Michaels," he said. "I'm very glad we were able to get you out safely."

"I am too. But it's not over. Tyler's not out of the woods yet. Where's Charles?"

"Your son went with two other agents to secure Manning and make sure he doesn't try to remotely detonate the bomb. We've received reports of men down at that location."

Mr. Morgan's breath caught. He waved the EMT's away. "Men down? Which men? Is Charles alright?"

"I don't know," Agent Michaels said. "The reports are that Manning is in custody, one man is dead and another is wounded. We should get more detailed reports momentarily."

Mr. Morgan frowned. "With all of the technology available today, you people ought to be able to get better information than that. What kind of-."

"Dad, stop terrorizing Agent Michaels. I've already done that enough today." Charles stepped from behind the bomb squad van, walked up to his father and hugged him tightly. "I'm so glad you're safe."

"Same here, son."

Charles pulled back, but kept his arm around his father's shoulders. "Did he hurt you?"

Mr. Morgan shook his head. "I'm fine, son. My pride

was hurt more than anything else. But Tyler's still in there. That boy took my place on the hot seat."

"I know." Charles' face was grim. "I saw it on a monitor in Manning's hotel room."

An unmarked sedan pulled up to the scene. The minute it came to a halt, Kathy jumped out and strode briskly up to Agent Michaels. "Is Charles here? Is he okay?"

"See for yourself," Agent Michaels said. He inclined his head in Charles's direction and then walked away.

Mr. Morgan watched Kathy turn her head and spot Charles. A smile lit up her face. She rushed straight into his son's arms and buried her face in his chest. Charles kissed the top of her head.

"I'm so glad you're okay," she said.

"I'm fine, Baby," Charles said.

Mr. Morgan raised his eyebrows. What have we here? He hadn't seen Charles interact with a woman like that since Patti's death.

Kathy pulled back and gave Mr. Morgan a smile.

"Hello, Mr. Morgan. I'm glad to see that you're safe too. I'm Kathy Brooks." She extended a hand.

Mr. Morgan shook it absently. "Nice to meet you. I wish it were under better circumstances."

She nodded. "I know what you mean." She turned back to Charles. "They said Tyler switched seats with your father. Is he still in there?"

Charles nodded. The three of them turned to watch the door to the warehouse.

Agent Michaels returned. "They've put liquid nitrogen on the bomb. That will give Tyler ten seconds to make the door of the warehouse. I hope that's enough time."

"He was the fastest runner in our unit," Charles said. "He'll make it."

Mr. Morgan watched Kathy take Charles' hand. As he said a silent prayer for Tyler, he felt Kathy pat him on the back. He looked at her. She sent him a reassuring smile. He returned it.

Agent Michaels raised the bullhorn he was holding. "Ready, set, go!"

Seconds later, Tyler sprinted through the warehouse entrance. Almost simultaneously, an explosion rocked the street and threw him into the air. He landed in a heap a few feet in front of them. Charles ran over to him and squatted down. "Hey man, you alright?"

Tyler rolled over, sat up, patted himself on various parts of his body as if to make sure they were still there, and then nodded. He looked a little dazed and had some minor cuts and bruises, but other than that, he seemed fine. "Yeah. But that's the last time I go into a rigged warehouse for your behind."

Charles threw back his head and laughed. He helped Tyler to his feet, grabbed him in a bear hug and spun him around.

"Hey," Tyler said, "put me down! I'm dizzy enough from the explosion."

Mr. Morgan walked up to Tyler and gave him a hug. "I'll never forget what you did for me, son."

"It's my pleasure Mr. Morgan. It was the least I could do after all you and Mama Morgan have done for me," Tyler said.

***

Two weeks later, Annette showed Charles into Kathy's office. He held a large bouquet of red roses.

"Oh Charles, they're beautiful," Kathy said.

"Special delivery for a special lady," he said. He kissed her on the cheek.

Annette stood there watching them, a goofy smile on her face. Kathy cleared her throat.

"Thank you Annette," she said.

"You are welcome." Annette wiggled her eyebrows at Kathy over Charles' shoulder before leaving the office and closing the door behind her.

Kathy shook her head.

"What?" Charles asked.

"Thank God your case is now completely over. You could have gotten me into a lot of trouble bringing that big ole bunch of flowers to my office. Anyone with two eyes could figure out we're still seeing each other."

"Yeah, it's pretty amazing how fast Peachtree's board of directors consented to a judgment against the company and dismissed the Bar complaint when their criminal attorneys saw how much evidence the F.B.I. had against them," Charles said.

"Even with the deal the company cut, Peachtree is finished as a defense contractor and Donald Peachtree's going to have to do a lot of prison time if they ever find him," Kathy said. "So, now that you've gotten your revenge and are a very rich man, what brings you here?"

"You do. I miss you." He walked over to her, pulled her into his arms and kissed her lightly on the lips. She felt a thrill travel down her spine. She always did when he kissed her.

"I miss you too. You've been pretty scarce these past two weeks."

"I had some thinking to do and some things I had to take care of," he said.

"Yeah? Like what?"

"Well for starters, I had to get this." He extracted a small box from his inner jacket pocket. He opened it to reveal a platinum engagement ring with a large pear-shaped solitaire diamond. He dropped to one knee.

Kathy's mouth fell open. Charles' amused gaze told her that she probably looked like a fish gasping for its last breath. She managed to close her mouth, but couldn't quite wipe the huge smile off her face.

"Kathy Brooks, I love you. I want to spend the rest of my life with you, to grow old with you. Will you marry me?"

"Yes," she said. "Oh yes." She got down on her knees, threw her arms around Charles' neck and kissed him. Then she pulled back and looked him in the eye. "By the way, I love you too."

He stared into her eyes. She could see the emotion swimming in his.

"Say it again," he said.

"I love you."

He pulled her to him and kissed her more deeply this time. She felt the thrill all the way down to her toes.

"Why don't we leave this joint and go somewhere a little more private to celebrate?" she asked.

"Sounds great. But first I have to go see Bill and tell him that I'm officially firing GRH."

"Sounds good to me. We'll stop by his office on the way out." She grabbed her purse, powered down her computer and followed Charles out of the office.

* * *

Giada carefully peeled the poisoned lip covers off her lips. She threw them and the disposable gloves she wore into the toilet and flushed. She extracted another pair of disposable gloves from her purse, put them on and wiped down any surfaces in the hotel room she might have touched.

She carefully applied lipstick and made a small adjustment to the wig she was wearing. Satisfied, she walked over to the desk and unplugged the laptop she had used to transfer funds from Peachtree's secret account into one of her own. She packed it into its case and took it with her. After all she had endured, the money and the laptop were the least Peachtree owed her.

She looked at his naked corpse sprawled across the bed and blew it a kiss. She then walked out of the hotel room and into her new life.

About the Author

The oldest of six children, I grew up in New York City. As a child, I escaped my noisy siblings by voraciously reading every book in my parents' collection and every romance novel I could check out of the public library. My tastes later expanded to include classics, spy novels, and thrillers. Inspired by the stories I read, I began writing poetry and song lyrics and even tried to write a fantasy novel at the tender age of 13. I began writing novels as an adult during National November Writing Month in 2007 and have been chugging along ever since. When I'm not writing, I practice law in Miami, Florida.

I hope you enjoyed my work. Either way, please don't forget to leave a review online. Also, please keep up with my new releases, events and appearances by signing up for my newsletter on my website and following me at the other social media sites below:

www.ljtaylorbooks.com

https://twitter.com/@ljtaylor99

https://www.facebook.com/LJTaylorbooks

http://www.linkedin.com/pub/lj-taylor/48/72a/a41

https://plus.google.com/+ljtaylor99

http://www.goodreads.com/ljtaylorbooks

http://www.pinterest.com/ljtaylorbooks/